SUPPORT
YOUR LOCAL
DEPUTY

5.10

D0752774

SUPPORT YOUR LOCAL DEPUTY

WILLIAM W. JOHNSTONE
with *J. A. Johnstone*

PINNACLE BOOKS
Kensington Publishing Corp.
www.kensingtonbooks.com

PINNACLE BOOKS are published by

Kensington Publishing Corp.
119 West 40th Street
New York, NY 10018

All Kensington titles, imprints, and distributed lines are available at special quantity discounts for bulk purchases for sales promotions, premiums, fund-raising, educational, or institutional use. Special book excerpts or customized printings can also be created to fit specific needs. For details, write or phone the office of the Kensington special sales manager: Kensington Publishing Corp., 119 West 40th Street, New York, NY 10018, attn: Special Sales Department; phone 1-800-221-2647.

PINNACLE BOOKS and the Pinnacle logo are Reg. U.S. Pat. & TM Off.
The WWJ steer head logo is a trademark of Kensington Publishing Corp.

ISBN-13: 978-0-7860-3116-0
ISBN-10: 0-7860-3116-6

First printing: March 2013

10 9 8 7 6 5 4 3 2 1

Printed in the United States of America

Chapter One

My deputy, Rusty Irons, was as itchy as a man ever gets. We were at the Laramie and Overland stage station, in Doubtful, waiting for the maroon-enameled Concord stage to roll in. Rusty couldn't come up with proper bouquets, not in the barely settled cow town of Doubtful, Wyoming, but he managed some daisies and sagebrush he had collected out on the range.

Rusty was waiting for his mail-order brides. That's right, Siamese twins, joined at the hip, from the Ukraine. He ordered just one, but they sent him the pair. He'd gotten a hundred and fifty dollars reward, offered for Huckster Bob, wanted dead or alive. Rusty got him alive, and collected, and applied the money to getting himself a wife.

And now we were waiting for the stage to roll in. It was an hour late, and maybe more.

Well, my ma always said there's nothing worse than a sweating bridegroom, and Rusty filled the bill. He had sweat running down his sides. His armpits had turned into gushers.

"Well, you get to be best man," Rusty said.

"If I don't arrest you first for bigamy," I said.

"I looked it up; there's no law in Wyoming Territory against it."

"Well, I'll arrest you for something or other," I said. "You found a preacher who'll tie the knot?"

"No, but I'm going to argue that all he has to do is marry me to one of 'em."

"What'll you do with the other?"

"I can't auction her off," Rusty said. "So she gets to be the spectator."

"They speak English?"

"Not a word. They're from Lvov, Ukraine."

"Well, that's a good start," I said. "You won't get into arguments. My ma always said the best part of her marriage was when my pa was snoring."

"Well, you're the result," Rusty said.

I wasn't sure how to take that, but thought I'd let it pass without a fistfight. His armpits were leaking worse than ever and I didn't want his sweat all over my sheriff suit and pants.

"You figure they're joined facing the same way?" I asked.

"Well, I wouldn't marry them if one was facing backwards. Here," he said, pulling out a tintype.

The image of two beautiful blondes leapt out at me. It looked like they were side by side, except they had a single dark skirt.

"This one here's Natasha, and the other is Anna," Rusty said.

"You know which one you'll hitch up with?"

"We'll toss a coin. Or maybe they've got it worked out."

"What if one wants you and the other doesn't? Or you want one and not the other?"

Rusty, he just grinned. "Life sure is interesting," he said.

Word had gotten out, and a small crowd had collected at the wooden stage office on Main Street. Some of the women squinted at Rusty as if he was a criminal, which maybe he was. One man looked like he wanted to propose to the other. But mostly they stared at Rusty, wondering what sort of twisted beast would want to marry Siamese twins. And now there were fifty of the good citizens of Doubtful, standing in clumps, whispering, pointing at Rusty as if he belonged in the bottom layer of hell.

Rusty, he just smiled.

"I'm glad you got me that raise," he said.

"You'll need it," I replied.

I'd gone to the Puma County Supervisors and talked them into raising Rusty's wage by five dollars, because of his impending wedlock, and his faithful service as my best and most useful deputy. That put him up just two dollars below my forty-seven a month sheriff's salary, but I didn't mind.

I saw Delphinium Sanders, the banker's wife,

glaring as hard as she could manage at both of us. And George Waller, the mayor, was studying us as if we belonged in a zoo, which maybe we did. I sure didn't know how this would play out, or who'd marry whom, but it made a late spring day real entertaining there in the cow town of Doubtful.

Hanging Judge Earwig was there, too, and thought maybe he'd do the marrying if no one else would. Judge Earwig was broadminded, and didn't mind it if people thought ill of him. He might even marry both the twins to Rusty, seeing as how there wasn't any law against it. That'd come later, when the next legislature got moralistic. Or maybe Rusty could take his gals to Utah and find a Mormon cleric to fix him up, but I didn't put much stock in it. Utah had outlawed that sort of entertainment.

That stagecoach sure was late. Dry road, too. Dry spring, no potholes or mud puddles. The waiting was hard on Rusty.

"Hey, Rusty, you got a two-holer, or are they gonna take turns?" some brat yelled.

I went after the freckled punk, got an ear, and twisted it.

"Cut that out or I'll throw you down a hole and you'll stink for a week."

"Aw, sheriff, this is the best thing hit Doubtful in a long time."

"You're Willie Dickens, and your ma didn't

raise you right. I let go of your ear, you promise to respect people?"

"Anything you say," Willie said, and yanked loose, smirking.

I let him go. This was turning into an ordeal for my deputy sheriff, instead of a moment of joy. It wasn't hard to tell what all of them good folks of Doubtful were thinking. This marriage would have a threesome in the bedroom.

And still no coach.

Then, about the time I was ready to head back to the sheriff office and look over the mail, we spotted the coach rounding the hill south of Doubtful, coming along at a smart clip, maybe faster than usual because them drays looked pretty lathered.

Jonas Quill, the jehu, pulled back the lines slightly, and the sweated horses gladly quit on him, while the coach rocked gently.

"Well, Rusty, here it comes," I said.

But Quill yelled at me, "We got held up, man."

"Held up?"

"Four armed men, masked."

By then the maroon door of the coach swung open, and six passengers emerged: four rumpled males, mostly whiskey drummers, and two frightened women, both gray-haired, in bonnets.

No Ukrainian Siamese identical female twins.

Rusty seemed to leak gas.

"Clear away from here," I yelled at the mob. "We got trouble."

"Where are they?" Rusty asked.

"Don't know, but we got business," I said. "Sheriff business."

"You passengers, stick close here. I'll want statements from all of you."

One woman looked annoyed and started off.

"You, too, Mrs. Throckmorton."

"I surrender to my fate," she said.

Rusty looked shell-shocked, so it'd be up to me. "Quill, tell me. What happened and what got took?"

"Nothing got took. Just the twins."

"My mind isn't quite biting this cookie, Quill."

"Three masked men on saddle horses, another in a chariot."

"A what?"

"A two-wheel chariot hung on two trotters. Man there was masked, too."

"A chariot like them gladiators used?"

"A two-wheel stand-up cart, with a lot of gold gilt and enameled red on it. They stop my coach, one has a scattergun aimed at me, and they open the door, and point at the twins, and say, 'Ladies, get out,' but the twins, they don't speak a word of English, so they prod the ladies out with their revolvers. That takes some doing, four legs, one skirt, but they get the Siamese twins out, get them into the chariot, and the man with the whip smacks the butts of those trotters and away they go, the three of them standing in that chariot."

"That's it?"

"The others wanted the twins' luggage, and they loaded it on a packhorse."

"And you didn't fight it?"

"They made us drop our weapons," one of the drummers said.

"What else did they take? The mail? Anything in a lockbox?"

"Nope," said Quill. "The foreign women and their bags."

"Did they give any reasons?"

"They said, 'Don't shoot,' we'd hit the women, and that was true. They headed due west, over some off-road route."

"Good, we'll have some tracks to follow," I said.

"Them were my brides," Rusty said.

"Real purty, they were," Quill said. "But sure hobbled up. I can see the direction your steamy little brain's taking, Irons," the jehu said.

This was getting a little out of hand.

"Rusty, you interview the male passengers, and I'll interview these women. Meanwhile, you people, clear out of here."

But no one moved. Half the town, it seemed, had flooded in.

Rusty and I got what we could from all those passengers. Nothing was taken except the Ukrainians. No one was forced to empty pockets. No valuables ended up in bandit pockets. The robbers were young, well masked, rode easily, wore wide-brimmed hats and jeans and dirty boots.

They were all polite; no apparent accents. None of them offered reasons. The Ukrainian twins went peaceably, not understanding a bit of it. They were even smiling. They were treated courteously by the bandits.

"Were they hostages? Would they be returned for a reward?" Rusty asked the drummers.

"Nope, no sign of it," said one in a black bowler.

"Who'd want female Siamese twins?" Rusty asked.

"They were real lookers," another salesman ventured.

Rusty whipped out his tintype. "These the ones?"

They studied the black-and-white a while. "Not sure, but seems so," one said.

"Did these women seem in distress?"

"Nope, they thought this was all pretty merry."

The passengers had been detained long enough, so me and Rusty cut them loose, cut the jehu loose, and headed for Turk's Livery Barn. We had some hard riding in front of us.

Chapter Two

Rusty, he wanted a posse. He was plumb irate. Them was his brides got stolen, and he was rooting around, looking for ways to hang the wife-rustlers at the nearest cottonwood tree.

"Hey, cool her off," I said. "Go saddle up and take some fixings. I'll get Critter, and we'll get this deal shut down in no time."

"Who'll run the office?"

"I'll send Burtell," I said, referring to a part-time deputy.

"I want a posse. That was Anna and Natasha got took. I want plenty of armed men."

"This'll be the easiest kidnapping we ever solved," I said. "Where can they hide? We got some dudes in a red-and-gold chariot, kidnapping beautiful Siamese twins in one skirt, and they speak Ukraine, whatever the tongue is. We got 'em cold, Rusty."

He didn't want to believe it, and I didn't blame

him. He got robbed out of two real pretty gals, and a lot of real fine nights once he got hitched to one or the other or both.

But my ma, she used to say that twins were double the trouble. She'd settle for twin cocker spaniels, but not any pair that would put her out some. In truth, if we got them joined-up twins back, I wasn't sure Rusty could handle the deal.

I headed for Turk's Livery Barn, fixing to saddle up Critter the Second. The first got his throat slit, and I looked hard before I found the Second, who was meaner than the first, so it worked out all right. I don't know what I'd do with a gentle horse. Horses are like women: If they don't buck when you're riding them, they're no good.

A while later me and Rusty met up at the livery barn, and fixed to ride out.

"Shouldn't we have a buggy or a cart?" he asked.

He was thinking about how to transport the Ukrainian ladies. You can't expect Siamese twins to climb up on a horse, but maybe a pair of horses would work if they crowded close.

I noticed he was armed to the teeth, with a saddle gun and a pair of mean-looking Peacemakers hanging from his skinny hips. He was gonna get his women back, even if he burned some powder.

"You got any idea why them gals got took?" he asked.

"It sure is interesting," I replied.

Critter was out in the yard, which wasn't good. He kicked down any stall he got put into, so Turk often put him outside. I got the bridle and went after him, and sure enough, he headed for a corner in the fence and waited for me, his rear hooves itchy to land on me. I tried moving along one rail and he switched that way, so I tried the other rail, and he switched that way.

"Critter, dammit, we're going to look for some women. Or one woman. I don't have it straight. So shape up," I yelled.

He turned and eyed me, and settled down and let me bridle and brush and saddle him without trouble. Critter was a philosopher.

"Dog food," said Rusty. "He needs to be turned into dog food."

"I won't argue with it," I said.

Turk spotted us. "You going after them stage robbers?" he asked.

"That's my woman they took," Rusty said.

"Double the feedbags," Turk said. "You sure got odd tastes."

That was my private opinion, but I wasn't voicing it. Rusty was the best deputy I had, and I didn't want to rile him up.

The town watched us ride out. Word spread through town like melted butter, and now they were all watching. Mostly watching Rusty, not me, because they were seeing Rusty in a new light. What sort of man would marry Siamese twins joined at the hip? Mighty strange. The women stood along Main Street with pursed lips, and I could read their every thought.

But soon we were trotting down the Laramie Road, heading for the ambush spot, so I could see what was to be seen, and we could see what the chariot wheels did to the turf. It should be easy enough to follow that cart, and with a little luck I'd have the bandits in manacles and heading for my lockup in a day or two.

Rusty, he sure was silent.

"What are you thinking, Rusty?"

"Maybe I won't marry after all. They'll be plumb ruined. I was marrying double virgins, and now look at it. It's a mess."

"You sure got big appetites, Rusty. Double everything—double marriage, double honeymoon, double household, double mouths to feed."

"Yeah, that's me," he said, a little smirky. Somehow he was seeing all this as proof that he was double the rest of us.

"What if they both expect babies at the same time, eh?"

Rusty was still looking smirky, so I didn't push it. Life sure was going to be interesting.

Critter loved to get out, and now he was pretty near popping along, and Rusty's nag had to trot now and then to catch up. We were riding through empty country, nothing but hills and sagebrush, and not worth anything except to a coyote. But that was Wyoming for you—ninety percent worthless, ten percent pretty fine.

It took us about three hours to reach the ambush place, well chosen to hide the ambushers behind a curve in the road. The jehu had given me a pretty good idea of it. There were signs around there, all right. Some iron-tire tracks, some hoofprints, some handkerchiefs, and plenty of boot heel dimples in the dun clay.

Sure enough, the iron-tire tracks led straight west, off the road, over open prairie, so we followed them.

"We'll nail 'em, Rusty. How can we lose? Look at them tracks, smooth and hard."

But the tracks were gradually turning, and finally came entirely around and headed for the Laramie Road, maybe a mile south of where the ambush happened. And there they disappeared. Those clean iron-tire tracks vanished. We messed around there a while, widening out, looking for the tracks, and there weren't any. It was as if that chariot had taken off from the earth and rolled on up into heaven.

Rusty was having the same sweats as me. That just couldn't be. Big red-and-gold chariots didn't just vanish—unless through the Pearly Gates. I wondered about that for a while. Were them Ukrainian ladies taken on up?

The road had plenty of traffic showing on it, and we scouted it one way or the other, checking hoofprints, poking at ruts, and kicking horse turds, but the fact was, the kidnappers had ridden off into the sky, and were now rolling across cumulus, or maybe thunderheads, to some place or other.

"You got any fancy theories, Cotton?" Rusty asked.

He sure looked gloomy, like he had been deprived of a night with two of the prettiest gals ever born.

"We could ride on down to Laramie and see what's what," I said.

"Who'd want 'em?" Rusty asked.

"Some horny old rancher, I imagine," I said.

"Well, there's no man on earth hornier than me," Rusty said.

It was dawning on him that he'd lost his mail-order bride, or brides, I never could get that straight, and he was sinking into a sort of darkness. I thought it was best to leave him alone.

"I'll get ahold of the sheriff, Milt Boggs, and tell him what's missing, and to let us know if we got a red chariot and two hipshot blondes floating around southern Wyoming," I said.

"We catch them, what are you going to charge them with?" Rusty asked.

"Now that's an interesting question," I said. "My ma used to say people confess if you give them the chance."

"Well, she inherited all the brains in your family," Rusty said, just to be mean.

Truth to tell, my mind was on what might

happen when we got back to Doubtful without two hip-tied blondes and a red chariot and a mess of crooks trudging along in front of my shotgun. They'd be telling me to quit, or maybe trying to fire me again. Seems every time I didn't catch the crook or stop the killer, they wanted to fire me. I've spent more time in front of the county supervisors trying to save my sheriff job than I've spent running my office.

Well, about dusk, we got back in, and all we raised were a few smirks. Like no one thought that kidnapping Siamese twins from the Ukraine was worth getting lathered up about. Especially when it was all Rusty's problem. He's the only one got shut out of some entertainment. So we rode in, by our lonesome selves, without a passel of bandits and bad men parading in front, and without those brides. People sort of smiled smartly, and planned to make some jokes, and maybe petition the supervisors to get rid of me, and that was that.

Me, I felt the same way. If Rusty hadn't mail-ordered the most exotic womanhood this side of Morocco, it never would've happened.

Turk showed up out of the gloom soon as we rode into his livery barn.

"Told you so," he said.

"Told us what?"

"That you'd botch another job again."

I was feeling a little put out with him, and if there were any other livery barns in town, I would have moved Critter then and there. Critter chewed on any wood he could get his big buck teeth around, and sometimes Turk sent me a bill for repairs, but I could hardly blame Turk for that.

Rusty unsaddled, turned out his nag, and disappeared. He was feeling real blue, and I didn't blame him.

"Hey," Turk said, "while you gents were out the Laramie Road, chasing Ukrainian women, a medicine show came up the Cheyenne Road and set up outside of town."

"Medicine show?"

"None other. Doctor Zoroaster Zimmer's Three-Way Tonic for digestion, thick hair, and virility. Three dollars the six-ounce bottle, thirty-five dollars a dozen. And you get to watch a juggler, belly dancer, an accordion player, and a dog and pony act, and then lay out cash for the medicine."

"Zimmer? Seems to me he's on a wanted dodger in my office. Whenever he hits town, jewelry and gold coins start vanishing, and dogs howl in the night. I think his tonic's mostly opium, peppermint, and creek water, but I'll find out."

"Yeah, sheriff, and guess what? I wandered over there to have a gander. He's driving a big red-enameled outfit with gold trim. But there's no chariots or Ukrainian blondes in sight."

Chapter Three

Doubtful, it had growed some, and was fixed in the middle of some of the best Wyoming ranch country around. So there were plenty of people in the Puma County seat, and also plenty more out herding cows and growing hogs and collecting eggs from chickens. There were even some horse breeders around town, most of them raising remounts for the cavalry.

And the town was half civilized. I knew the rough times were over when some gal named Matilda opened up a hattery. I don't know the proper name of a hat shop, but it don't matter. Hattery is what she operated, and she did nothing but sell bonnets and straw hats full of fake fruit to the town's ladies. And gossip, too. All the local gals went in there to gossip about the rest of us. Sometimes I got a little itchy about sheriffing in a halfway civilized town and thought I should pack up and head for the tropics.

But my ma, she always said don't shoot a gift horse between the eyes, and that's how I looked at my job. That eve, Rusty quit early on me, and headed off to his cabin to nurse his disappointment. He had his heart set on marrying the Ukrainian beauties, and never having to have a conversation with his women because he didn't understand a word they said. I thought it was a fool's dream, myself. What if they was saying mean things about him, in their own tongue, maybe even at night with the pair of them lying beside him?

The town was drawing everything from whiskey drummers to medicine shows these days, and I intended to get out to the east side to have a close look. Half the shows rolling through the country roads of the West were nothing but gyppo outfits, looking to con cash out of the local folks, while swiping everything that wasn't nailed down tight. And if they could get a few girls in trouble while robbing citizens and peddling worthless stuff, they did that, too, and smiled all the way to the next burg.

I'd wander over there. But first I'd patrol Doubtful, as I did every evening, wearing my badge, walking from place to place, rattling doors to see if they were locked, and studying saloons closely to see if there was trouble. Sometimes there was, and the barkeeps would be glad I wandered in at a moment when some drunken cowboy, armed to the teeth, was picking a fight.

So I did my rounds, seeing that all was quiet at

Maxwell's Funeral Parlor, and no one was busting the doors at Hubert Sanders's Merchant Bank. I peered into Barney's Beanery, and saw that it was winding down for the eve, and peered into the dark confines of Leonard Silver's Emporium. I checked the office of Lawyer Stokes, and saw no one rifling his file cabinets. McGivers' Saloon was quiet, and so was the Last Chance, where I saw Sammy Upward yawning, his elbows on the bar, looking ready to close early.

There were a few posters promoting Dr. Zoroaster Zimmer's show. The man had a string of initials behind his name, but I never could figure out what all they meant, but the Ph.D. meant he was a doctor of philandery or something like that. The "KGB" puzzled me, but someone told me it was British and had to do with garters and bathtubs. You never know what gets into foreigners. At any rate, this Professor Zimmer had them all, and they followed his name like a string of railroad cars. I thought I'd like to meet the gent.

Denver Sally's place, back behind saloon row, looked quiet, the evening breezes rocking the red lantern beside her door. Most of her business came on weekends. The Gates of Heaven, next door, looked as mean as ever. Who knows all the ways a feller wants to get rid of his cash?

Doubtful was peaceful enough, that spring evening. So it was time to drift out beyond saloon row, east of town, and take a gander at this here

medicine man show. There were a mess of these
shows wandering through the whole country, setting
up in dark corners of a little town, running an act
or two across a stage set up on a wagon. Then the
medicine man would step out and peddle his
stuff, and when he gauged that he'd done all the
selling he could, he'd pull up stakes and head for
the next little town and do it all over again.

Sure enough, east of town, on an alkali flat,
there were a couple of torches going, two fancy
red-and-gilt wagons, a makeshift rope corral with
some moth-eaten drays in it, and a lamp-lit stage
on a wagon. There were maybe twelve, fifteen
suckers watching some jet-haired woman in a
grass skirt wiggle her butt and make her bosom
heave. I'd never seen that, and it seemed entertaining, but I had sheriff business to do. Namely,
look for a red-and-gilt chariot, and two blonde
Ukrainian women joined at the hip. I took a quick
prowl around the rear of the place, and into the
other wagon, to satisfy myself that no one was
hiding a chariot or Siamese twins, blonde or any
other color. Whoever kidnapped the ladies, it
wasn't this miserable outfit.

I spotted a gent smoking a cigar back there, and
thought he might have some answers. He saw the
glint of my badge even before we spoke. He sucked
on his gummy cheroot, and knocked off the ash.

"You looking for something, sheriff?"

"Just keeping an eye on things. How many people you got in this outfit?"

"Six and the professor."

"Any women?"

He stared at me as if I were an idiot. "That's Elvira Smoothpepper out there. And we got Elsie Sanchez, the Argentine firecracker."

"No Ukrainian blondes?"

"You got eyes, dontcha?"

"Who else's in the show?"

"Sheriff, there ain't anyone with a wanted poster on him. There's me and another teamster. He's the accordionist, and there's a tap dancer named Fogarty, and the professor."

"What does the professor sell? What's his medicine?"

The gent smiled. "Try it sometime and come back and tell me."

"Any chariots around here?"

"Any what?"

"Oh, never mind."

"You all right, sheriff? Want to lie down? That second wagon, it's got bunks. Had a little too much?"

"Who's the professor?"

"He's whatever he is at any moment. Right now, he's a medicine man, and he's working the rubes for a few bucks."

"Yeah, well I'll go watch the show," I said.

"It beats pissing on a fence post."

Half of the crowd was cowboys, out from the

saloons. I recognized a few, most of them the ones that hung out at Mrs. Gladstone's Sampling Room. They were tied up with the Admiral Ranch, other side of the county. But there were some locals, too, including the mayor, George Waller, who looked embarrassed when he saw me.

"I just came to view the competition," he said. Waller was a merchant, and any outfit that sold anything was competition, as far as he was concerned. "Maybe you should arrest the whole lot," he said.

"What for?"

"They're all crooks."

"Well, that's progress. You show me one act of crookery, and I'll pinch the person straight off."

Elvira Smoothpepper was making her belly roll and the grass skirts sway, and that was pretty entertaining. The accordionist got to wheezing away, and pretty soon the act creaked to a stop, and out came Professor Zoroaster Zimmer, in black silk top hat, tux and tails, and a grimy white vest that looked a little worse for wear.

I'd never seen the like.

He spotted me at once, and welcomed me. "Ladies and gents, here's the sheriff of, ah, what? Puma County, Wyoming. Come to see our little show, and maybe endorse my product, namely, the Zimmer Miracle Tonic, guaranteed to cure piles, insomnia, gout, St. Vitus Dance, and all bowel troubles. Welcome, Mr. Sheriff.

"Now, esteemed friends, I want to tell you about a product that should need no introducing, since it sells itself. You need only ask your neighbor, who has the remedy on his shelf, ready to use, and you'll see how effective it is. Mr. Sheriff, please come up."

"Me?"

"Of course, you. Step right up, my friend."

"I haven't got anything ailing me, doc."

"Oh, my friend, do you have restless nights? Toss and turn nights?"

"Naw, I sleep like a log."

"Do you ache after a long day on your horse?"

"Now, you're talking about Critter, the orneriest critter on four legs. Yes, I'll allow that I ache some after a long ride on that beast."

"Were you out on him today, sheriff?"

"Pretty near the whole blasted day, professor."

"Then you must feel weary, right down to the bone."

"Well, we were out looking for some blonde Ukrainian women that got attached at the hip and plain disappeared."

That got mostly dead silence and a couple of snickers from some of them cowboys.

"I think you are very weary, sir, after a day of searching for blonde Ukrainian women. Are you a bit worn?"

"I am done in."

"Well, perfect. I would truly like to have you

sample Doctor Zimmer's Tonic, and report the results to all these fine folks."

"My ma, she used to say, one drink is enough."

"Oh, this is not drink, sir. This is an elixir to balm the soul, elevate mood, celebrate life, and rejoice in your own splendid body. Now how old are you?"

"I forget; past thirty, anyway."

"Ah, the shady side of thirty. Let me tell you, my friend, that is when Doctor Zoroaster Zimmer's Tonic works wonders the fastest. It works wonders at any age, sir, but especially after thirty."

The maestro of this here event reached for a bottle of the stuff, which was sitting on a little shelf, with a gold halo around it, so the bottle looked like a saint.

He sure was smiling. He grabbed that stuff, and pulled the cork, and poured a little into a tumbler, and handed it to me, while all them cowboys and Mayor George Waller watched.

I remembered what my ma used to say, no guts, no glory, and I downed the stuff in one gulp.

Well, it took a moment and worked through me, like a glow of a lot of fireflies, and then I plumb keeled over. The accordionist caught me going down.

Chapter Four

I think the professor was a little surprised, but he took advantage of it.

"There, you see. Sublime happiness! Look at the sheriff smile! Not an ache in his carcass! Step right up, folks, only two dollars the bottle, and if you buy five, you get one free."

All them cowboys were staring at me, sitting there on the stage, looking like some drunk, but eventually I got myself up, teetered around, and gazed happily at the whole universe.

"There, you see? Sheriff, will you testify? Will you tell these fine folks what a marvel the Zimmer Tonic is, and what joy awaits them?"

I wasn't at all sure I could manage that, seeing as how my tongue wasn't operating right, but I sort of nodded, and lifted my old hat, and that did it. Them cowboys lined up and forked out payday cash for a bottle or two of the stuff, and wandered off, enjoying the young night, sipping as they went.

Me, I didn't know whether to go back to Belle's Boarding House, or arrest the man. So I just stood there, while the outfit shut down for the night.

"Whatcha got in them bottles, Zimmer?" I asked.

"It's a proprietary secret, my friend, but I'll confide in you, the lawman. There's tincture of opium, wintergreen oil, creek water, and a secret substance I shall never divulge, even on my deathbed, because it holds the secret of eternal bliss. Now, I'm going to sell you a bottle for half price, one dollar cash, for you to take back to your bed. Dr. Zimmer's Tonic is an improvement on love, women, alcohol, tobacco, and religion."

"Oh, all right," I said. "If it's an improvement on religion, I'll buy it. My ma used to say that religion's all right except when you need it, and then it quits you."

"A wise woman, your ma, and she raised a bright boy."

"Well, she always said I was a little slow, but I'm quick with a gun, which adds up to exactly what's needed in a sheriff."

"Ah, I see, my good man. Now here's the bottle of my elixir, and you just dig into your britches for a greenback, and we'll call it even. I like doing favors for lawmen; we're brothers under the skin, trying to make the world safer and happier."

"We are?" I asked. Zimmer sure had some strange ideas.

The crowd had vanished into the mild night.

There was only Zimmer's crew, stowing away the show stuff.

"Say, professor, I got a few questions. Do you know anything about a couple of blonde Ukrainian twins, joined at the hip? They got took off a coach and loaded onto a red-and-gold chariot, same colors as you got here."

The maestro lifted his silk hat and settled it, his gaze keen upon me. "Let me check you for fever," he said, running a hand along my forehead. "No, no fever. I think you're the sort who responds to a good tonic with more enthusiasm than usual. My learned advice is, go to your bunk and sleep it off. You'll feel better in the morning. And don't indulge in my elixir while you're on duty."

"Just thought I'd ask," I said, feeling grouchy. Chasing down Rusty's missing brides wasn't my notion of a picnic. "You keep things clean around here, and I won't trouble you. Minute I hear of trouble, I'll come down on this outfit like a swarm of red ants."

"I knew you'd see it my way," he said, a mysterious smile on his ruddy face. The crew was dousing the oil-fed torches, and suddenly it was plenty dark in there.

I floated along to town, scarcely knowing how I got to Belle's Boarding House, where I had lived ever since arriving in Doubtful. I had that bottle in hand, and thought to pitch it down the two-holer I would use before heading for my room, but then I thought better of it. That stuff might come in handy someday.

I slept the sleep of the innocent, and awakened with only a mild headache. The elixir didn't last until dawn.

When I finally dragged into the sheriff office, Rusty wasn't there. But a note on my desk explained that. "I'm going out to look for my mail-order women," he wrote. "And if you don't like it, fire me."

I didn't like it, but I wasn't the one marrying Ukrainian blondes connected at the hip, both big, bosomy dolls. I didn't know how I'd explain all this to the county supervisors, especially Reggie Thimble, who was a natural-born skeptic. If Professor Zimmer didn't buy it, no one would.

So I patrolled. I knew enough about road shows to know that anything not bolted down would vanish when a road show came through. While they were entertaining the suckers, their thieves were pocketing anything they could finger. So I started at the west end, and worked east, telling merchants to watch out, and take inventory, and tell me when anything didn't add up.

I stopped in at the Mercantile, and found Leonard Silver unloading jars of pickles.

"Hey, Leonard, we got a medicine show camped here, and they're born pickpockets. I'd say, keep a sharp eye on your goods, and if you see anything, let me know. Anyone with itchy fingers, get me fast."

"I've been worrying my way along," Silver said. "I'm waiting on any stranger personally, and I've got Willard watching the door. I suppose you could always raid their wagons and find whatever got took."

"They're usually too smart for that," I said. "They cache the stuff and pick it up later, when they're pulling out."

"Well, thanks for the word, sheriff."

I made a point of stopping at the smithy, where One-Eyed Jack shoed horses and hammered iron.

"Hal, them outfits, they like nothing better than to filch horseshoes and nails. They're on the road, and they need to keep their draft animals shod, and they don't want to pay for any of it if they can help it."

"I allus keep a red-hot poker ready for business," Hal said, grinning.

"Yeah, but that's daytime."

"Maybe I'll just hang around here at night," Hal said. "Or have The Sampling Room send me a few boilermakers and wait for the medicine show to come. I'll tack shoes on their bare feet."

Hal would take care of himself, all right. He had piles of horseshoes, mule shoes, and even ox-shoes for whoever needed them.

I got the whole business bunch alerted that day, but that didn't mean the homes around Doubtful were safe. I didn't know where Rusty had got to, but he was making himself scarce, and I needed him. I thought of deputizing a few citizens just to be on the safe side, but I knew the county supervisors wouldn't shell out a nickel for them. So I was on my own.

But Rusty did finally drift in, and found me doing rounds on Wyoming Street.

"Thanks for all your hard work," I said.

Rusty, he just smiled. "What did your ma tell you about people who don't show up for work?"

That sure got me. I'd have to ask her sometime. My ma, she knows just about everything there is to know.

"They git fired," I said. "Sheriff doesn't like no-account help."

"I got some good stuff. I rode way out the Laramie Road, to the Douglas turnoff, and found a few freight outfits, and asked the teamsters if they'd seen some real purty Ukrainian blondes joined at the hip, in a red-and-gold chariot."

"What'd they say?"

"They said, fella, we don't have a drop left, but Doubtful's got some fine saloons, and you'll do fine over there. So I told them I was engaged, and would be marrying one, if not both, depending on whether the justice of the peace was in a fine mood."

"Yeah, well, we got a medicine show in town. Professor Zoroaster Zimmer is pushing his elixir.

And you know what that means. Nothing's safe around here."

"Maybe I'll like the tonic," Rusty said. "He got some samples?"

"Two dollars a bottle."

"That's too rich for me, Cotton. But I found out something today. There's a carny show moving through the area. They didn't know the name of it, but it's a big show, with a dozen heavy wagons, lions, tigers, freaks, fat women, two-headed goat, boa constrictors, hootchy-kootchy girls, and stuff like that."

"I hope they don't show up in Doubtful. By the time Zimmer pulls out, the town's gonna be a lot poorer."

"Well, I need to find that show. A pair of real pretty Ukrainian women joined at the hip, why that's worth two bits a peek."

Rusty was right. That probably was where his brides ended up, and since they couldn't talk English, the carnival felt safe abducting them. I'd send out information to all the counties around Wyoming, and maybe we could get Rusty's mail-order brides back.

"Rusty, you get some chow, and we'll go on out to the medicine show. After that, we'd better start patrolling."

"Sure, Cotton," he said.

The evening was going to be much like the last

one, except there were more cowboys in town. I saw a mess of horses at the hitch rails, especially in front of the Last Chance. They'd get boozed up and head out for the free entertainment east of town, and there'd be a lot of hooting and hollering. The brands were mostly Admiral Ranch, which was all right; there were worse outfits out in Puma County, some of them just looking for any trouble they could get into.

Doubtful depended on the cowboys and ranches. There were a couple of mines at the far edge of the county, but mostly it was a cow town, and most of the businesses in Doubtful supplied the ranches.

Rusty showed up at the sheriff office and jail, and went for a shotgun, but I told him no; that's just asking for trouble. This was a billy club deal, a nightstick deal. A lawman good with a billy club got more respect than one armed to the teeth.

"I don't know what all they've got on stage; an accordionist, a fiddler, some female in a big grass skirt who does a hootchy-kootchy, and the professor himself, pitching his joy juice at two dollars a bottle," I said.

"That's a lot of money. Them cowboys earn forty a month."

"When you taste what's in them bottles, Rusty, two dollars is cheap."

But even before we got to the show, there came Zimmer himself, silk hat, tux and tails, gold walking stick, orange chin-whiskers. He sure was looking agitated.

"Sheriff, I'm glad I found you. Grief. Pain. Misery. Someone in your fine city of Doubtful is a thief. My strongbox is busted, and I've lost every cent I possess."

Chapter Five

Me, I'd rather face a gunslick wanting to put me in my grave than to track down a burglar. Catching a thief is a skill I never got born with. It takes a lot of figuring to track down a thief. You've got to see what got took, and figure out who took it, and that's harder than it sounds, especially for someone born a little slow, as my ma used to say. So I always gave the thief business to Rusty, or one of my part-time deputies. But Rusty, he's been swooning over his lost Ukrainian mail-order women, so I got stuck with it.

"All right," I said to Professor Zimmer, "let's have a look."

He took me over to the second wagon. The show was rolling in front of the first wagon, and a mess of townspeople and cowboys were watching in the torchlight that spring eve.

He led me inside the second one, dark as pitch,

but he lit a lamp. It was mostly hammock bunks in there. Them show people sure lived poor and crowded. But Zimmer had a corner to himself, and on the floor was a strongbox, bolted down tight. But the cover was opened, and there was a sawed-up padlock on the floor. The burglar had gone to work with a hacksaw while the show was running, cut through, scooped up the loot, and beat it.

"I know to the penny," Zimmer said. "That scoundrel, that swine, lightened my purse by two hundred seventy-nine dollars and forty cents."

That was a heap of money. But he had payroll and all the costs of manufacturing his tonic, and his transportation to pay for, so maybe it wasn't so much.

"Now I'll have to buy a padlock. I don't suppose there's one available in Doubtful. Nothing's safe. I'm near broke!"

"Ah, professor, you mind telling me when this happened?"

"How should I know? You think I'm a witness? You think I have eyes in the back of my head?"

"Well, when was the last time you checked?"

"Why, this is our dressing room. This is where I don my costumes. Everything was perfectly proper at the start of the evening."

"So it happened just now?"

"I admire your powers of deduction, sheriff."

"You get a look at this crook?"

"He's probably standing out front right now, mixing right in. You might arrest the whole lot and frisk them."

"I need a little more to go on, professor."

"All right. Whoever buys a lot of bottles, arrest him. My tonic is so much in demand that people buy it by the case, the carton. There's nothing like Zoroaster Zimmer's Tonic to cure the ills of all creation."

"You sure it wasn't one of your own people sawed this padlock?"

"Do you think my people run around with hacksaws?"

"Well, it's a handy little tool, Your Honor."

"Ah, finally some respect from you, sheriff. How did you know I once was a judge?"

"You look sort of judgey, if you ask me."

"Well, I was a Supreme Court Justice of the state of West Virginia, second circuit, three terms, before I answered a higher calling, which was to make the world a happier place, and to offer the suffering some relief at just two dollars the bottle."

An accordion act was winding up on the other wagon, and there was a scatter of applause.

"I've got to go make the pitch, tell the world about miracles and blessings," Zimmer said, and hastened into the darkness.

The lamp on the wagon cast an eerie glow. It was hard to imagine how a company of six managed to live in such tiny quarters. I studied the padlock, which had been expertly sawed apart. The cashbox, tiny like everything else here, lay empty. I didn't even know what sort of bills and coins had been in it; probably pretty small ones. There wasn't anyone around Doubtful that could pull a twenty out, or even make change for a twenty.

It sure was not anything I was going to solve very soon, but I'd give her a wrestle. If someone had cash, then someone would probably spend it pretty quick. That's how it went in Doubtful. Them cowboys came to town on paydays, and spent every last dime before riding out. So I figured I'd just start asking around a little. Some unseen crook, big or little, was probably going to push some bills across the bar tops.

I watched Zimmer pitch his tonic to the grinning crowd. He wasn't making much headway until he switched to new ground. The cowboys looked like they were ready to head back to the welcoming saloons along Saloon Row, and I spotted a yawn here and there. The chill night air was eddying through the small crowd, reminding them that summer was yet a month off.

"Now, friends, listen close, because this may affect your happiness more than anything you've ever come across," Zimmer was saying. He was leaning forward, almost falling off the wagon into his audience, the lamplight throwing light and shadow over his craggy red face.

"I also have compounded, from my own secret and priceless recipes, a special Manhood Improver and Conditioner. Now, this precious liquid, well, you'll find yourselves transported to heavenly bliss, beyond your wildest imaginings, and your romantic partners will thank you and bless you and shout hurrahs to you. Now, this is absolutely guaranteed. Ask anyone who's tried it. If I only had some tiny bottles I'd give each of you a free sample, knowing that you'd soon be flocking back to buy out every bottle in stock. But alas, gents, I have no samples. But I do have countless testimonials, which are written in this brochure, here, for you to read.

"Now if you are looking for a true manhood expander and gateway to the highest peaks of human experience, then you'll want Doctor Zimmer's Private Stock Manhood Improver. It will take you to places you've only dreamed of. Now, it's not cheap. It costs four dollars the bottle, but it lasts and lasts, and improves with age. Why, year-old Manhood Improver is even more powerful than day-old Manhood Improver. This is absolutely guaranteed. On each bottle is a return address. Send the bottle back, if it fails you in any manner, and you will soon receive a gift certificate from Doctor Zimmer for any of his products."

That sure was entertaining, and them cowboys, they sure were listening hard. They didn't have much opportunity to make good use of Zimmer's Manhood Improver, since they lived in bunkhouses on ranches around Puma County, but that wouldn't make any difference to them. A cowboy's a cowboy, even if he's fifty miles from the nearest female.

Sure enough, about then one of them performers, the big lady in the grass skirts, she carries out a carton of the Manhood Improver, and those cowboys, they're already digging into their jeans for loose cash, while Zimmer kept on yakking on stage. I squinted at that bunch, looking for a big spender, but they were having trouble coming up with the bucks, and some were going fifty-fifty on a bottle.

I sure had to hand it to Zimmer. Broke one moment, coining profits the next.

That reminded me I had to start hunting down a thief, which for me was like eating sour apples. Zimmer's show was going to wind down pretty soon, so I drifted back to Doubtful, past the cottonwoods along the creek, useful for a good hanging, and began with the Last Chance Saloon, because Sammy Upward was my friend, and he often helped me out.

The place was mostly empty because Zimmer's show had drawn the usual saloon crowd. But that was fine; it gave me a chance to talk quietly with Sammy, who was washing glasses behind the bar.

"Sammy, I'm looking for big spenders," I said.

"Someone's got something to spend?"

"A lot to spend, and it ain't his."

Sammy grinned. He was a redhead, with a good freckle-faced grin. "Gotcha," he said.

I did the same at the Lizard Lounge, Mrs. Gladstone's Sampling Room, and McGivers' Saloon. The barkeeps listened to me skeptically and nodded. They weren't going to squeal on a paying customer setting up drinks for the crowd, not if they could help it, but they also knew I'd come after them if I found out they were going along with a thief.

"Something got stole?" asked George Roman, who ran Lizard Lounge.

"If you're smart, you'll keep cash in the bank, and not around here," I said.

Roman eyed me, a faint smile building. "Maybe the town needs new blood in office," he said. He was referring to me.

When I got back to the sheriff office, there was Rusty, lying in a cell, staring at the ceiling and leaking tears.

"You found your missing twins?"

"They're gone forever. Happiness is gone forever. My life is ruint."

"There's a lot more Ukrainian blondes there. Just order a new one."

"But they ain't joined at the hip, Cotton. Two fer one; best bargain I ever come acrost."

"Well, dry your tears. We got a crime to solve. Zimmer, he's been robbed of pretty near three hundred smackeroos."

That got Rusty's attention. That was almost a year's deputy salary. "What happened?"

"He's got a lockbox in the wagon, and someone sawed through a padlock while the show was rolling, and made off with the profits."

"Yeah, sure," Rusty said.

"You saying it ain't so?"

"I'm saying maybe Zimmer robbed himself."

"You got no faith in human nature, Rusty. The loss of your blondes has made you downright cynical."

But Rusty, he just grinned. "Watch and see, Cotton. We'll find out who got robbed of what, and why."

"You're just saying that because you're feeling mighty blue, Rusty."

"You want me to solve it? Tomorrow I will."

Rusty was sure acting strange, like he was disgusted with me or something.

"I'll tell you what's going to happen next. There's going to be robberies and thefts all over Doubtful."

"You mean that burglar that cleaned out Zimmer's not done?"

"He's just getting started, Cotton. And he's going to be hard to catch, even if I know who he is right now."

"So who is he?"

But Rusty only laughed at me. He sure was being ornery, but that's what lost love does to people.

Chapter Six

My ma, she always used to say, "Early to bed, early to rise, makes a man healthy, wealthy, and wise." Some smart Pennsylvanian named Franklin was responsible for that, according to her. Me, I've been an early riser from the get-go, but I sure didn't get wealthy or wise from it. The real good thing about early rising is that I can get out to the crapper behind Belle's Boarding House before a line forms when the sun comes up. There's nothing worse than getting up and waiting in line to use the biffy. The seat's frosty, and there's nothing worse than settling down on some cold wood, but that's the price paid by the early bird.

Zoroaster Zimmer, he's an early riser, too. I hardly got into my office and cleaned up the puke of the drunks in the jail before he showed up and wanted me to solve the burglary.

"That's the life and death of my show, sheriff. I can't pay my cast when there's nothing in the till."

"We're working on it," I said, which was a stretch. All we'd done is ask the barkeeps to tell us about big spenders.

"I'm expecting you to find the culprit before we leave."

"How much time we got?"

"Tomorrow. We'll have our grand finale tonight and roll out."

"So we're supposed to catch this crook, collect what you lost, and put it back in your britches before then?"

"I insist on it. This has been a terrible ordeal. We haven't sold many bottles of the elixir. We're not drawing crowds. Doubtful is very doubtful."

"You got yourself a new padlock at the hardware?"

"No, I can't afford one, sheriff. I'm putting our paltry cash in with my chemicals. I have another, larger lock cabinet, with my tinctures and bottles and secret miraculous ingredients."

"You want to give me the old lock, doc? My friend George Waller, the hardware man, thinks maybe he can tell whether the padlock was sawn through with a coarse blade or a fine one, and we'll look for hacksaws with the right blade on them."

"No, no, no, sheriff. We'll buy a replacement in a large town, where we have a choice."

"Well, just leave it behind and we'll maybe figure out a thing or two."

"I commend you for your diligence, sir, but that's not going to put a crook in your little jail, is it?"

"Well, professor, I've put my best man on it, Rusty, and he'll maybe nab someone."

"He's the lovelorn groom?"

"That's him."

"If you find those Ukrainians, let them know I'd be glad to hire them for my show. It's a good life. They'd get a nice salary between them, and I'd build a special bunk in the wagon, and they'd get to see the country."

"They're plumb gone, professor."

"A pity," Zimmer said. He clamped his black silk stovepipe hat over his graying locks, and beat it. He'd do his first show after lunch, and another late afternoon, and the big show in the evening. The lunch show got the women out, and he pitched his elixir for female complaints and vapors. The night show, that was for cowboys, so he pitched his elixir for virility. But that just meant the old men in town lined up for a bottle or two.

I wandered over there to his camp on the edge of town, just to see him give another of them stem-winders. There sure were a mess of women there. I didn't know we had so many women, of all shapes and sizes and ages. And there was Zimmer, silk stovepipe hat, swallowtail coat, holding a bottle of his magic potion in hand.

"Ladies, this is your last chance. I implore you, buy while you can. Don't suffer regrets that you failed to purchase not one, but six, bottles of my elixir. Remember this: My elixir regulates female cycles and improves health. Are you worn down? Zimmer's Tonic will lift the aching heart, bring up the chin, brighten the eye. Are you weary of child-bearing? Take Zimmer's Tonic each morning, and you will see magical results. Do you yearn for more children, or the attentions of your handsome and gifted husband? Why, take a double dose, two teaspoons, late in the evening, and your smile will radiate through the whole room, and win smiles from your happy mate. Do you hurt? Are you melancholic, at times? Zimmer's Tonic does wonders for the spirit. Now, as my parting offer, I am going to give you the bargain of a lifetime: two bottles for the price of one. Two bottles for two dollars cash. You'll have one for the future, or one to share with your husband when he's worn down. Just two dollars buys you a cornucopia of joy."

The women looked undecided. Some had para-sols, and twirled them in the warm spring sun. They were consulting, weighing, hesitant. But then a woman Cotton hadn't seen before laughed and said, "Save two for me!"

He looked closer; it was the grass-skirt lady in the show, but all dolled up in a blue dress and bonnet. She pushed forward, waving two green-backs, scooped up two bottles from one of the teamsters who took her cash, and strutted off. That sure started it. A mess of them ladies lined up, pulled dollars out of their reticules and pockets, and began snapping up all that stuff in the green bottles.

Zimmer smiled and waved his accordionist up to the stage, and pretty quick the feller was pounding out a jig, while the ladies snapped up bottles.

I spotted Rusty coming at me like a clipper ship, and he waved me aside.

"We got trouble. George Waller's says he's been robbed."

"What? When?"

"A whole list of stuff. He's still trying to figure it all out. He took some shipments two days ago, and now stuff's gone and no one in the mercantile sold it."

"Burgled or robbed?"

"He says the store's been locked tight at night, but someone's sneaking stuff out when no one's looking. He says arrest all these medicine people."

"He got any proof?"

"He says they're here in Doubtful, and that's all he needs."

I hurried over there, only to run into Hubert Sanders, who owns the Merchant and Stockmen's Bank.

"Little problem, sheriff. My tellers tell me there's cash missing. We're doing an audit; seems someone opened the cash drawers and made off with coin and greenbacks, when no one was looking. It's impossible; my people are always alert. But someone did it."

This was getting serious.

"George Waller's got some trouble, too. I'll put Rusty on that, and I'll see what's happening at the bank. When did you find out?"

"It's three o'clock, closing time, and my tellers, they're counting the cash, and something's haywire in two cash drawers."

"Hardly seems likely a light-finger thief would go into your drawers, Hubert."

"If you're insinuating that one of my tellers did it, then we need a new sheriff," he said.

I'd heard that sort of sentiment pretty near once a week in Doubtful. But I still had a job.

We rushed up those sandstone steps into the bank, and the clerks were waiting.

"Drawer A is lacking forty dollars and twenty-five cents. Drawer C is lacking seventeen dollars and two cents, sir. We've double-checked, and it's clear someone nipped cash, maybe when one or another of us was at lunch or occupied."

"But it's all in plain sight. I see every person coming in and going out." He turned to me. "It's the medicine show."

"They're having some trouble, too, Hubert. Zimmer lost every cent he had, his strongbox opened up."

"Huh," Sanders said. "Do you believe it?"

"I'm checking it all out."

"What have you done?"

"Talked to Zimmer's people, and asked all the barkeeps in town to tell me about big spenders."

"Sherlock Holmes you definitely are not," Sanders said. "Get that money; solve this, or else quit."

I talked a little with those two tellers, McAffee and Barnes, trying to get some handle on when it happened, and when those two weren't in their teller cages. And trying to figure how someone could reach through the teller window, open the cash drawer, scoop up some money, and slide the door closed without being spotted. From the sound of it, the best time was around the lunch hour, when Sanders was gone and one or another teller was gone, leaving just one man in the bank. But both men swore they were constantly vigilant. And neither saw anyone, male or female, from the medicine show lingering around the place.

They enacted how it had to happen, with McAffee acting the part of the thief, reaching through the window when no one was around, sliding the drawer away from him, nipping some money, and sliding the door closed. That accounted for one window, but two? It sure was a headscratcher, I thought.

"All right, you fellers think of anything else, you get ahold of me or Rusty. I gotta talk to George Waller. He says his store's been hit."

"Him, too?" Barnes asked.

"So he says. He says the medicine show people did it."

I found Waller and his clerk, Gasper, along with Rusty, in the gloomy mercantile. There sure wasn't much light in there. I'd hate to spend the day in a place with just a little window light coming in, and heaps of merchandise everywhere, but hard to see. If someone was nipping stuff from the store, it wouldn't be hard in a place like that.

"George, what you need is some of them skylights in the roof. Maybe this wouldn't happen if you let some light in here," I said.

Waller glared. It was a fire-the-sheriff glare, and I'd seen it a few times. But I was right, so I thought I'd rub it in.

"Women, they come here for cloth, and the first thing they do is haul it to the front of the store so they can see what they're buying."

"I've just been robbed, and you tell me how to run my store."

"Yep, maybe the two fit together. Dim store, no one sees the nipper."

"Blame the victim!"

"Maybe you need some blaming, George. But I'll check this out, and if you got a list of stuff that got took, I'll head over to them medicine show wagons and turn the outfit inside out, and if I find any of your stuff there, they'll all end up in my little iron-caged hospitality house."

That lowered the boiler pressure a little.

He was missing some ready-made skirts, women's stockings, men's underdrawers, a box of candles, a jug of lamp oil, some ready-made wire-rimmed spectacles, some bars of Fels-Naptha soap, four horseshoes and a box of shoeing nails, a carton of saltine crackers, a bottle of dill pickles, and a red blanket.

"Probably more. It's hard to keep track," Waller said.

"All right, me and Rusty, we'll head for the medicine show and have a look."

"You won't find a thing," Waller said. "They're too smart for that."

"If they got it cached, we'll find the cache," I said.

Nothing but trouble now in Doubtful.

Chapter Seven

That evening, the orphan train rolled in. I'd never heard of it, but there it was, three wagons, each drawn by a four-horse team, a mess of boys and girls and two adults, a man and a woman. That sure was one strange outfit rolling in. The boys, most of them little squirts, they seemed to be handling the teams just fine.

I thought I'd solved the burglary problem. It was pack rats. The whole town was full of pack rats, and there wasn't a one-inch crack somewhere they didn't come through. I was thinking maybe pack rats made off with all that stuff, but Rusty thought I was nuts, and it was two-legged rats cleaning out the mercantile. Pack rats are cute little buggers, and they like to show off some, sitting on windowsills, especially at night, and stealing anything they can. I've seen pack rat nests loaded with coins and paper money and rings and spoons and corks. But Rusty, he thinks

I'm joking. I've seen a pack rat haul stuff ten times his size and weight, and I'm not joking. Rusty, he's too young to know about pack rats. I'm thirty-one, and he's twenty-seven, and no one under thirty knows anything.

I was fixing to tell Zoroaster Zimmer that he was robbed by rats, and any pack rat can gnaw right through metal. But just as I was about to go over there, this here bunch of wagons rolls in with a mess of little farts on board. They roll right up to my office, too, like their first business is a talk with the law. I looked them over, wondering how one couple could have seventeen children pretty near the same age, maybe six to twelve. That'd be a mess of triplets, but the woman didn't show any wear and tear.

Those big wagons halted out front. They were peculiar looking, with high canvas bows so someone could stand inside. This here man and woman, they come on in, skinny folks, but clean and trimmed.

"Sheriff? I'm Hatfield McCoy, and this is my wife, Judith. We're members of the Children's Aid Society. Are you familiar with it?"

"I'm Cotton Pickens. My ma, she always used to say, if you don't know something, listen hard, so I'm listening."

"Well, good, I've a chance to talk about our mission. The society was formed back East to help the thousands of orphans in the big cities, especially

New York, children who have lost their parents or are simply running free, unsupervised. Did you know, sir, there were thirty thousand of these? It is the society's mission to place these children on western ranches where they'll become valuable additions to the homes and businesses that adopt them. They are hard little workers, and even at a tender age entirely competent. You see the little fellows handling the teams. The girls cook and clean. The boys do the teamstering, the girls the housekeeping. What we do, sir, is bring these children west in trains, and then take them out to towns where they might be adopted. I suppose you know of a dozen ranches in the area that might welcome additional help."

"Well, that sure's the truth."

"These are sturdy little folks, with good muscle and teeth, though a few need spectacles, and all they need is a home and some good parents. We can arrange adoptions, and have all the papers on hand. So what we want, sir, is to let the ranches know that we're here, and the farmers and ranchers can see for themselves what fine additions to their families we've got here."

There was something a little odd about all this. "You just sort of sell 'em off?"

"A small fee, sir, is charged to underwrite our cost."

"And them ranchers, they just get the pick of the litter and walk off?"

"That's correct, sir."

"And these little people, they got no say in it? Not even if they fear and dread some new parent?"

"They're minors, sir, under adult supervision. We are their legal guardians."

"And what happens when friends are separated? Are some brothers and sisters?"

"That's a sad prospect, sir, but we usually allow only one child to any new parent."

"And these new parents, can they do whatever they want with the children? Work 'em hard? Turn 'em into little drudges?"

"It is better than running loose in a big city, sir, turning to lives of crime and desperation. Most of them could survive in the cities only by pilfering and violence. The society is their salvation, sir."

"What if some of them are troublemakers?"

"A firm hand is needed; spare the rod, spoil the child. Once in a while, there's a small discipline problem, but that's rare, sheriff. Most adoptions go well."

Well, this sure was something new for Doubtful. There weren't very many children in town. Cowboys don't breed, and some folks say they can't breed, after being crotch-hammered in the saddle. They hardly know what a woman is. My ma, she always said that cowboys and women don't fit together. The merchants in town don't breed neither, being too busy making money instead of babies. So now it looked like Doubtful would get a whole mess of little ones, and probably there'd be some trouble in it.

But I took kindly to this. My ma, she always said if it wasn't for her and Pa, I'd be an orphan. So I studied on those little fellers, sitting restlessly on wagon seats, eyeing the town and wondering about their fate. There was one little freckle-faced boy, nose pointy like a rat, I thought needed a good home in Doubtful, Wyoming.

"How does this here work?" I asked McCoy.

"Well, tonight we'll put them on display at the courthouse, and tomorrow we'll sell them to the highest bidder."

"You mean they're for sale?"

"No, but somebody wants a good little worker and is willing to pay more than the regular five-dollar fee, we look kindly on it."

"You check this out with the Abolitionists?"

McCoy laughed. "It does look that way, doesn't it? Actually, the child can be adopted, or indentured. If someone wants to indenture the child, he agrees to raise the child to age sixteen, and teach him a trade."

"What if a little feller don't like it?"

"He's got no say in it. The contract's between the buyer and the Children's Aid Society, one copy filed at your courthouse. We act in loco parentis, as legal parent."

"What if someone wants one of these little girls to abuse her?"

"We screen our customers, sheriff. We prefer to place our young females with couples."

"Well, what if some wife mistreats the girl?"

McCoy sighed. "The children are better off. If you knew what hell they lived in, back East, you'd realize that we're doing them a great kindness."

That seemed all right with me, even if I was a little itchy about it. "Well, we got a medicine show on the east side of town leaving tomorrow, so you and your orphans ought to camp on the west side, nice grove of cottonwoods there for you."

"Medicine show? We'll camp over there. The more people see our orphans, the better the adoptions go. That's perfect. Maybe the manager will adopt a couple orphans for his show."

That sure sounded peculiar, but I saw no trouble with it. If Zoroaster Zimmer wanted a few orphans to display, and the orphans liked his tonic, maybe that was better than running around on the streets of New York, the worst city on the planet, apparently, except for Laramie.

"All right, sir, and madam, you just head on over there and get yourself settled."

"We'll set up, and bring the orphans back here for the showing," he said.

"Sure beats all," I said.

I watched the orphan-master point toward the east side, over beyond Saloon Row, and pretty soon them little buzzards got the three wagons rolling that way.

"We selling orphans now?" Rusty asked.

"Nice outfit, seems like."

"I caught five pack rats and fed them to the dogs. That should eliminate our crime wave."

"Naw, Rusty, there's thousands of pack rats, and we got to get them all. They're all little burglars."

He was smirking at me. I meant it, and he was funning me. Some people never do see the truth of things. Pack rats make a crime wave.

Pretty quick, Zoroaster Zimmer, he came boiling up.

"What's this? What's this? That's my turf, over there. Get them out."

"It's just one night, professor. They're selling orphans, and want a large crowd on hand to look over their merchandise."

"Selling orphans? Those are a bunch of little thugs off the streets, Pickens. Orphans? They're little hooligans. You run them out of Doubtful or none of us'll be safe. And while we're at it, have you made any progress getting my cash back?"

"It was pack rats, professor. The Mercantile, it got attacked by waves of pack rats. They're real saucy little suckers. They'll strip the corn off a cob while you're eating it."

"In other words, no. You don't know which of your locals in this crime-ridden little burg stole my livelihood."

"It'll show up. I got the barkeepers watching. And professor, the McCoys, they thought maybe you'd like to indenture an orphan or two for your show. Those boys, they're real good with draft animals."

Zimmer stared, his orange whiskers quivering up and down, his black silk stovepipe hat bobbing on his generous locks. He didn't reply; just whirled around and headed back to the east side. It sure was going to be interesting out there this evening.

Sure enough, about the time the stores were closing up, the McCoys herded all their orphans to the courthouse steps, and that sure drew a crowd. Seems like word got around fast that an orphan train was in, and just about every adult in Doubtful showed up. I even saw Sammy Upward from the Last Chance Saloon looking 'em over, and a couple of madams were on hand, too, Denver Sally and Mrs. Goodbride. I was gonna have to make sure they didn't adopt any girl. That's just my prejudice; I didn't know of any law against it. I suppose a madam has a right to adopt an orphan, same as anyone else.

There was such a hubbub as I ever saw in Doubtful. Them children, they'd been through it all, and just stood quiet, maybe a little fearful, as people looked them over, looked for flab, squeezed their arms, pried open their mouths to look for bad teeth or no teeth. Nothing ruins an orphan like bad teeth.

"No, no adoptions today, friends," McCoy was saying. "Tomorrow, right here on the courthouse steps, beginning at ten, we'll put these fine young people up for adoption or indenture. Bring cash; we do not accept bank drafts."

The boys, they were looking wild-eyed, but the girls, they just looked downcast and stared at their toes, even as people poked and probed and pried open their mouths.

It sure was a sight, I thought, and it'd be interesting to see what Doubtful families would grow the next day.

Chapter Eight

There sure was a ruckus east of Doubtful that evening. The medicine show was going full bore, with one act after another, but now there was the orphan wagons parked nearby, in some cottonwoods. It looked like the whole town of Doubtful was on hand, and so were a mess of cowboys off the ranches.

All them orphans, they were cut loose to go wherever they wanted. The girls, they clumped together and seemed timid, but the boys, they roared around looking for ways to get into trouble. Mr. and Mrs. McCoy, they just roamed placidly, keeping an eye on the orphans.

The accordionist, he finished up a jig on that little wagon stage, even as the two teamsters lit some oil lamps as dusk settled. The stage, backed by one wagon, was all lit up, drawing attention to the show. I wandered around behind the stage, looking for trouble, but most of them medicine show people, they just sat on folding chairs and smoked cigars, including the women.

The professor appeared, all fixed up in his tux and tails and stovepipe hat, and now he climbed a few steps and got out in front of that mob. This would be his last pitch; whatever he didn't sell tonight, he'd have to sell in the next town.

"Ah, my friends, my new lifelong friends in this noble town of Doubtful, Wyoming, we come to the moment of parting. Tomorrow, Doctor Zimmer's medicinal exhibit will pack up, not only all of our things, but all of our sweet memories, and hasten away.

"Now I've told you all about what my famous elixir does for the mortal body, but I have yet to speak of what it does for animals. The tonic is known to put new life in old horses and mules, to put joy into a venerable dog, and it has a special effect on draft horses, making them eager to pull and tug, and turning them young again. A spoonful for your horse, and the plowing goes better.

"My friends, animals have their own sorrows of body and soul. They age and grow weary. They faithfully carry the cowboy on his daily rounds. They draw heavy wagons, and pull plows, and drag buggies. And they hurt, just like we mortals hurt after a hard day. Any cowboy who knows his horse knows how much the horse has given to him that day, all-out help, every hour.

"Now, long ago some cowboys discovered that a

little dose of Doctor Zimmer's Tonic comforts their faithful and noble horses. It needn't be much; maybe two teaspoons of it, mixed with the grain, and lo, behold, their animals are young and frisky again, and ready for the next hard day. It's an act of charity, an act of kindness, to treat your faithful horse or mule or dog to this tonic that restores youth and vitality in them.

"Now, to prove my point, I invite someone to bring his horse up to the stage, and I will supply an absolutely free dose of my tonic, and you will soon see that old horse sigh, smile, and dance. Are there any takers?"

Sure enough, several cowboys were running to fetch their horses, and in a moment, one showed up. Zimmer expertly opened the horse's jaw and pumped a spoonful of his tonic into the beast, which licked and slurped, and then farted.

"Now, friends, it takes a little time for you to see the results, so while we wait, I'll be pleased to sell you two bottles for one, as my going-away offer, two dollars for two bottles of Doctor Zimmer's Medicine Tonic."

Sure enough, a mess of cowboys lined up in front of the teamster who was doling out the bottles and collecting the cash. He must have sold twenty bottles or so when the horse began weaving, rocking, swaying, and finally settled to earth, sighed, rolled over on its back, and pawed the air.

"There, you see? One happy horse," said Zimmer,

who sounded a little worried. "Listen to him pass gas; the mark of true happiness in any livestock. Show me a farting horse, and I'll show you a happy horse."

But he stared anxiously at the downed animal, until at last the beast got up on its forelegs, and then staggered up on his rear legs, and shook the dirt off.

"One happy horse," Zimmer bellowed.

The cowboys flocked around the beast, patting it, tweaking it, studying it, and mostly agreeing. The tonic had wrought joy in the old plug.

"There, you see? The salvation of man and beast!" Zimmer announced. "Buy now, because it may be a long while before I return with my fine company of performers. Buy now, because the sand is flowing through the hourglass, and in the morning, we'll be on our way, heading to the next town, to give them all an opportunity to enjoy Doctor Zimmer's famous tonic. Buy it now, to relieve the sorrows of dogs, babies, horses, mules, goats, women, schoolteachers, merchants, law officers, and hoboes. And to improve all night-time activities."

Well, I had to credit Zimmer. Those cowboys ponied up in a long line and began to shell out their hard-won cash for the tonic, instead of blowing it all in the saloons. But then an old gray cowboy reached into his britches to buy some of that joy juice, and came up empty.

"I been robbed," he bawled. "Some light-fingered whelp's made off with my purse."

That sure caused a commotion, and pretty quick, most of them cowboys were digging into their pants, making sure they still had their cash and private parts, and a mess more came up missing their pay.

"Some little whelp's gone and dug into my pants," yelled another son of the prairies.

I didn't doubt what started the crime wave, and headed straight for them little orphan buggers, who were racing around there. I'd had my eye on one, a carrot-topped little punk that looked mean as a lobo wolf, and pretty fast. I snatched him by the collar and flattened him on the dirt, and dug into his pockets, and sure enough, there were three purses he'd purloined while working that crowd, and by then Rusty had snagged another punk, this one with blond hair and a big jaw, and he proved to be another light-finger genius, with four more cowboy purses stuffed into his pants.

Them cowboys saw all this, and snared the rest of the orphan boys, and dug into their pockets, while the McCoys sounded like a pair of squawking pigeons. But the cowboys came up empty. Rusty and me, we'd got the two pickpocket punks. It took a while to get the purses back to the right owners, and have them count up the cash, but in time we got it all squared away, and they got back into line and bought Zimmer's Miracle Elixir for their horses and their own carcasses. There wasn't a man or woman or merchant around there that wasn't checking purses and wallets and pockets. And the orphans, male and female, vamoosed over to their own camp and hid out. I sure wondered how the adoptions would go the next morning on the courthouse steps.

Zimmer, he got his performers to strike up a tune, and pretty soon the next acts, the fat woman in the grass skirt and the fiddler, were hard at it in the yellow light of the lamps.

Rusty and me, we dragged those two little hooligans off to the jail and set them down for some serious palavering.

"You first," I said to the red-haired one. "What's your name?"

"My name's whatever you choose. I don't got none, but Mickey'll do. And if you want me to fess up, you got it. I've been snatching purses since I was six, and I almost got enough to retire tonight."

"You with that orphan train?"

"Them turds. I almost got away tonight."

I turned to the blond kid. "And you?"

"Call me the Big Finn, copper. I got more loot than Mickey, and I'll whip his ass any time."

"Where'd you grow up?"

"Nowhere. Hell's Kitchen, but you're too dumb to figure that out."

"Where's that?"

"I don't know. That's where this orphan outfit

caught me. Regular snare net come down over me and they hauled me off to here."

"You want to spend the rest of your days behind them bars there?"

"Beats getting adopted and having to work my ass off for a living. That's what it is, pal, slave labor. That's a slave labor outfit, selling us out."

"You been doing this all your life?"

"Since I was old enough to spit, copper."

"You want to go to the pen, the big brick pile, and hammer rocks the rest of your life?"

"Hey, they feed me, right?"

"Yeah," said Mickey, "toss us in there. We get three squares a day, and don't have to lift a finger."

"You got any remorse?" Rusty asked.

"What's that? If it's worth something, I'll cop some for you."

"I stole a bottle of Zimmer's dope," the Finn said. "It's in the wagon. I'm gonna go on a wild ride."

"Where'd you get that?"

"Right off the table when that big galoot was making change."

"What do you want to be when you're grown?" I asked.

"A paid clock-stopper. Them gents get a hunnert dollars for each hit. I'd kill me half a dozen and live like a king. I'd slit their throats; beats having a gun."

By this time, I sure was wondering what to do, and the most likely thing to do was get these two out of town as fast as the orphan train would take them. I couldn't think of anything that would slow this pair down.

That's when King Glad walked in. King, and his sister, Queen, ran the Admiral Ranch outside of Doubtful. They were both tough customers, as hard as any people got, but straight shooters. Their pa had started the outfit, and employed the roughest hands in Puma County, including Big Nose George, Spitting Sam, Smiley Thistlethwaite, and Alvin Ream. They sure weren't men to mess with, and most of them were recruited from jails back East. The Glads ran their outfit with an iron hand, and smart people left them alone.

"I heard about the ruckus," King said. "These the little punks?"

"Yep, this here's Mickey, from off the streets somewhere, and this one's the Big Finn, from Hell's Kitchen, wherever that is."

"Perfect," said King. "They're just what I'm looking for."

"Naw, they're not. This one here, he wants to stay in jail because he gets meals and no work; this other, he wants to be a contract killer and live easy."

Glad turned to the punks. "My kind of fellers," he said. "I'll indenture you tomorrow, when they have that hoedown on the courthouse steps."

"You know what you're doing, King?"

He grinned at me. "Sheriff, I run the best reform

school in Wyoming. A few days with Spitting Sam and Big Nose, and they'll be the best little workers around."

"I'm locking them up tonight, King."

"I'll buy them tomorrow," he said.

Not a bad deal, I thought. Except maybe the brats would steal the ranch.

Chapter Nine

I went to see the medicine show off at dawn. I sort of hated it; I hadn't figured out who nipped the boodle in Zimmer's cash box, and I hadn't come up with any suspects at all. I wished I could set it right with him.

I wrestled myself out of my cot at Belle's Boarding House and got out there just as the outfit was fixing to roll.

"You, is it?" Zimmer asked. "You found some hard-won and easily nipped greenbacks that belong to me?"

"No, sir, I reckon I ain't. Not even a likely prospect. But I want an address so if I get aholt of it, I can return it."

Zimmer sighed. "I have none, sir. I hope to retire in Ames, Iowa, when I've advanced a few more years, but my home, sir, is only a soft and seductive dream."

The feller sounded sort of lonely. It would be a strange sort to run around the country peddling tonic all his life, with nary a hope of home and family. But the world's full of odd sorts like him.

"You do well here?"

"I would have, but for the theft, sheriff."

"You sure it ain't someone in your company? Someone who wouldn't be noticed sawing away on the padlock in your wagon?"

"It pains me to see you drive a wedge between my loyal people and me, sir. No, they are stalwarts. The visit to Doubtful was a wash, thanks to some culprit in your town. And now, sir, we make haste for Douglas, up north a way."

Those people were standing around, waiting for me to let them loose, it seemed, so I waved them off. For once the professor wasn't in his tux and tails. He wore soft britches and shirt, and was going to drive one wagon.

The whole business seemed unfinished to me, but that's how it is with law enforcement. Stuff goes unresolved. For all I knew, this outfit pilfered all the stuff from George Waller's mercantile, and maybe more.

"One last word, sheriff. People in towns like yours are suspicious of road shows like mine. There's a sentiment that we're knaves and thieves, and that we're not to be trusted. I've run into it time after time. So, if there's doubt in your bosom, feel free to examine any of my wagons and their entire contents. Maybe that'll put to rest whatever's bothering you; whatever brought you here at dawn to look us over."

"Well, Rusty, he had a look already, so you just get on the road now. I got a mess of new troubles, including an orphan sale this morning."

Zimmer smiled. "I'll sell you a bottle of tonic for fifty cents, sheriff."

"Naw, my ma always said, don't use crutches if you can walk upright."

Zimmer nodded, clambered up to the high seat, cracked the lines over the croups of the draft horses, and the wagons slowly rumbled away. I watched them go, itchy and unhappy, wanting to finish business that lay hanging over me. It put me in a bad mood, and when I thought of those little hooligans I had to go back to the jail and feed, I got myself into an even badder mood. Them two, unless King Glad could square them up, was headed for a hanging, and likely their own.

The brats were awake and rattling the cage. When they saw me, one reached for the slop bucket, and I knew what he had in mind.

"Toss that at me, boy, and I'll put a bullet between your eyes."

That was a slight exaggeration, but it stopped him. Some people, force is the only language they understand. He edged away from the bucket, which stank from the night's accumulation.

"You want some chow, do you?"

"Nah, we don't need nothing," Big Finn said. "When do we get outta here?"

"When I feel like it," I said. "You have to get on the good side of me to get what you want."

"There ain't a good side to you," Mickey said.

"You got that right, boy."

Rusty, he came in with two bowls of oatmeal from Barney's Beanery, eyed the prisoners, smiled, and looked over the logbook.

"Hey, we want the feed," Mickey said.

"You gotta work for it," I said.

"Doing what?"

"Talk," I said. "Tell me all about yourselves and you'll get your chow."

"Talk?"

"You bet. Start yakking away. Talking's hard work. Who are you? Where'd you grow up? Who are your folks? Who are your grandparents? What do you want from life? You got any dreams? You talk, work hard at it, you eat. You slack off, you don't eat."

Mickey and Big Finn stared at each other.

"I got nothing to say," Big Finn said.

"Tell me everything that's happened to you."

That met with silence. Rusty, he was enjoying this.

Neither boy talked. The clock ticked. The boys eyed the cold gruel malevolently. I finally relented, handed them their gruel and spoons, and they wolfed it down.

"You want to talk now?" I asked.

"We ain't worth it," Mickey said.

"You're worth it. I want to know all about you."

"Yeah, so you can throw the book at us."

"Think whatever you want. Mostly I want to know who you are. I like me, but you don't like you, is that it?"

I wasn't making any headway with the bone-heads, but pretty quick I was rescued by King Glad. He had indenture papers in hand, had made the legal arrangements with the McCoys and the Children's Aid Society, and had come to collect.

"They're in there. You got some help? You'll need it," I said.

"Big Nose George and Spitting Sam are right outside."

"Yours, then," I said. I unlocked the cell, while the brats watched, ready to bolt, but King Glad and I, we collared the pair and marched them to the door. Out there, Big Nose and Spitting Sam were waiting with two empty saddle horses.

"Who's this? What's he want?" Big Finn asked me.

"This is King Glad. He's got a big ranch near here. He's indentured you both."

"Indentured? What's that?"

King Glad replied, "I get to stuff food into you

until age sixteen, and you get to work for me and learn a trade until age sixteen."

"Work? I ain't gonna let you sucker me into that."

"That's fine. I won't let you sucker me into feeding you."

"We'll bust loose, sucker."

"I'm sure you'll try. Want to try right now?"

The hooligans, they eyed me, and eyed Glad, and eyed the door, and allowed themselves to be taken outside, where the horses were waiting, along with Glad's men.

"You're gonna hafta drag us," Mickey said, and immediately quit walking. So we dragged him down to the street, and then dragged Big Finn, too.

"This here's Big Nose George, he's my ramrod, and this here's Spitting Sam, he's my second ramrod. You boys climb up on those nags and we'll head out," King said.

Instead, Mickey and Big Finn sat down in the street. "Make us," snapped Finn.

Them hooligans never knew what landed on 'em. Next they knew, they was stretched out in the horse dung, on their bellies, and the ramrods were sitting atop them. Spitting Sam, he dug into his pockets for some chaw, put a pinch into his mouth, and handed the tin to Big Nose, who took some and slid it under his tongue.

"You had breakfast yet, Sam?" Big Nose George asked. "A rank horse sure makes me hungry."

"We'll send someone to the Beanery," Spitting Sam said. "I got a bucking bronc here."

"Hey, let us up," Big Finn snapped.

"You hear something, Sam?" asked Big Nose.

"Just the crickets," Big Nose said.

By then they were attracting spectators, who eyed the odd scene with displeasure.

"Don't mistreat the orphans," said one lady. "This is inhumane."

"I only weigh a hundred forty, ma'am," Spitting Sam said. "You mind telling me how I'm mistreating these fine young fellers? We're just having a chew and some breakfast."

She glared at him and stalked off. The rest of them folks, they just snickered.

This whole deal lasted about ten minutes, and then Big Finn said, "Yeah, let me up and I'll get on that plug."

"Glad you see it our way, boy," Spitting Sam said, and stood up. Big Finn rose slowly, and climbed on the horse, looking whipped. Mickey followed. In moments, King Glad and his foremen were riding out of Doubtful with their two indentured boys riding slow plugs just in case they got notions. Neither of them had ever been on a nag before, so the ride out to the ranch was going to be an education that would improve their butts. I didn't think it was going to go well for anyone, but I'm not very good at predicting the future. The thing that clawed at me was a hope that the little hooligans were treated fair, and not hurt. They didn't know any better, and I hope King Glad understood that.

It was time for the adoptions, and there were a mess of people, mostly curiosity-seekers, milling around the courthouse steps. I was glad most of them didn't see what was going on in front of my office. I saw the McCoys over there, with their orphan wagons, and all them young folks looking for a new ma and pa, or maybe not wanting one. But they didn't have any say in it, being minors, so most of them were just standing there, half afraid, awaiting their fate. The girls were quieter and sadder; the boys were scared, anyone could see that. The girls didn't look at the people, but stared at the clay, while the boys, some looked bitter, and others were real hopeful, and wondering if they were entering heaven, or hell, or no place at all.

The McCoys, they got their show on the road right at ten.

"All right, friends, these are orphaned youngsters, or children without shelter, and they're looking for good homes and parents who'll protect them, love them, raise them up straight and true, and welcome them into their families. You've had a chance to look them over. They're all sound of limb and teeth, and speak English. They'll all be good little workers and affectionate and obedient young people. So, let's begin. Are there takers?"

Chapter Ten

This here time when a lot of desperate and lonely little tykes was about to be adopted sort of got me riled up. That's because some of those people circling around the children wasn't interested in giving the children a home; they was looking for slave labor that'd cost nothing but food and clothing.

It was real quiet there on the courthouse steps. Adults, they were staring at the children, and the children, they were fidgeting and looking like they wanted to be somewhere else. The first to take the plunge was Reuben Cork, who had a mule-raising outfit on the west edge of Puma County. He was a skinny old bachelor, fifty maybe, graying, with cruel eyes and a good eye for horseflesh. He had two ex-jailbirds working for him, mostly to stay out of sight from the rest of the world. I knew him only because he drove his wagon to town to load up now and then, and he brought in mules to sell or ship out.

He was eyeing a skinny kid named Thomas, who looked about as bitter as Reuben, and wasn't enjoying being poked and prodded.

"You like animals, boy?" he asked.

Thomas shrugged.

"You ever seen a mule before?"

Thomas didn't answer. There was no need.

"I'll take him," Reuben said to the McCoys. "Indenture him. He's what, nine? I get him for seven years, do I?"

Seven years of hell, I thought. If the kid didn't run away first. Kit Carson, he was indentured and he ran away and stayed in the mountains, and they never did catch him. The kid, he didn't move, and looked defeated. He was not the master of his fate. He was a minor. If it wasn't Reuben Cork, it might have been a fine fate for a city kid, getting out into the healthy fresh air a lot. But Reuben, he was as likely to use a buggy whip on the boy as he was on a mule.

There wasn't any law against it, and all I could do was watch the transaction, as Cork laid out a few dollars, put his X on some papers because he couldn't read or write, and motion the boy to climb onto a saddle mule and that was that.

People were watching, and not with gladness as far as I could see.

Next a girl named Sally got plucked up by Alphonse Smythe, the postmaster, and his wife, Mabel. They poked and prodded, and checked teeth, and then anted up the ten dollars, and signed some papers.

"Well, Sally, welcome to our house. We've always wanted a daughter, and now we have you, my dear. I think you'll find your life with us a happy one, if you're not lazy or contrary," Mabel said.

Sally clutched the few rags she owned, and quietly followed the Smythes up the street. They lived a few blocks away. People watched them, mostly wondering privately how it'd work out, and whether anyone would be happy with the adoption. At least Sally got adopted. That was a good sign.

A couple of boys got indentured to Puma County ranchers. That looked fair enough to me. Most ranchers were bachelors, and they had a bunkhouse full of drovers, and were always short of help. It wasn't home, and those boys wouldn't see much of any mother around, but they'd be sheltered and fed and probably come out fine at age sixteen.

The number of orphans was dwindling some, but there were plenty remaining, and they looked more and more miserable. Then the town's banker, Hubert Sanders, and his wife, Delphinium, showed up and immediately closed in on a frightened girl in pigtails, who wore a blue shift and ancient shoes that didn't fit her little feet.

"We've been looking at you, my dear," Delphinium said. "What would you think about joining our family?"

"I don't know, ma'am."

"We have high standards, my dear. You would need to meet them and live respectably, and strive for a well rounded nature."

The girl stared.

"What's your name, my dear?"

The girl glanced at the McCoys, but said nothing.

"She's Minerva," Mrs. McCoy said. "We found her wandering free along the Hudson River, half-starved. She said her name is Minny, and that's all we know."

"How old are you, Minny?" Mrs. Sanders asked.

The girl shrugged.

"We think about eight, and that's what we put in the Children's Aid Society form."

"Are you respectable?" Mrs. Sanders asked.

The girl shrugged.

"We're looking for a good little worker, who can do scullery tasks, and soon can cook and clean. Would you like to do that?"

Minerva shrugged.

"Who was your mother, dear?"

"Big and fat," the girl said.

"What happened to her?"

"She . . . The coppers took her away."

Mrs. Sanders pursed her lips. "You have much to overcome. Would you like to overcome these things?"

The girl shrugged again.

The Sanders retreated a way, and I watched them engage in a lot of whispered talk, and then they returned to the courthouse steps.

"We'll adopt her, and hope for the best," Delphinium said. "I do need a maid."

Soon Hubert had filled out the adoption forms, a copy to go into the courthouse, and a copy for themselves, and a copy for the society.

"You want to come with us now, Minny? We'll have you set a nice table, and serve us a nice lunch, and then you'll have your first meal with your new parents. You'll call me Mrs. Sanders, and call him Mr. Sanders. Never 'Mother' or 'Father.' We won't allow that."

Minny shrugged, but let Mrs. Sanders catch her hand, and I watched them walk toward the north side, where the town's biggest homes and richest folks seemed to collect. I sure didn't know whether I'd like to be adopted by people like that. I guess mostly I'd just want a ma and a pa smiling at me.

An hour or so dragged by, and no more children got took. The rest of them, they were doomed to go on, shuffling from place to place until someone adopted them. Maybe the ones that got taken were the lucky ones, even though they faced a hard life, and not much more caring than when they were orphaned or found running the streets.

The McCoys were looking about ready to pack up and leave. McCoy was talking to Turk, our liveryman, about buying one wagon and team, since they didn't need three outfits anymore.

That's when I noticed the kid, standing in misery, tears leaking down his face. He was freckled, with cauliflower ears, auburn haired, and miserable.

"Hey, kid, what's wrong?" I asked, knowing what was wrong.

"I just want a mom," he said.

"Well, maybe next town, you'll find just the right mom."

He shook his head. "Three towns already. No one wants me."

"What's your name, sonny?"

"Riley."

"How'd you get that name?"

"My ma."

"Somebody's gonna want a Riley. That's a good name for a boy. I wish I was a Riley."

"You gonna arrest me?"

"For what?"

"For crying. They always say stop that."

"Feller can cry all he wants, in my book. My ma always used to say, a boy without a good ma is a boy who'll never grow up."

"I'm slow," Riley said. "That's why."

"Boy, join the club. My ma, she always called me slow."

"How'd you get to be sheriff?"

"I'm fast with, ah, my hands."

"Like shooting?"

"That's what got me my job. But I don't shoot people if I can help it. I just try to keep people safe here."

"I wish you could find a ma for me," Riley said.

I spotted Rusty, and just then an idea popped into my head.

"Hey, Riley, would you settle for a pa?"

He looked alarmed. "I never had one."

"Pa's are as fine as ma's are, and can teach you a trade when you get old enough."

"They can?"

"You bet. Now I'm going to go talk to that feller over there for a minute, but I'll be back, hear me?"

I got aholt of Rusty, who was looking over the orphans and the crowd.

"Hey, seeing as how you didn't get any Ukrainian brides, how about a kid?"

Rusty, he was as shocked as if I had fired him on the spot, almost as shocked as if I had just given him a two-dollar raise.

"Who wants a kid?"

"Well, you were fixing to start a family, weren't you? Siamese twins? You were even going to rebuild the outhouse for them, so they could sit together. Seems to me, Rusty, if you're willing to rebuild your outhouse, you could adopt a boy. That there boy, Riley, he's just aching to belong to someone, and that someone's gonna be you."

"What did I do to earn this?"

"I'm just trying to console you, Rusty, because you lost your two Ukrainian twins."

"I'm not fit for fathering."

"Then try mothering."

"How'm I gonna raise a kid? I got to be on duty."

"The whole sheriff outfit, we'll pitch in. We'll get the kid raised. We'll make Riley a deputy soon as he can handle a gun."

"Well, don't this beat all," Rusty said. "I been snookered."

That was Rusty's way of saying yes, so we headed back to Riley, who was still leaking tears.

"Boy, here's a pa—if you want him?"

Riley, he stared upward, looked deep into Rusty's face, and then ran to Rusty and threw his arms around my deputy and hung on hard as he could.

Rusty, it was all he could do to hide what was crawling over his face.

Twenty minutes later, the Puma County sheriff's office had a new little deputy, with a star on his chest and two or three daddies.

Chapter Eleven

No sooner had the orphan train pulled out, with a lot of tears flowing, than a mess of cowboys landed in my office. They were all waving bottles of Dr. Zimmer's Miracle Healing Tonic, and they weren't happy.

"This stuff, it don't work," one said. "I get more mule kick out of a one-bit shot of red-eye. I tried a little dose, and a big dose, and it ain't worth the glass it came in."

"Yeah, that's right! This stuff, it's creek water, and maybe a little flavoring. And to think I paid good money for it. I got suckered," yelled another.

Rusty chimed in. "I tried a swallow or two, and I sure didn't get any trip to heaven out of it. Looks to me like I got stuck with nothing."

That was the verdict of eight cowboys and Rusty. Me, I had that sip when the show rolled in and it flattened me, and started the world spinning round and round and round. They carried me home.

"It sure kicked me in the butt," I said. "But I was up there, on that little stage, before he really got to peddling the stuff. Looks like there's more than one version of the tonic."

"Looks to me like we got took," Rusty said. "Anyone who bought the stuff late in the game, we all got suckered."

I sampled one of the bottles, and sure enough, it was creek water, pure as the mountain snow, with maybe a dash of wintergreen flavor in it. It sure didn't start any tincture of opium buzzing in my innards.

"You want to do something about it?" I asked Rusty.

"You bet I do," he said. "I'm sorely put out. He seemed like a nice fellow, polite and cheerful, all the while he was cheating us."

"We can catch up and squeeze some cash out of him," I said. "I want a hundred, and I'll refund it to anyone that's got a complaint."

"You gonna bring him in and charge him?"

"Hell, no. The sooner he's out of here, the better off we are. Puma County's gonna see the last of him. But we'll collect enough to make good on everything."

"So what do we do with our new deputy here?" Rusty asked.

Sure enough, there was Riley, about one hour into being Rusty's boy, staring real sad at us.

"Saddle up, Rusty. And bring a spare rifle as well as your side arms. I'll meet you at Turk's in a bit."

I knew exactly what I was going to do with Riley. "Come along, boy. We're going to meet my land-lady, Belle."

I was soon hammering on her apartment door. She had about half of the first floor of her board-inghouse, and rented out the rest. She opened, eyed Riley, and started to shut the door.

"Sheriff, I'm not in the orphan racket."

"I ain't selling orphans, Belle. You get to be a mama for a few hours if you lay down a straight flush."

"This is Rusty's kid. I've heard about it about six times now."

"This is Riley. Hey, kid, meet your ma. At least, she'll be working at it. She's never been a ma in her life and she's itching to try."

Belle eyed him. "Hey, kid, you got cauliflower ears and slope shoulders."

Riley, he started to cloud up some.

"That's how I like 'em," Belle bawled. "Hand-some man shows up at my door, I kick ass. Come on in, kid, and face the music."

Riley edged into the warm apartment.

"Hey, Riley, see that white jug with the orange butterflies on it? Go over there and lift the cover and take two. That's the cookie jar."

Fearfully, Riley did as he was told, extracted two sugary cookies, and waited.

"Eat, dammit," Belle said.

Riley ate. Then he started crying.

"Hey, kid, come here," Belle bawled.

She took Riley into her ample arms, and held him quietly until the storm had passed.

"We got to go, Belle. I'll pick him up in a few hours," I said.

I headed for Turk's Livery Barn, where I kept the most recent version of Critter in a box stall. Rusty was waiting, saddled up and ready to go. Turk watched malevolently.

"You always show up when I'm getting Critter saddled up to get on board," I said.

Turk grinned. "I'm one of them types likes to watch a good hanging, especially after the drop, when the neck's busted and life's leaking out."

That was Turk for you.

I began by talking to Critter, but not opening the stall door.

"Critter, we're going for a nice little trip. You get bored in here, dontcha? Well, we're going to see some country, and you'll see some nice spring grass coming up."

Critter cut loose with a rear hoof. It hit the door so squarely the whole barn shuddered.

"I see you're feeling just fine, Critter," I said, opening the door a crack.

Both rear hooves smacked the door, driving it all the way open.

I used the moment to slide in beside him, and

slip a bridle over his snout. He let me do it before the Big Squeeze. That was always his second maneuver. He began to push me into the side of the stall, harder and harder, intending to reduce me to bag of broken bones.

I kneed him in his gut, which didn't do much; he just increased the pressure, until my ribs hurt and my pelvis, it was ready to crack in two. So I grabbed both his ears and twisted until he quit. He bucked, but the door was open and he had nothing to kick, so he settled for a big old fart, and I knew I'd caught him once again.

"That's my day's entertainment," Turk said. "It's downhill from here."

Critter, he let me brush him, throw on a blanket, tighten a saddle over his quivering back, and lead him out into the aisle. We were ready to roll.

"He's getting tame," Rusty said.

"You could sell him to the French," Turk said.

"Now what's that supposed to mean?"

"French like horse meat."

That's how it went at Turk's barn.

It was already well along so we trotted north on the trail to Douglas, hoping to catch up with the medicine show at its first camp, nine or ten miles out of Doubtful. It sure was a fine spring day, with all the dandelions blooming and all.

Critter got into the spirit of things, and I had to hold him down to a jog. Critter is notional. He wanted to get into a race with Rusty's old plug, but

I resisted. He got so fractious I finally reined him into a tight circle until he got the message, and then we made good time. The soil was soft and there were ruts where the medicine wagons had passed through.

We raised the medicine camp late in the day. The outfit was parked at a spring with a few cottonwoods around it, a place that had been much used as a stop. They watched us ride in, and I saw a couple of teamsters slip toward their wagon, where a couple of scatterguns lay.

They were cooking dinner in a tin stove.

"They know how to live, Rusty. My ma always used to say, you want to eat soon, don't cook over an open fire. That takes forever to cook up something."

"You ma had the smarts in the family," Rusty said.

I didn't take that kindly, but I was too busy keeping an eye on that bunch to make any objections. My ma, she always said I was slow but made up for it. I'm real quick with my hands, especially when it comes to hefting a revolver.

Zimmer, he had good vision, and he saw who was coming, and raised one of his white hands. We rode in, saw the meal cooking, and saw the bunch eyeing us warily. This wasn't gonna be easy.

"Why, sheriff, I imagine you have good news for us. You've recovered the stolen funds."

"Well, no, professor, that ain't it. Truth to tell, we

got lots of complaints. This stuff you're peddling, it don't do nothing."

"Why, every bottle is bonded and certified, sir."

"Rusty, gimme that bottle. Professor, you uncork this and sip for a little. In fact, you drink her down, entire."

"Why, I couldn't do that, sir. I've taken the Temperance Oath. Lips that touch whiskey will never touch mine. Now, as it happens, the tonic is ten percent spirits, so I mustn't touch the bottle you generously offer me."

"Drink her up."

"That would offend my person, sir. We must never violate another's person."

"Drink her up."

Zimmer stared upward at me. Critter was getting restless. He prefers to kill anything in his way rather than stand still.

"We got about fifty people, they say there's nothing but creek water and wintergreen flavoring in these here bottles, so I said I'd fetch a refund. You willing to pay up, or do I have to haul you back to Doubtful?"

"Now, don't be hasty. There might have been a few bottles that were accidentally filled without the usual certified quality check, sheriff. What I'll do is send you back with ten bottles of simon-pure, double-checked, certified tonic, guaranteed to produce instant joy and sublime peace in the partaker."

"Nope, Zimmer, it's cash on the barrelhead, or

I take you back and charge the whole outfit, and let the judge decide what to do with you."

I was keeping an eye on them two teamsters, who doubled as musicians in the show. They were hovering around one wagon, ready to reach for their persuaders.

"You fellers, you come over here," I said.

They dallied a moment, and then did, and I felt like Rusty and me, we were in a little more control. Rusty, he hung back, his hands not far from his artillery.

"I'm taking a hundred dollars back, to cover any claim against you. Someone brings me a bottle of worthless creek water, he gets two dollars. If there's cash left over, it'll be kept for you when you come back."

"This is certainly arbitrary and hasty,"

"That's what my ma always said," I told him. "Call me Hasty Pickens."

"I will give you fifty. We sold most of those at a discount, one dollar for two bottles."

That was true. "All right, you give me fifty," I said.

I got down off Critter, who eyed the bunch with laid-back ears and clacked his teeth. Critter was worth about two deputies in a deal like this.

Zimmer looked forlorn. Like surrendering greenbacks was the same as an attack of gout, or getting a cold enema.

We entered the dark confines of the bunk-wagon and he headed for the strongbox, which had a fresh padlock on it.

"You got you a new padlock," I said.

"Oh, it's one I remembered I had."

He unlocked the padlock, and lifted the hinged top. There were greenbacks galore in there, and something else, the sawed-off padlock.

"Whatcha keeping that, for?" I asked.

"Oh, it might be repaired."

He swiftly counted out fifty dollars in gummy greenbacks, and I stuffed them into my britches.

"I want a receipt," he said.

That stumped me. I could manage it, but it would take some doing to print it out and put my X on it.

"Hey, Rusty, come on in," I yelled.

Rusty, he didn't like it, leaving that outfit to do whatever it wanted. But I thought it'd be all right. I had the cash to repay the gypped cowboys.

Rusty, he looks around in there, and sees things I didn't.

"Cotton that's the stuff that vanished from George Waller's Mercantile," he said.

But by then it was too late. Just outside, there were them teamsters, each with a scattergun aiming our way. Zimmer had somehow slid away, so it was bird hunters against two partridges.

Chapter Twelve

Well, my ma, she always said there's no better way to win an argument than to poke a twelve-gauge shotgun at some offender's mouth. It stops all conversation. And that went double this time, with one of them scatterguns aimed at me, and one at Rusty.

The main thing to do is keep your trap shut, so me, I just went real silent and wondered if this was the last sight I'd see.

But the professor didn't see it that way. He seemed actually melancholic about it.

"This poses a sad dilemma, with no good way out," he said.

"We're going the way of the carrier pigeons," I said. The last of those little buggers got shot away years before. They once sold by the wagon load for pig feed.

"No, not quite. If we were to feed you to the

magpies and crows, my friends, the Zimmer Medicine Show would come to an immediate halt, and every person here would flee for his life. For there would be no doubt about who to pursue, and every lawman in several states would do so, with great zest. So, you see, I would face not only the departure of these friends, and my show, but also my way of life, which I cherish."

This feller was sure talking like someone in some college somewhere.

"On the other hand, if we let you go, we face tribulations, and another set of sorrows that would doom the show, and maybe remove our liberty from us. We all cherish our liberty, sheriff. We wouldn't belong to a traveling road show if we were content not to roam, and live within the bleak confines of some dreary city."

This sure was getting long-winded. I wished he'd just wind it up.

"Well, friend sheriff, what are we going to do? I am awash in sadness."

"Pass around some of your joy juice, the real McCoy."

"Ah, sheriff, your humor excels, but your practicality is wanting."

"You got any ideas?" I asked.

"Perhaps a trade-off?"

"What for what?"

"Well, suppose we return the goods that someone accidentally left in our wagon, and suppose we pay fifty dollars to the customers who bought our elixir after the tincture of opium ran out, and suppose we pay a twenty-dollar fine for disorderly conduct, and then you go on your way and we go on our way."

"I got to uphold the law. Feller does something wrong, I got to haul him in so he will face the music."

"Ah, but we are remedying the wrong, you see?"

Rusty, he was tired of staring into the bore of a twelve-gauge, and was getting itchy. "I'm tired of this. I'm getting on my nag and heading back to Doubtful, and if you're gonna shoot me, then do it."

"Hold up, deputy. Drop your gun belt, and you can go. Adam, take the rifle from the sheath."

I wondered if Rusty had something in mind, but he was playing his cards close to his vest, so I didn't even get a look at his face. He got onto the livery stable nag, and eased out of camp.

"And you, sheriff?"

"Me, I'm sworn to uphold the law, so I'm stuck here until I uphold her. Professor, this here Mexican roulette ain't gonna change. Either you kill me or I take you in. Your choice."

Zimmer, he sure did look sad. But finally he caved in. "Adam, saddle a horse. I'll take my medicine."

That sure was something. I collected Critter, and Zimmer cleaned out his cache of money, and climbed onto a horse that a teamster saddled for him. They gave me Rusty's artillery to take to him, and two burlap sacks full of purloined items from the Mercantile. But the shotgun on me never wavered.

"I'll be back whenever Fate decrees it," Zimmer told them. "Enjoy the night."

We rode under a starry sky, making swift time back to Doubtful, and pulled in around nine or ten. Rusty wasn't far ahead of me, and was rounding up a posse when we got in. George Waller was pleased to get his stuff back. Or most of it. What came back didn't quite match what got took. There were some ladies' items that had gone missing, but I wasn't inclined to ride out there and check what was on the southern parts of the grass skirt woman cooking dinner out there.

I pitched the medicine man into a cell, which he eyed dolefully, and sat down with a pencil to draw up some charges, while Rusty went to find Hanging Judge Earwig, and get him to open up court.

There wasn't any attorney around to prosecute, but maybe it wouldn't matter if Zimmer pleaded guilty and coughed up a fine.

Old Earwig, with his gray muttonchops and bald head, he even looked like a judge most of the time, when he was sober. He grumbled and whined, and didn't like being dragooned from his evening toddy, but I got real serious about it and said if he didn't show up fast, the county might have the expense of trying about seven members of the troupe, and feeding them, until it all was settled. So he finally hiked over to the courthouse in his bedroom slippers, lit up some lamps, and waited for me to bring in the current prize locked up in one of the two iron cells.

Zimmer, he looked even more doleful than Earwig. He was wearing his travel clothing, not his show outfit, and looked like a little dumpling rather than some fancy impresario. The courtroom filled up real quick; Doubtful can't hold a secret five minutes, and word sure got around, and pretty quick half the cowboys in the bars filled the room, and most of 'em had tonic bottles they wanted to exchange for some greenbacks.

By midnight we got the show on the road. Earwig banged his gavel.

"Will the culprit rise?"

I prodded Zimmer, and he stood up.

"You fixing to make restitution and pay a little fine?"

"If Your Honor so declares," Zimmer said, woefully.

"You gonna declare yourself guilty as hell?"

Zimmer sighed and groaned and passed a little gas, and nodded.

"You got to say it," the judge said.

"Guilty as hell, your lordship."

"All right, now we can divide the spoils," Earwig said. "Now what are you guilty of?"

"Watering the tonic, your lordship."

"How many bottles?"

"I got one," yelled a cowboy.

In all, there were twenty-three cowboys in there wanting their money back.

"That's forty-six simoleons," Earwig said.

"But your lordship, they bought these for less than list price."

"Don't matter. It's two dollars a bottle they'll be getting. Now what else are you confessing to?"

"I confess to nothing, sir. But I am willing to make whole any injured party, within reason, of course, even if I am entirely innocent of all wrong-doing."

Hanging Judge Earwig turned to me. "What are the rest of his sins, sheriff?"

"George Waller's store lost some merchandise, most of which was recovered when I raided the medicine show this evening. But he's still missing some, ah, ladies' unmentionables, mostly because of the difficulty of making a proper search for the items."

"What say you, Zimmer?"

"Well, your lordship, I am bereft of knowledge of all that, but believe she may have been making repairs to her grass skirts. When we are short of grass, on the road, my animals feed on her grass skirts, and modesty requires that she have something else on. So my surmise, sir, is that she was simply attempting to protect her womanly modesty."

"She ain't all that modest on the stage, Your Honor," I said. "Fact is, these here unmentionables got took from the Mercantile, and still abide somewhere north of Doubtful, on the south side of the woman in question."

Hanging Judge Earwig discovered the merchant in the crowd. "Waller, what are they worth?"

"A dollar and ninety-eight cents, sir."

"All right, I'll fine this feller two dollars for the undies, and he can pay you when we're done, or spend thirty days contemplating the error of his ways, guest of Sheriff Pickens. That suit you, Cotton?"

"Your Honor, I've always disliked the name Cotton, but Pickens is all right. That was my ma's joke, calling me Cotton Pickens, but it's been an anvil around my neck all my days."

Hanging Judge Earwig banged his gavel. "You're out of order, sheriff. This court refuses to listen to tales of woe. We're after justice and money here, not tales of misery."

I must have really ticked him off. He hardly ever assails me, but once he banged his gavel on my head when I got cranked up in the witness chair.

"Sheriff, has the culprit agreed to be fined?"

"Yes, sir, and I propose twenty-five dollars for the whole lot. I could run up a list of offenses, but as long as Zimmer here is agreeable, it'd save Puma County a mess of work and bookkeeping if he just paid up."

Hanging Judge Earwig leaned over the bench. "You good for twenty-five more?"

"Your lordship, that would be hard indeed on my loyal staff, who would not be paid if I am forced to squander such a sum as this. They have toiled and the toilers deserve their reward. But if you would lower the bar, so to speak, to seven dollars and a half, I could see my way clear to satisfy all the demands of justice in Puma County, Wyoming."

"That suit you, sheriff?"

"Well, my ma used to say, don't niggle the details."

"Done. This culprit is nailed for seven and four bits, and will trade twenty-six bottles for two dollars each, and will pay George Waller two dollars for some vanishing undies. Does that do it?"

"Your lordship," said Zimmer, "this has been a pleasant and momentous occasion, and upon the conclusion of these transactions, I wish to treat you to a libation at the Last Chance Saloon, and will stand a drink for the rest of the gents here, in this progressive and noble city, blossoming in Wyoming."

"Zimmer, if you've got a bottle of the real McCoy on you, I'll buy it as a parting gesture."

"I just happen to have one, your lordship."

Well, quick as greased lightning, the cowboys turned in bottles and got two bucks, and Waller got his two, and the county got its fine, and we headed to the east end of town, where the Last Chance Saloon stood, and Sammy Upward was soon pouring the staff of life, and pocketing all the loose change that was floating around.

Zimmer and Hanging Judge Earwig, they got themselves a fine corner table and set about toasting each other, and swearing eternal friendship, and talking about future business partnerships. Me and Rusty, we went back to Belle's to pick up Riley, who was asleep on the couch, with Belle waiting and watching in her stuffed chair, an odd smile on her weary face.

Chapter Thirteen

Next morning, I ran into the Puma County supervisor, Reggie Thimble, and he started jacking my hand like it was a pump handle.

"Well, ya finally caught some crook," he said. "I was beginning to think the county didn't have a lick of crime in it."

I sure didn't know how to answer that one. So I told him the straight truth of it. "Reggie, it wasn't me. Zimmer simply caught himself. He got himself into a real bind. If he'd shot me and Rusty, especially for a few miserable dollars, his show would be ruined and all them people in his outfit would scatter, so he decided to face the music and come in and get her done with."

"That's not what I heard, sheriff. I heard you singlehandedly captured the whole evil lot and brought the ringleader back here to face Hanging Judge Earwig."

"I hope Rusty ain't spreading that manure," I said.

"What's this about him adopting one of those orphans?"

"Riley, yes. He nabbed one, mostly because I pushed him into it."

"Well, fire him. You can't have a deputy running around with some orphan he latched on to."

"We got it all fixed," I said. "Belle, she's gone catawampus over Riley, and Rusty's gonna have a tough time prying the boy loose now and then and give him a little fathering."

"Belle must have lost her marbles," he said.

Reggie didn't much care for it, but he didn't have any real comeback, so he just growled a little about duty and loyalty, and don't charge the county for anything not right, and stalked off.

But all that morning people came roaring up to me, shaking my worn-out paw, telling me how glad they were that I'd brought the archfiend Zimmer to justice. I spent the whole day, pretty near, explaining that Zimmer marched himself in, that all I did was stare into the muzzles of two twelve-gauge shotguns loaded with buckshot, and I didn't much care for it, preferring that someone else stare into the muzzle of my shotgun. But that's life for you. They made a hero out of me when all I did was try to stay alive.

At least, I wasn't likely to be fired. Most days around Doubtful, some leading citizen or official was planning to evict me from my sheriff office, and hire someone more to his liking. But I managed to hang on, one way or another. My ma, she always said just live a day at a time and keep plenty of corncobs in the outhouse. I prefer cobs to Monkey Ward.

A couple of days later, a tent preacher came in, with his own show, and set up shop right where Zimmer's Medicine Show was playing. He put up a big, worn canvas tent, and a sort of pulpit he could thump with his fish-belly-white fist. This feller, Mr. Elwood Grosbeak, was a sinner-collector. And a first-rate pulpit-thumper. He was looking for sinners under every bush, and inviting them over there to hear all about their evil ways. And he had other things to talk about, too. He said the world would come to an end in three weeks, before sundown, May 28, and woe to anyone who wasn't real prepared. That sure scared the crap out of a lot of people. But there wasn't any crime emanating from his shabby tent, so I just stayed away. Mostly, he was attracting townspeople; I hardly saw a cowboy off the ranches anywhere near. They were too busy looking after the crop of new calves to worry much about the world coming to a halt or all the elect sailing off into the wild blue heavens, never to be seen again, at least on earth.

But a teamster down from Douglas told me that Grosbeak had been pulpit-thumping up there, only he told those folks the world would end on May 1, and that had scared the dickens out of some. Come May 1, and Grosbeak was nowhere to be found there, and the sun came up and the sun set, and all that happened was that Grosbeak had cleaned Douglas out of about four hundred smackerinos, before rolling into Doubtful. Now that was an interesting scenario. I sort of wondered if it was proper to scare the hell out of people and run off with their cash.

I asked Lawyer Stokes, who doubled as county attorney when Puma County gave him some business, whether Grosbeak was doing stuff illegal, and he said let it alone. So Grosbeak was holding his camp meetings each night, and hammering his pulpit, and saying May 28 would be the last day on earth, and scaring the crap out of some folks around town. And they were filling the collection plate he passed around in the middle of all this.

I don't take kindly to it when I see the people I try to protect being fleeced, and I didn't have much of any notion how to slow it all down. I stopped in at the Last Chance Saloon, where my friend Sammy Upward tended bar, and asked him what he planned on Doomsday and he said he was handing out free drink tokens that could be redeemed the evening of May 28 after the sun set. I told him about the deal up in Douglas, and he enjoyed that, and said he'd maybe he'd invite Grosbeak to the Last Chance to deliver his tub-thumper right there in the barroom and entertain the cowboys at the finish line.

Well, the whole idea just bloomed, and pretty

soon all the saloons in Doubtful were passing out
tokens for a free drink on May 28, after the sun
set. Barney's Beanery got into the act, and offered
a free breakfast to survivors who were still around
the next morning. And then the madams got into
it, and offered one free lay between midnight,
May 28, and dawn the next morning. That sure
got the cowboys interested.

Rusty, he had the best idea. "We'll offer one
free hanging at dawn, May 29, and we'll announce
a ballot to select who gets to enjoy the noose. Now
if the world ends on the twenty-eighth, like the
man says, no one gets hanged."

"I got an idea, Rusty. We'll invite Grosbeak to
stand there with a noose. If he's right, he'll vanish
into the heavens. If he's wrong, he gets hanged."

Rusty, he whistled. That was Rusty for you. When
he really liked an idea he didn't just say so, he
whistled. And now he was chirping like a canary.

That sure was good scheme, all right, and I was
wondering how I could pull it off. There were a
few in Doubtful that deserved a good hanging,
but getting them up on the gallows would take
some doing. Getting Grosbeak up there might be
a lot easier. If he believed in what he was talking
about, he'd gladly step right into that noose.

I decided it was time for a little talk with Elwood
Grosbeak. He was staying at the Wyoming Hotel.
It wasn't much of a hotel, but it was the best in

town. His six staff people, I don't know where they were staying. There were rooms for rent over most of the saloons and likely they were parked in those. Sometimes a visitor could arrange a room at a cathouse.

They had a little dining room there in the hotel, so I tried that first. Sure enough, he was sipping java in there. He was a formidable man, with hair slicked back with goose grease, and a fresh white shirt, and one of them huge cravats, red paisley, and a pretty nice suit coat and britches with a knife-edged crease in them. He didn't wear that stuff in his revival tent, but just a plain gray outfit. The first thing you notice about him was his eyes, big and burning, and lips that seemed to mock even when he wasn't saying a word.

He saw my star, and rose at once.

"Sheriff Pickens, I believe?"

"You got her," I said.

"What brings you to my table, sir?"

"Well, there's fellas around here who don't think the world's coming to an end, and they're getting up some entertainments to celebrate when nothing happens and it's time for a drink."

"There's always skeptics," he said. "I deal with them regularly. They don't grasp my message, which is not that the earth beneath our feet will vanish, but that the elect will be whisked away to their eternal reward. One hour you see us; the next hour, we're gone. The lady down the street has vanished. The man you called a friend is departed. The child you watched grow up has gone away. That's the story, sir, and that's what I preach."

"Yeah, well, are you going up the golden stairs?"

"If I am called, and I am sure I will be, I'll be gone. Do not look for me on this earth on May the twenty-ninth, because I will have joined the angels, and the seraphim and cherubim."

"What are those? You got me there."

"It's too long to explain, sir, but call them helpers. They are assistants in heaven."

"Well, Rusty—he's my deputy—he has a dandy idea. The sheriff office wants to join this here party, and what we propose is to put up our gallows, and have you volunteer for a hanging on May 29. Comes dawn and you're still around, you get hanged. If you got taken up, there's only an empty noose dangling in the sunlight of a new day."

That sure took him aback. He stared with the smoldering eyes until I felt a little put upon.

"You mock me, you mock my beliefs, you laugh at the powers above."

"Well, my ma used to say, put your money where your mouth is. She also used to say, actions speak louder than words. You want to prove your beliefs? You can come to the necktie party. Your very own party."

"I am speechless, Pickens, absolutely speechless. You should be recalled or fired."

"Seems like a good idea, this gallows party. Think what it gets you. A mess of believers everywhere."

"You forget, sir, I am a man of the cloth, a prophet, and you must not insult anyone who's been set apart to bring people the good word."

"Well, they tell me up in Douglas, you collected about four hundred dollars before you vamoosed in the night, on May 1, and now you're here, and the greenbacks are landing in your collection plate, and I just was sort of wondering if we'd see your outfit on May twenty-ninth. If you all are on your way to heaven, I guess you'd leave behind your tent and wagon, right?"

"Are you done insulting me, sir?"

"I ain't very good at it, but I am getting better, the longer I'm in office. Maybe, before they fire me, as they're fixing to do, I'll get real good at insulting. You could prime me a little."

Grosbeak, he just glared, and seemed to shut me out. It was like he was no longer sitting there eating his eggs Benedict, oatmeal, tea, toast, and strips of bacon.

"Where are you going next?" I asked.

"What business is it of yours, sheriff?"

That was as much a confession as I needed, I figured.

"I got a saloonkeeper friend, Sammy Upward. He says he's having a big End of the World fiesta the afternoon of May 29, and you're invited. He's giving out tokens for free drinks, and says you'll get one. He says you can come on in, and spread the word, and he's got a whole bar full of cowboys waiting to listen to the whole mess. You gonna come on in?"

But Grosbeak, he was methodically eating and ignoring me, and I saw how it'd go.

"You got many of the town's ladies going out there in the afternoons? They laying out a lot of quarters and dollars to get themselves in good shape to be hauled up to heaven?"

He ignored me.

"If I was you, Reverend, I'd think about giving all that cash back, or donating it to the Doubtful Chamber of Commerce. They could always use a little infusion."

"You are a crass materialist, sheriff. You haven't the faintest notion of spiritual matters."

"Well, my ma used to say, being spiritual is what you do if there's money left over after paying your bills. I'm thinking, Mr. Grosbeak, maybe you should pull up stakes and get on the road, just as fast as you can, before someone gets his neck broke."

Chapter Fourteen

Well, that done her. By the time I got out to the campsite, them doomers—that's a good word for it—the doomers were packed up, and fixing to go. They didn't even bother to come over and complain. They just loaded up that ragged canvas, heaped stuff in another white wagon, and drove off. I noticed that Elwood Grosbeak, he had a fine ebony carriage, but the rest, a ragamuffin bunch, mostly walked beside the mule-drawn whitewashed wagons.

"You heading for greener pastures?" I asked Grosbeak.

"You won't escape your reward," he said, mysteriously.

And then they rolled away, on the rutted road to Laramie, and I thought them nice folks in Laramie were in for it. I watched them go, with a lot of cash they'd extracted from the good citizens of Doubtful. Grosbeak had been passing the collection plate for days, and scaring people half to death for days, and it probably didn't matter to him if he skipped town a little ahead of Judgment Day.

Me, I was feeling pretty good about getting rid of a parasite, and thought I should ask the Puma County supervisors for a raise. But then I spotted something I didn't want to see. A whole mess of Doubtful women, every last one of them dressed in white, head to toe, even white hats and veils, was coming along on Wyoming Street, and they each had a little basket, and I knew what was in them baskets. It would be money. Greenbacks, mostly, but silver and gold and jewelry, and I knew what all this was about, and I knew what would have happened if Grosbeak had hung around instead of skedaddling.

So I just waited there on that field, with all the spring grass trampled down by crowds, and the sun playing tag with puffball clouds. I just waited there for them ladies in white, all dressed to the nines, a mess of fevered-up ladies, fixing to pave their way through the pearly gates.

They flooded onto the flat, saw that it was empty, and there was only Sheriff Pickens standing there. They hadn't expected it. Finally, one of them approached me. It was Reggie Thimble's third wife, Matilda, and she was the leader of this bunch.

"Mr. Grosbeak has departed?"

"Yes, ma'am."

"And was he taken up to heaven?"

"No, ma'am, he got out of Doubtful just as fast as he could pack up and vamoose."

She contemplated that for a moment. She was flanked now by a few more of the ladies, making a kind of white wall in front of me. I knew them. They were merchants' wives mostly, and a few maiden girls waiting for handsome and promising husbands. They sure looked nice, all gussied up in white, with flowery white hats.

"Did you cause the reverend to depart, Mr. Pickens?"

"No, ma'am, but I did make a suggestion or two. I said, says I, Mr. Grosbeak, you should put your money where your mouth is. I'll set up the gallows and you step right up and put that noose over your neck, and if you ain't taken up by the morning of the twenty-ninth, says I, we'll drop the trap. He sure got offended, and said I was disrespectful, and I said a person's got to act on his beliefs, and if he wasn't gonna get took up to heaven, then a hanging wouldn't scare him."

Well, Matilda, she stared and stared at me. "You have desecrated the sacred," she said.

"Well, ma'am, this outfit come down from Douglas, and I got word of how it went up there. Grosbeak, he says, doomsday is May 1, and he preaches it and gets them folks upset and they heap cash into his collection plates, and then the last hours of April, he and his bunch, they harness up and pull out, with a mess of greenbacks in their britches. And they come here, but now the date's May twenty-eight."

"The devil has you by the throat," she said.

Me, I wasn't going to argue with her. There's no arguing that stuff. You either accept it or not, but facts don't matter none. I rubbed my Adam's apple a little to let her know it was still operating.

She turned to the whole mess of ladies, and she says, "This doesn't matter. The Hour of Salvation is at hand, even if this evil man has driven away our prophet. His words are true, and we must have faith. So, instead of cleansing ourselves of all worldly possessions by placing our baskets on his table, we will proceed to the creek, and we will divest ourselves of everything, and then await the chariot of fire that will carry us upwards into glory."

"Ma'am, don't do that. Give it to the Sheriff Department Retirement Fund, or whatever."

"You are loathsome, Mr. Pickens. We will toss our filthy lucre away, and prepare for the end and the beginning."

"Ma'am, you been bamboozled, you been conned. You just take all that stuff to Barney's Beanery and get a good bowl of oatmeal, and then go on home to your folks."

"You are unspeakable." She turned to the rest. "Come with me," she said.

She led that whole lot of nice ladies in snowy outfits toward the creek. I had an awful sinking feeling in my gut, but what they did with their own money was up to them, and there wasn't anything I could do about it.

The ladies, looking determined and soulful, like Joan of Arc about to be burned as the English heaped kindling at her feet, these sainted women began their stately walk toward Doubtful's dubious creek, which supplied water to the town, and removed other stuff. There, in a sort of grassy glade, the women collected along the bank, and plunged into mournful silence.

About then, Cronk, the faro dealer at Mrs. Gladstone's Sampling Room, he waited on the path with questions written all over him. He was out early, enjoying his morning dog-turd-colored cigar and the fresh air.

"What are they up to?" he asked.

"They are surrendering all their worldly possessions, to prepare themselves to be swept up to the pearly gates in a day or two."

"What's in them baskets, sheriff?"

"You leave that stuff alone, hear me? I'll fetch their husbands in a bit, and try to get it all back."

"Any law keeping me from trying?" Cronk asked.

"My law," I said. "That stuff, it's going back just as quick as I can get it back."

Cronk, he just smiled and puffed away, enjoying the May weather.

Them women in white, they all raised their arms and waved at the sky, and then one by one they approached the creek and tumbled the contents of their baskets into the purling water. I sure saw a mess of green fluttering down. Them greenbacks, they didn't sink, like the coin, but simply floated leisurely down the creek, which ran behind Saloon Row and the red-light district, and toward the Platte River, miles distant.

Cronk sighed. But he knew if he dove for that loot, I'd buffalo him so fast he wouldn't know what bounced off his skull.

One by one, the shining white-clad women tilted their baskets over the creek, and loosened a small fortune. I thought I saw a few gold rings and maybe a gemstone or two in there, but I was standing a respectful distance. And Cronk, he was smiling to beat the band, just sucking on his fat cigar and smiling, like he had a sudden vision of retirement from the shadowy confines of the saloon where he ran his faro game month after month.

There sure was a mess of greenbacks bobbing downstream. I shoulda guessed what came next. When the bills got near Denver Sally's place, a mess of women in wrappers and kimonos came boiling out. It was early for them gals to be up; their business day didn't start for some while, but somehow they got wind of this, and were heading toward the creek to harvest the crop floating in.

Cronk, he was just standing there with an arched brow. "They get in, but you keep me out?" he asked.

He sure enough had a point. "You steer clear of these women here," I said.

Cronk, he went running toward the belles of the evening, planning to improve the day's take from his faro game. Me, I stood on the riverbank and watched them beautiful women in the whitest white unload their worldly goods, and when it was over, I headed for the courthouse. I wanted to talk to the supervisor, Reggie Thimble, about what his latest wife was up to, and suggest that maybe a few husbands around Doubtful might want to reclaim what was left of the family stash.

Them women, they were in no hurry, and headed back to the empty field for some reason, probably to await their ascent into the cloudless skies. That suited me fine. I'd get the husbands out to the creek and let them collect what they could, and hope they wouldn't get into a brawl doing it.

I started into town, but I was too late. There were ladies of the evening, and barkeeps, and even a few old drunks down there on the creek, scooping up the loot, much of which shone brightly in the pebbled bottom of the creek. Oh, there'd be some unhappy households this eve, and there'd be a few people from the sporting district who would be partying.

I spotted Rusty on the way, and told him about it, and Rusty just shook his head. "I think you got your tail in a crack," he said.

So I clambered the courthouse stairs and found Reggie Thimble sharing a little toddy with Silas Jones, who owned the Blue Rib Ranch, way west of Doubtful.

"Sheriff?" Thimble asked, looking annoyed.

"Need a private word, sir."

"There's nothing needs saying that old Silas shouldn't hear," he said.

"It's about Mrs. Thimble, sir."

"Well, fire away, then."

I sure didn't know how to tell him that his wife had led a group of white-clad women and they had pitched the family fortunes into the creek. I tried that one about three times before I just settled down and narrated the whole shebang, while Thimble glared at me, accusation in his face.

"So you've driven the tent preacher out, is that it?"

"He packed up and left, yes, after I let him know I was keeping an eye on him."

"You telling people in Doubtful what their religion's gotta be, is that it?"

"Nope, just warning a crook to behave."

Thimble, he glared at me. That was his wife leading the pack of white-gowned ladies, and now the family fortunes were at least somewhat depleted. I wondered what he was thinking.

"I reckon we can recover some of the cash from all those sports in the district," I said. "Rusty and me, we'll have to turn 'em upside down and shake the bills and coin outta their pockets, and they'll whine some."

Thimble shook his head. "Finders keepers," he said. "If you hadn't chased the tent preacher out of town, there'd be no trouble."

"If the world doesn't come to an end on May 28."

"If it didn't, he'd simply return the items the next day with his apologies," Thimble said. "But now it's lost. A small fortune changed hands because of your boneheaded behavior. Looks like we'll have to fire you, Pickens. This time you've gone too far."

Chapter Fifteen

Spitting Sam, one of the Admiral Ranch foremen, raced up to my office on a lathered horse, and came roaring in.

"Trouble, sheriff. Them two hooligans, they've got King and Queen captive and are holding out for ten grand."

"Captive? Ten grand?"

"The orphans. Little bastards. They worked this out. There's guns all over the ranch, and they collected a bunch, and caught King Glad and his sister at dawn, and are holding them in the big house, and say they want ten grand and a getaway buggy, and if they don't get the dough, they'll kill King and Queen."

"There ain't ten thousand dollars in Puma County."

"You gonna come out there or what?" Spitting Sam said, an edge to him.

"I should bring the money? Get Hubert Sanders to give it to me?"

"It's your baby, Pickens. We can't even get near the big house. For city brats, they know how to shoot."

"And the Glads, you're sure they're in there, alive?"

"No, we're not sure of anything."

"Those boys, Mickey and Big Finn, they set any deadlines?"

"It's a mess, and if you're going to help us, come on out. If not, the hell with you. We'll play it our way."

"They gonna let me talk to them?"

"Who knows? City boys don't hear a damned thing."

"I'll get Critter and we'll go talk."

I buckled on my gun belt, and checked the loads, and collected a scattergun. If I had to use any of those, I'd lose. And the Glads would be history. Spitting Sam nodded, and I knew he'd meet me at Turk's where I'd get Critter saddled if I was lucky, and get my leg broke by a flying hoof if I wasn't.

I sure didn't know about this one. If it came to shooting, the owners of the Admiral ranch, brother and sister, would soon be buried, and maybe a bunch more of us, and likely those two little rug rats that came in with the orphan train.

I wasn't going to take any ransom money; not

now. I wasn't even sure Sanders would open his vault to pay the ransom without collateral. There was a mess of things to think about, and I'd have a little time riding out there to look at some possibilities. But I knew the first thing was not to underestimate those two orphan hooligans, who knew more angles than a hungry carpenter.

Spitting Sam and Turk stood silently in the barn, waiting for me to back Critter into the aisle and get him ready for travel. I got a piece of two-by-four and went up to that bronc and told him I'd whack him between the ears, because I was in a hurry, and he'd better behave.

"I'm a horse whisperer," I said to Turk.

Turk smirked.

"More like a horse shouter," Spitting Sam said.

But Critter was listening. He tried one ritual kick when I opened the stall door, and then backed out like he was wanting to be sociable. In quick time, I got him bridled and saddled.

"That's a record," said Turk. "It's a bad omen."

"He'll throw you into prickly pear," Spitting Sam said.

But we trotted out smartly, and when Critter was warmed, we slid into a rocking chair lope that would get us there in half an hour. Critter, he was enjoying it more than Sam's Roman-nosed nag.

"There's been some shots fired?" I asked.

"Oh, yeah. They was trying out the hardware, and keeping us well away from the house. We tried circling around and breaking in the rear door, but they were wise to it."

"They got food and water and plenty of rounds?"

"Who knows? But them punks is smart, and they got it all schemed out."

"What's the deal?"

"Bring money, put a buggy in front of the house, one with a top on it, and they'll take a hostage and kill him if they're followed."

"Can we put some slow plugs in harness?"

"No, they want two saddle horses, too, tied behind the buggy."

"They know where they're going?"

"Hell, no. They're off the waterfront. They don't know which way is north."

"They talk about their destination?"

"They don't know Wyoming from Florida. They just want to beat it with ten grand in their satchel."

"You think they'd kill the Glads?"

"At their age, it's easier than if they were older. Yes, and Queen first, just to show off a little."

"You say they're off the waterfront? In New York?"

"Yeah, that's a good place for little thugs like that to learn the racket, stealing, slipping past ship's pursers, cleaning out freight warehouses, latching on to food. The longshoremen, they don't care. Half of them were waterfront rats before they hired on."

"Is one of those boys a little softer than the other? Listen to reason?"

"Mickey, he's sometimes friendly. Big Finn, that one was born in hell and is going back soon."

We covered ground, loping for a while, then jogging, then loping. In time, we raised the Admiral Ranch, which rested solemnly in a green basin, with mountains rising to the west, and a good creek watering their beef.

"Well, my ma used to say, treat a child like an adult, and he'll toe the mark."

Spitting Sam, he just shook his head.

The Big House, as the impressive building was called, rose in majesty, well apart from the barns, bunkhouse, corrals, and sheds that one usually saw on cattle outfits.

There sure wasn't any straw bosses or drovers standing around in the open. The windows of the house were dark, and revealed no sign of anyone peering out, but I didn't doubt that we were being watched.

"You figure out what we should do?" Sam asked.

"Go talk," I said. "I can't make any sense of it until I talk to them."

"It's hard for you to make sense of anything, Pickens," said Big Nose George.

I've heard that talk all my life, and don't bother to get mad anymore.

"Get me a white flag on a stick," I said.

George, he sort of smiled. "Chicken, ain't ya? If

I had my druthers, I'd surround that Big House and charge, and leave two bodies behind. We got a dozen tough drovers here, and a few more."

"You got big balls, George. Me, I do things my way."

"Give him his chance, Big Nose," said Spitting Sam. "Then when he gets shot up, or can't budge those little turds, we'll do it our way."

They wasn't saying much about trying to keep their two employers alive. The fastest way to put the two Glads into their graves was to start a war.

"Long as you're all bulletproof, including the Glads, your plan might work fine," I said.

Spitting Sam headed for the bunkhouse, running across an open area where he might take a hit, and pretty quick came back with a sheet on a stick. The thing was all sheet and no stick, but it'd do. I took it, told them kibitzers to watch their topknots, and headed out, waving that monster sheet on the dinky stick, like I was flagging a horse race. I got maybe twenty paces toward the Big House and a shot hit the dirt ahead of me.

"Stop there, sheriff."

"Who am I talking to?"

"Pair of no-good orphans."

"All right, you gotta tell me what you want, and who's in there."

"We got them Glads, and we'll put enough bullets in them so they bleed out in thirty seconds if you don't follow what we ask."

"Who are you, boy?"

"Who do you think?"

"I bet you're Big Finn, right?"

There was wild laughter in the window. Neither boy was visible. They were back in the shadows, like good smart gunmen. They'd been around the block, seems like.

"Finn, you gotta show me the Glads, one by one. I got to see if they're alive and well. If you don't show them, then we figure you've got no hostages, and it's all over for you when we come in."

That met with a mess of silence.

"We ain't gonna show them to you," Big Finn finally yelled. "Keep you guessing."

"How about you cutting them loose and sending them here to me? That way, you get out of the house alive."

"Sucker bait," the kiddo yelled.

"How about you sending me Queen Glad, and keeping women out of it? Just let her out the front door."

"She's worse than he is. We ain't gonna spring her or him, sheriff."

"How come she's worse?"

"She's hell on earth, sheriff."

"Then cut her loose."

"What do ya think I am, King Arthur?"

That stumped me. I'd never heard of that dude. "Hey, kiddo, ask her what she's queen of. I always wanted to know. Her old man named her. His name was Admiral. That was his real name."

"Cut the crap, sheriff. You get us a horse and buggy with a top on it, two saddled horses, and ten thousand clams. You got until sundown."

"Where you going, boy?"

"San Francisco."

"When you gonna get out there, boy?"

"We ain't saying."

"What'll you do when you get there?"

All I heard was a bunch of cackling. For two boys about eleven or twelve, they sure could snicker away. This sure was shaping into something strange. Two half-grown boys threatening a ranch family, and wanting to clean out the till, and the pair of them ready to shoot. That's what troubled me. Boys that age could be good shots, and know all about handling a weapon, but they didn't have an ounce of judgment. My ma always used to say, men ain't men until they're thirty. That means I barely made the grade myself, and I was more than twice the age of those two brats threatening to bring tragedy down on a lot of good people.

"Big Finn, how are you gonna stuff food into you when it runs out there?"

"We'll eat Queen Glad first, sheriff, then King, and then you."

"That don't work, boy. You kill off the hostages, there's nothing holding us back, and once we come in, boy, you can measure your life in minutes."

For a response, he fired another shot. It plowed the earth twenty feet away. Sure was making me itchy.

"Hey, I want to talk with Mickey," I said. "He's dumber than you."

"Dumber? I heard you was the dumbest lawman in Wyoming."

"Well, my ma agrees with you, boy, but how are you gonna get out of there?"

"Ten grand, in small bills, sheriff, by sundown. Plus that buggy and fast saddle horses, and you get to be our insurance."

"There isn't that much cash in the bank, boy."

"That's the deal, sheriff. Bring the dollars or Queen's gonna croak."

"Show me she's alive, boy, and King, too."

That met with a mess of cackling again, and I was getting real itchy. I hadn't seen hide nor hair of the Glads, and no one else had, either, and it sure made a feller wonder what was going on inside that ranch house.

I backed away, slowly, and they let me. I had some calculating to do, and fast.

Chapter Sixteen

About then, Rusty showed up on a livery barn plug.

"Belle baked this apple pie," he said. "She says it's for King and Queen Glad, and don't let those little skunks have it."

That was Belle for you. Full of kindness and not a bit practical.

"Hubert Sanders, he says it can't be done. There's not that much cash in Wyoming, and it'd have to come up from Denver. And he'd want a transfer of deed from the Glads. He can't just empty his bank without some collateral."

"That ain't good news, Rusty. Those hooligans may be boys, but they're grown up enough to kill, and fixing to do it if they don't get what they want."

"Would fake money do it?"

"They're smart boys, Rusty."

It was a waiting game, but the brats controlled

the clock. I grabbed that white flag and waved it, and made sure it was being seen in the late afternoon light, and then headed for the house with the pie.

"Stop there, sheriff. You got money?"

"Nope, I got a real good apple pie sent by folks in town for the Glads. You want to deliver it to them?"

"No, they can starve," yelled one of them. It sounded like Big Finn.

"Hey, put it on the porch. I want it," Mickey yelled.

"You can't have it. It was baked for the Glads, not you," I said.

"Then I'll steal it," Mickey said. "Put it on the porch or get shot."

"And we need water. Bring us a bucket," Big Finn yelled.

The pump was in the yard.

"Toss out a pail and I'll fill it," I said. This was getting better and better, and I was getting closer and closer to that building.

Pretty quick, a tin pail got pitched out the door and landed on the porch steps, so I eased forward, a little prickly because boys with guns get careless, but pretty soon I got the pail.

"Where's that pie?" Mickey yelled. The door was open and he was back in the shadows somewhere.

"That apple pie, best pie I ever ate, it's for King and Queen Glad, boy. You don't get one thin slice."

"Where's the money?"

"We're getting things together, Mickey."

"Get some water."

I took the pail, hung it over the pump spout, and began jacking the pump, and pretty soon water gushed out. They had good water on the Admiral Ranch. Some places, people had to drink gyp water or some such, but the Glads struck it rich, with real fine water. I carried the bucket back to the porch, while a mess of stinking cowboys were watching from around the bunkhouse and sheds. I was wondering where they'd have me put the water.

"Stop there, sheriff," Big Finn said. "Set down the pail, drop your gun belt, and carry the water to the door, and set it in shadow inside the door, and then back out. Then go get the pie and bring it."

I hefted the tin pail up the porch steps, across the porch, and into the doorway. The sun was blinding me so I couldn't see in, but they were there, and they were armed. I backed off, started to pick up my gun belt, and a shot stopped me. I eased back to the sheds, got the fragrant apple pie from Rusty, and headed in again.

It was the same routine. "Leave the pie in the door, sheriff," Big Finn said.

"Naw, I'm gonna deliver it to King and Queen. If they don't want it, I'll give it to you," I said.

"Are you crazy? Put that pie down."

"You heard me, boy. Belle baked this for the Glads, not for you."

My eyes were getting used to the gloom. I could see them in there. Both had drawn revolvers. And the Glads weren't around.

"You get Queen, and I'll give the pie to her," I said. "It's for her. Otherwise, I'll just take it back, and we'll slice it up at the bunkhouse."

That was an odd thing. Those two, they didn't know what to do. If it was gold or greenbacks I was carrying, they'd kill for it. But they didn't know what to do with a nice, fresh, still-warm apple pie. So I just stood there, thinking they'd make a move one way or another. I could maybe throw it at one and rush the other, but that was probably hare-brained, so I just waited to see how it'd play out.

"Get the old lady," Mickey said. "When she gets it, we've got it."

Queen, she was hardly thirty, but these were boys talking.

Big Finn, he knew what the muzzle of a gun does to a man. He smirked. "Set it down on the floor, you big dope." He waved a .45-caliber muzzle at me.

I set that pie down, real gentle, on the plank floor.

"Hey, you dope, pick up that bucket of water and carry it to the kitchen," Big Finn said. He waved his revolver at me to make the point. So I eased slowly back to the front door, lifted the pail, lifted it by the bail with one hand and the bottom of the bucket with the other, but he didn't notice.

Mickey, he shoved his revolver into his belt, and

grabbed the pie off the floor, which suited me fine. I headed for the kitchen at the back, under Big Finn's gaze, but as I passed him, I twisted a little and tossed that water into his smirky face. He coughed, fired a wild shot, and I booted him in the gut, swerved, and caught Mickey in the middle with my fist, and caught the pie midair. That was for Queen, and she was going to get it. I set it down as Big Finn was coming up for air, and trying to aim. I whanged his hand, and the revolver went flying, caught Mickey as he pulled his out of his belt, and knocked him halfway to China, and then kicked him as he sailed backwards, and then I landed on Big Finn, and that was when King Glad landed on Mickey, and the party was over.

"Got some pie for Queen," I said. "Belle, she baked it special."

That's when Queen appeared in the stairwell, and smiled. "That's very kind of her, Cotton. Give her our regards. You want a piece?"

"In a little bit, Queen. We got us a couple of wiggling tadpoles here got to get tied down."

King, he collected the revolvers, unloaded them, and set them on the kitchen counter.

We heard shouting out there. They'd heard the shot Big Finn fired. But no one dared rush the Big House. Not yet.

Queen found a couple of lariats, and we hogtied them two little hooligans so tight they couldn't even stand up without help.

I edged to the front door, wary of a wild shot. "Come on in and have some apple pie," I yelled.

Ten guys were waving revolvers out there. They stared.

"Put away the guns, boys," I said, still sticking to shadows. Those cowboys were a wild crowd, a little loose with the trigger finger.

"Rusty, you come on ahead," I said.

"You got a couple of Ukrainian beauties for me?"

"Nope, just a pair of dimwits," I said.

Sure enough, Rusty edged up the porch steps first, wary of a trap, but in one glance he took in the brats tied tight, King, who was guarding them, and Queen slicing apple pie into thin pieces since it would have to stretch to a dozen men.

"It was the pie that done it," I said. "We got to thank Belle for it."

Big Finn, he was wrestling with the rope, flopping like a just-hooked bass, but Mickey, he just stared at us, his dream over, and maybe any hope of a good life, too—if he ever dreamed of one. You never know. Sometimes the worst feller around wants nothing but a little cottage with rambling roses and a sweetheart and a job as a janitor somewhere.

About then, all the Admiral Ranch hands rolled in, including Spitting Sam and Big Nose George. It took them a single glance to see the two waterfront hooligans hogtied, and Queen dishing out skinny slivers of apple pie.

"Best pie I ever ate," I said. It was gone in two bites.

"You tell that Belle, she's gotta bake one for me," said Spitting Sam.

We all had a slice, and a lot of smiling was occurring without permission.

"What are we gonna do with these little turds?" Spitting Sam asked.

"Use 'em for bait," Big Nose said.

"Like minnow bait?"

"Yeah, over at Lake Booger, where the alligators live, we could troll these two, with a hook in their mouths, and wait for a bite."

"What's the biggest gator you ever caught that way?" King Glad asked.

"Well, that's the ten-footer we skinned out."

"And what were you trolling with?"

"A little pig with a hook in his snout. That gator, he swum up from under, and downed the pig in one gulp, and the hook got set in his jaw and we reeled him in."

"I'd rather hang!" yelled Big Finn.

"I want to go to San Francisco," Mickey said.

"That'll be up to Hanging Judge Earwig," I said.

"Hanging judge?"

"He's even more famous than Hanging Judge Parker down in the Indian Territory. He packs 'em off to the gallows about as fast as the hangman can wind a new noose."

"And we're going to be taken to him?"

"That's what I'm planning on. You any objections?"

"They can't hang boys," Big Finn yelled. "It ain't allowed."

"Well, Judge Earwig prefers to hang girls," I said. "But he doesn't exempt boys."

"He'd hang a billy goat if he caught the goat stealing," King Glad said.

"He favors schoolmarms," Queen said. "He's hanged more teachers than anyone I ever heard of."

"He hanged a preacher a few times," Big Nose said.

"Well, they deserve it," Rusty said. "We pretty near hanged one a few weeks ago, but he skedaddled just ahead of the noose."

The pair of hooligans, they looked a little pale around the gills.

"All right, Rusty, let's pack up this pair and lock them up. We'll fetch Hanging Judge Earwig, list a few dozen charges, and let them plead."

"I didn't do nothing," Big Finn yelled.

"That's what I used to tell my ma when I got caught red-handed," I said.

Chapter Seventeen

We started for Doubtful along about sunset, with the two hooligans on Admiral Ranch nags. A posse of cowboys, led by Spitting Sam, came along, to make sure that the sheriff, a man of dubious competence as far as they were concerned, delivered the goods to the county jail. I didn't mind. I always enjoy good company. Rusty, he'd been sort of sour ever since he lost his Ukrainian bride and her Siamese twin. I'd be sour, too, losing two brides for the price of one.

So we headed along the lonesome road as twilight gained on us, but we didn't get far before the hooligans started bickering.

Big Finn started it. "I told ya not to go for that apple pie," he snapped at Mickey. "Look what it got us."

"Aw, shut up," Mickey replied. "It was your idea. You pushed me into it."

"It woulda worked if you knew what you're doing. I just got stuck with an idiot."

"As if you knew what you were doing," Mickey replied. "You can't plan your way out of a flour sack."

"I'll kill you, soon as we get out of this. You and your apple pie. If you hadn't took that pie, and let him come after me, we'd be on our way to Frisco, with ten grand."

"Go ahead and try it," Mickey said. "You can't even button your fly."

"Just you wait," Big Finn growled. "Man, you're already six feet under."

"You fellers sound real friendly," I said. "How long you known each other?"

"We met in the orphan wagon. Now look at us."

"Yep, you're up to your buns in trouble, boy."

Big Finn stared. "There ain't no jail holds me, sheriff."

"We'll see what Hanging Judge Earwig says about that," I said.

"Shut your traps," Rusty said.

"Let 'em talk," I said. "It's all sort of a confession, I figure. These here poor little orphan boys got snookered by an apple pie. It's pretty entertaining."

Spitting Sam added his two bits. "I'll pay my respects to Miss Belle. Her pies are better than a load of buckshot."

"She'll appreciate it, Sam," I said.

We made town about at full dark. Word had gotten ahead of us, and a lot of citizens were lining Wyoming Avenue to see the little criminals we were dragging in. I saw Belle standing there with Riley in tow, and lifted my sweaty Stetson as we passed.

Burtell, who was manning my office, spotted us. "Hanging Judge Earwig's in court and waiting for you," he yelled.

"You mean we don't have to lock up these suckers?"

"He's already got the lamps lit and his gavel in hand."

That gavel was a menace. He sits above the witness stand, and if he doesn't like the witness, he knocks him on the head with the gavel. It sure gets their attention.

"Guess we go to the courthouse for the trial," I said. "We're going to need a few charges."

"He'll supply them," Rusty said. "He's real good with charges. And besides, we heard them confess as we rode into town."

That sounded about right. We were collecting a crowd, following along as we steered our tired nags to the courthouse. Critter, he laid his ears back and threatened to kill anyone who got within six feet, but the whole town knew about Critter; he'd injured half of them, so they got real respectful around my horse. I'd gotten offers for him from dog food makers, but I turned them all down. This was my second Critter. Critter, he was a part of me, and reflected my true self. If anyone wanted to know who I was, I always said I'm the human version of Critter. That little observation, it always did wonders, and maybe that's why I'm still sheriff, even if half the town doesn't like it.

We got to the courthouse. A light was burning upstairs in the courtroom. I nodded to Rusty. We both knew what was about to happen. Those two hooligans were going to dismount and run for it. Spitting Sam eyed me, and nodded slightly. He knew. The rest of them cowboys knew.

Sure enough, the hooligans dropped like rocks off their nags, but I caught Big Finn by his shirt, and Spitting Sam clobbered Mickey and then picked him up out of a manure pile, and everything went fine.

"Just you wait, sheriff," Big Finn growled. "It ain't over. We're orphans."

He was expecting special treatment, orphans being deprived and oppressed, but he wasn't familiar with Hanging Judge Earwig, who specialized in oppressing the helpless and hopeless. He was a man after my own heart. I always said it was Earwig: He was the secret of law and order in Puma County. The only people he didn't jail or hang were the rich and privileged, the ones he played cutthroat poker with on Wednesday nights. My ma, she always said Earwig was worth two or three sheriffs and a dozen deputies when it came to making the county peaceful and safe.

The judge was waiting. And so were the privileged, who crammed the seats.

He was in an affable mood, had his hair slicked back and his beard combed. He always was happiest when he could impose the maximum, and this time the sky was the limit. He watched the two hooligans enter, his bushy brows climbing up his forehead. When everyone was in, he rapped his gavel, which sounded like a shotgun blast.

"Court's open for business," he said. "Are these the little crooks?"

"These are the pair, Your Honor," I said.

"And what are the charges, sheriff?"

"You name them, Your Honor."

He turned to the boys, who were finally looking subdued. "What are your names, eh?"

The boys mumbled their names.

"Mickey who?"

"How the hell should I know?" Mickey replied.

"Big Finn who?"

"Big Finn Earwig. You're my old man."

Never had I seen such delight crease the judge's formidable face.

"What did you do? Finn, you start."

Big Finn, he had some bluster in him. "We got some revolvers, raided the house, stuffed them two owners in the water closet, and told Spitting Sam to bring ten grand and a getaway rig."

"Did you threaten the lives of the Glads?"

"You bet your ass. Money by sundown, or they were dead meat."

"You, Mickey, you wave a gun around, did you?"

Mickey, he looked scared. "Just a little," he said.

"Where were you gonna go, boy?"

"Back to Hoboken."

"What would you do there?"

"Work for someone."

"You was gonna kill the Glads, boy?"

"Not me. I wouldn't hurt a fly. It was all a mistake. Big Finn, he scared me into it."

"He's chicken," Big Finn said.

Judge Earwig eyed me. "How'd you spring the Glads, Pickens?"

"With Belle's apple pie, Your Honor."

"That would do it, all right. Best apple pie this side of Salt Lake City."

"Do we have a confession here?" Earwig asked the boys.

"I didn't do nothing," Big Finn yelled.

"That's a double negative, boy. If you didn't do nothing, that means you did something, which is the same as a guilty plea. Good. That'll save us having to lasso a jury and go through all the rigmarole. Now, Fatherless Mickey, how do you plead?"

"I got pushed into it," he said.

"Same as guilty. You just confessed. Doesn't matter whether you got pushed or walked into it. You did it. All right, that will save us a half hour, and the county will get off cheap this time. I was hoping I wouldn't have to lock up these little farts and bring in the Glads and swear a jury, and summon Lawyer Stokes to bore us for an hour. We've got it locked up clear." He studied the pair. "Step forward for sentencing."

The boys stood frozen in place.

Judge Earwig seemed puzzled a bit. He tugged at his beard, studied the kerosene lamps, peered, annoyed, at the silent spectators. "Trouble is you're too young to hang. You gotta have some weight on the noose or the neck don't break. If you had another thirty pounds, your necks would snap just fine, but that would mean jailing you until you got big enough, and that would cost the county a heap of money, and Cotton Pickens would get bored with it all. No, there's got to be a better way."

His brow furrowed until great ridges crossed his forehead. I rarely saw Hanging Judge Earwig at a loss for a sentence, but this time he was.

"Too bad we're not on the coast," he said. "You two should be shanghaied. You need to get stuffed into a good clipper ship and taken to sea. There's no way out. If you jump ship, you feed the sharks. But this ain't the coast, so I gotta come up with something that will work around here. Anyone got any suggestions?"

"Ship 'em out," yelled Turk.

Hanging Judge Earwig didn't like that. "Then these little farts would learn nothing."

"Send them to college," Reggie Thimble said. "What could be worse?"

"Not a bad idea, Reggie," Earwig said. "Learn or be guillotined."

"What's that word mean?" Big Finn asked.

"They stick your neck into a big meat cleaver," Earwig said. "And after they cut it off, the executioner holds up your head so everyone can see your last blink."

Mickey, he was looking pale.

Earwig leaned over the bench. "You fellers, what do you want for a sentence?"

"I want to be a hundred miles from Big Finn," Mickey yelled.

"Yeah, and I don't want this fruitcake near me," Big Finn yelled. "He cost us ten grand."

"Belle's pies do that," Earwig agreed.

He seemed at a loss for a moment, but then he spotted One-Eyed Jack among the spectators. Jack was the town blacksmith. "Ah!" Earwig said. "I think I have it. Hey, One-Eyed, step forward please."

Jack stepped forward. He stood six feet tall and about three wide, at least across the shoulders. He'd lost an eye in the Civil War, and wore a black patch over it. His hair was graying now, and he viewed the world through one sulphurous, smoldering eye.

"You good at leg irons, Jack?" the judge asked.

"Leg irons? I've made a few."

"Can you make some no one can wiggle outta?"

"You bet, Leonard."

I was reminded that Jack and Leonard Earwig played poker on Wednesdays.

"You think you could hammer a little iron for these two?"

"I can. The secret's a long cylinder above the ankle, so tight they can't get the heel through."

"Do you think you could make a chain they can't chisel through?"

"That's a little harder, Leonard. But with a little daily checking, it'd hold."

Hanging Judge Earwig seems to light up like a burning Christmas tree. "I got just the thing. It's worse than a hanging. It's worse than a beheading. You put a leg iron on their legs, and connect these buzzards with a three-foot chain. I'm sentencing them to be paired together with a leg iron for one year. If they kill each other, that's fine. If they learn to get along for the year, they'll be reformed. And meanwhile, the Glads can put them back to work."

That sure took my breath away. In fact, that was the most beautiful justice ever meted out by Hanging Judge Earwig. People whistled and applauded. It was sublime justice. It was reform. It left the fate of those two hooligans in their own hands. Get along, or kill each other. Learn to live in harmony with others, or quit living entirely.

"All right, One-Eye, you go fire up the forge, and

when you've got these two in irons and chained up good, summon me for inspection, and I'll release them to the Glads," Earwig said.

"Let's have a party," Spitting Sam said. "I'm happy. The Glads, they'll spring for a drink."

Chapter Eighteen

Rusty Irons, he sure was sour, moping around my office like the whole world was against him. I knew the feeling. I didn't have my heart set on any Ukrainian mail-order bride who was a Siamese twin, but I'd eyed a few ladies in my day, like Pepper Baker, only to have her father rush her off to finishing school. That pretty near finished me.

So Rusty was looking grim. He had a kid to raise and no woman. I deputized Riley, and gave him a badge, and the kid strutted around my office with an empty scattergun. Might as well teach them about weapons at an early age. We had him swab out the two jail cells, and told him he could be a jailer when he grew up, but he needed to know how to do it, and we'd help him practice.

Well, Puma County Supervisor Reggie Thimble blew his cork. He came roaring in, eyed Riley, and started yelling.

"What do you think you're doing, Pickens?

Making a little kid a deputy? Trying to screw the county, is that it? Trying to get us into big trouble? He's too young to be handling weapons. You pull him off the force right now, or you're fired."

Reggie had been working for years to get me fired, but after I rescued the Glads, he clammed up a little, for a few days. But then he found a way to get around it: It wasn't my ability that nailed the little hooligans, it was Belle's apple pie, and Cotton Pickens had nothing to do with the rescue. Mickey the hooligan smelled the pie, and that was the end of it. Pickens just happened to be on hand to shut the little swine down. That's what he spread all over Doubtful, and pretty soon half the town agreed. It was Belle's pie that nailed the little turds.

I've heard that stuff all my life, and maybe it's true, at least a little. My ma, she used to say . . . well, I couldn't remember what she said. She was a fountain of wisdom, and I blotted it all up whenever I could, which wasn't very often.

The Glads put the little criminals to work building fence. If they cooperated, they could dig the postholes, set the posts, and string wire. If they fought, then the fence wouldn't get built and the Glads wouldn't pay them wages. I heard somewhere that fences make good neighbors, but maybe they make good fence-builders if the two didn't kill each other with spades or wire cutters.

Riley, he was a different sort of orphan, and between Rusty, and me, and Belle, we gave him a home and a way to grow up and get ahead. Belle and Rusty schooled him, since they didn't trust me to do it. I always had to look up the big words. Rusty, he said I should join Riley's class and maybe I'd learn to spell like he was. But I was in law enforcement, and didn't need any classes in anything. What lawman ever went to school and got anything out of it?

It was going to be a peaceful summer in Doubtful until one June day the Pike Brothers Carnival rolled into town, twenty enameled red and blue and gold wagons, with Seventeen Sensational Exhibits and Forty-four Ways to Improve the Mind. There was Cleopatra, in the flesh, wearing exactly what Cleopatra wore when she was with her Roman lovers. There was Little Egypt, doing her famous dance. There was a genuine, live, two-headed calf, and the Blonde Bombshells, and the petrified remains of Irish Revolutionary Thomas Francis Meagher, who had turned into solid rock. The show ran two city blocks, the wagons drawn by slobbering oxen, and they paraded down Wyoming Avenue, stirring up some excitement, especially among the town drunks. After a lot of brown and tan and a little green that spring, some gold and red color brightened up the place.

The men wore white shirts with black vests, and bowlers, except for the majordomo, who wore a silvery coat with purple lapels. They were all smiling and waving at the rascals who were tossing horse apples at them and thumbing their noses. I thought maybe this outfit had seen that before. Two trumpeters and a trombonist were blatting away, making military sounds from the top of a gold wagon with PIKE BROTHERS CARNIVAL lettered on the sides.

I was all for it. Doubtful, it was a nice town, but a little remote from the rest of the world, and now a genuine carnival show was setting up, and we'd have a fine few days. Probably a minor crime wave, but that came with the territory, and I'd deal with it. Sure enough, they rolled in, dusky Cleopatra in pantaloons and a sort of vest and fez, and the two Blonde Bombshells side by side on a wagon, smiling at the gathering crowds, and a veiled wagon that said TWO-HEADED CALF INSIDE, and a wagon rigged up as a hearse that was supposed to contain the petrified body. Little Egypt swayed languorously and rotated her hips. A sign said EDUCATIONAL EXHIBITS FREE; RARITIES AND ODDITIES, TEN CENTS. I figured the outfit would make a few dimes in Doubtful, and pull out in a day or two. There weren't a lot of dimes around town, and maybe they'd be spent on flour and beans rather than two-headed calves or peep shows.

"Open at dusk!" the majordomo shouted into a megaphone, "Sensational sights, and uplifting exhibits."

I wondered where they would set up camp, but shouldn't have. They needed a creek, and set up along Doubtful's little stream, which was fine except for the mosquitos. I eyed the Blonde Bombshells, certain thoughts trailing through my mind, and decided to have a closer look at them. They sure were sitting tight together, and when they stood up, acknowledging the crowds, they rose and sat together. Could it be? Had they been kidnapped by this here outfit?

I'd know soon enough, and maybe get them back to Rusty, assuming he'd want them and they'd want him. Carny ladies didn't enjoy the loftiest of reputations, and Rusty might have second thoughts. On the other hand, heartbroken Rusty Irons might just have his heart mended before this outfit blew out of town.

I drifted along with the show, and watched them settle on a spot, and begin throwing up the tents. These lined both sides of a concourse, grassy now but soon little more than clay. The roustabouts put up tents with amazing speed. A tent went up every few moments, and soon there were big signs in front, advertising its exhibits. You could pay ten cents to see any exhibit, or a dollar to get a pass that would let you into them all. There was also stuff for sale, and a beer garden, food, and candy. The stuff for sale, it was mostly gimcracks, like decks of cards with half-naked girls on them. I didn't know how a feller could concentrate on poker if he was looking at acres of bosom, but each to his own tastes, I thought. They probably would be popular with cowboys, and would vanish into the bunkhouses of all the local ranches.

There were games of chance, too—hit the bottles with a ball and collect a prize of some sort, or a box of licorice. There was a game like horseshoes, in which you had to flip a ring over a spike, and if you tossed three rings just right, you got a teddy bear, or maybe a stuffed monkey. Those all cost extra, and didn't come on the pass that got you into all the exhibits.

Pretty quick, a rough customer in a bowler headed my way, and I knew I was about to meet the manager. He had a corrugated face that looked like it had been picked over by smallpox.

"Sheriff?" he said. "Something wrong?"

"Nope," I said. "Pickens here, and you?"

"Heliotrope Pike," he said. "My show. We run a clean outfit."

"You having a good season?"

"Nah. Country's gone to the dogs. Depression. I got performers quitting me because I can't pay them on schedule. These are tough times."

"We've had a mess of shows through here this summer. Even an end-of-the-world outfit."

"That's what I should do. Scare the crap out of people and walk away with the loot. That's as good as it gets. Well, sheriff, if there's anything you want, you holler. You get a free peek. Just flash your badge. You'll like Cleo; she's got a lot of tit."

"Sounds like a good evening," I said. "Say, tell me about the Blonde Bombshells."

"Oh, them. Hot stuff. Pair of Russians, joined at the hip, and they like to show it a little."

"Where'd you get them?"

"Bought them, I don't know where."

"Well, think about it. I'd like to know who sells Russian blondes."

Pike smiled. "Everything's for sale," he said.

"I'll be talking to ya," I said.

That was the first clue I'd gotten since the pair were kidnapped coming this way. I wondered how I'd talk to them. I didn't speak Ukrainian, and never heard a Russian, so I'd need some help for sure. I wondered whether to fetch Rusty, and see his heart break, and decided not to for the moment. He'd find out soon enough.

Heliotrope Pike was off a way chewing out someone for putting up a tent backward. But mostly this outfit seemed to know what to do, and the midway rose with amazing speed. It looked dreary in late light, but I could see roustabouts carrying oil lamps out, one in front of each tent, at the ticket window, and one for the show inside. There wouldn't be enough light to get a gander at Cleopatra in her undies, but maybe the next day I'd do better.

Sure enough, about dusk the workers lit all the lamps, a hundred or so, and the whole midway got lit up, and looked almost merry. That's when I spotted Rusty boiling my way.

"Where are they?" he asked.

"We get to see them when the shows open, few minutes."

"About six people told me these are my women."

"Well, these women have been sharing their charms for a while, Rusty."

He glared at me. But I was glad he would be forewarned.

About the time the Doubtful people came boiling in, the barkers got set up, with their megaphones, and began barking.

"Step right up, folks, show your pass or part with a dime, and see the greatest sight ever to surprise mortal eyes," said one. He sounded like he was from the South. "We got a sight in here never seen before in Wyoming. We got Cleopatra herself, in all her beauty, the one and same as romanced Caesar, and Marc Antony, and ruled with an iron hand the great nation of pyramids. Come see Cleopatra, and see the self-same curves that enticed the emperors and caesars to her bedside. It's something never before seen, a tableau out of history. Women can see her for five cents, but all men must pay the full price, no discounts allowed. Step right up, folks."

Fellers were lining up to lay out a dime. Some had tokens, ten for a dollar, that couldn't be redeemed anywhere else, but them cowboys sure wanted to see Cleopatra, and I was tempted myself.

But Rusty, he just glared, and went hunting for the tent that sheltered the Blonde Bombshells. That was down the midway some, but we got her located. It was a big, lofty tent, and had two lamps at the door flap, and a dapper little huckster and ticket taker outside.

"See a sight you've never seen, folks. See two beautiful ladies, their flesh connected at the hip. They'll show you how it is, pull back the drapes and let you see this wonder, this freak of nature, this marvel. Brought especially from Europe for the Pike Brothers Carnival. We should be charging twenty-five cents instead of one thin dime, folks. It's worth fifty cents if it's worth a penny. And we're raising the price tomorrow, but tonight, our big opening in Doubtful, Colorado—ah, Wyoming, it's one thin dime to see one of the wonders of the world."

Rusty, he balled his fists, but I put a hand on him to quiet him, and got us in on our badges. The ladies were sitting on the stage in there, smiling at their audience. And Rusty couldn't stop staring.

Chapter Nineteen

Rusty, he looked so wound up I thought he was a clock spring ready to break. The blonde beauties were sitting on a makeshift stage in that dark tent, not quite side by side, but facing each other a little. They were plain good looking, with ample curves beneath two gowns that somehow were slit at the side. Grecian gowns, you might say, diaphanous and womanly. One wore a nice seashell necklace. Both had rings on their fingers.

I couldn't say what Rusty was thinking, but he didn't doubt these here were his Ukrainian mail-order brides, and now they were on display in a freak show, and it was shameful.

When the tent was full up, maybe thirty people sitting on wooden benches, that huckster at the door came in and climbed onto the platform.

"Now, ladies and gentlemen, you will see one of the wonders of the world, two beautiful women, joined from now to eternity, at the hip, and fated to live their lives in sublime union. Look hard; they will show you this wonder for only a few moments. And then tell your friends and neighbors to come here and see for themselves."

He eyed the silent crowd, gauging its interest.

"Now, they don't speak a word of English. They've come over the seas to these shores, so you can't talk to them. They get about three proposals a day, but they turn them all away, because their fate in life is with each other, beloved twin sisters, bound together. Now, we don't know their names, so their friends here in the carnival call them Tiddlywinks. On the left, there, is Tiddly, and next to her is the beauteous Winks."

"That's Natasha," said Rusty.

"Now, folks, it is time to prove that this phenomenon is real. There is a bridge of flesh; indeed, they share some organs, the doctors tell us. And I will ask them to stand and draw apart their robes just enough so you can have one discreet look at this oddity of nature."

He stepped aside and gestured. The twins stood, and each tugged the split gown away from her side, baring the connection that began at the ribs and continued through the rest of the torso of each.

"Step right up, folks, and have a closer look. You don't need to be glued to the seat. Come up and see for yourself, but don't touch. We're a respectable company, and this is an educational exhibit."

Several of the audience, all male, sprang up,

studied the oddly shaped bond that connected the women, as if it were gun cotton ready to ignite. Then they drifted back, satisfied that the joining was real, and not some carny trick.

The women stared nonchalantly at the spectators, even as the citizens of Doubtful stared back, and then they rearranged their skirts. It wasn't indecent, but it violated them anyhow, and it made me boil up. Rusty, he just clenched his fist, struggling to keep from hammering that huckster, who was smiling blandly.

"Now the ladies will walk in a circle, to show you how beautifully coordinated they are, and that will conclude this amazing exhibit, the most amazing sight ever seen in, ah, Doubletree, Iowa."

Again the twins walked a tight circle on their little stage, and sat down together, and people stood up, stared at the women, and drifted out in a pensive mood. Then the women exited through the rear of the show tent.

Rusty, he corralled that huckster, who was standing blandly as the tent cleared.

"Where'd you get them?" Rusty asked.

The huckster eyed him, and eyed me, and saw the badges.

"We purchased them not long ago, and no, the act is not for sale. It's the top draw in our lineup. Man, it's the hit of the carny."

"What do you mean, you purchased them?" Rusty asked.

"Oh, I'm sure Mr. Pike has the contract in his files," the huckster said.

"These women are wanted by the law," Rusty said. "They were stolen off a stagecoach."

"Well, I wouldn't know anything about that. I'll refer you to our manager, and he can answer your questions. They ladies certainly enjoy the attention. They earn a nice income for doing nothing at all but draw the draperies aside a bit. Man, that's a rare sight."

"You're a pimp," Rusty snapped.

"Oh, I'm worse than that," the huckster said. "That's the least of my crimes."

"These ladies were kidnapped, and we're holding them here," I said.

"Go talk to the manager. He's over in the Little Egypt tent. That's his sweetie."

"Come on, Rusty, we'll talk to the women later. We got law business to do," I said.

Rusty, he just sat on that bench, poleaxed. But I pried him up and we headed down the midway to the Little Egypt tent, where we spotted Heliotrope Pike selling tickets and chewing on a cigar.

"Pike, we want to talk to you, right now," I said.

He started to protest, saw the look on my face, and nodded. Some lackey stepped in to sell tickets to the belly dancer show.

"You got a couple captive women that got kidnapped off a stage to Doubtful, and we're keeping them here."

"But you can't. That would be entirely illegal, sheriff. They're an act we purchased."

"They got removed from a coach at gunpoint, and vanished until now," I said. "We're taking them in."

The manager nodded, and we followed him to a sort of office wagon, and he led us in. He lit a lamp, opened a file drawer, and extracted a handwritten page. I couldn't make heads nor tails of it, and it sure wasn't using any letters I'd come across.

"This is their contract. They were sent to us by a booking agent in the Ukraine. It details their salary, term of service, and special quarters. We've got them for three years at ten dollars a week plus feed. It's expensive, feeding two women."

"They were kidnapped off a wagon, Pike. They were to be mail-order brides."

Pike beamed, and pushed his bowler back. "That's an old racket. Get some love-struck groom to pay the passage. Then when you get here, ditch him."

Rusty, he sure was looking thunderous, but he kept his trap shut.

"Who talks Ukraine around here?"

Pike shook his head. "No one in the outfit."

"We're going to find a way to talk to them ladies, and I'm bringing over some witnesses that saw them get taken off the stagecoach, and if those ladies got kidnapped, they're staying here until we get it sorted out. That clear, Pike?"

"No, it's not. I paid good money for the act, and I'm keeping it."

"I want that contract. You'll get it back. But I am going to get her translated."

"It ain't yours, copper."

"I have the feeling if I don't take it now, we'll never see it again, and it'll vanish from sight."

Pike, he stared at me, stared at Rusty, who was looking like hell unloosed, and handed over the contract—if that was what it was. It was a sheet with a lot of foreign stuff on it.

"Is there a translation?" Rusty asked. "You got a contract in your file you can't read, and you say no one in this outfit can speak Ukrainian?"

Pike, he sort of smirked. "Show people, we got our own language," he said. "Look, gents, this is no big palooza. This is carny biz. These lovely gals, they're happy as corks in wine bottles. They can speak a little bitta English; go on over and have little talk with 'em. Now, I gotta get busy. We got a nice crowd here, and I got work to do. So if you'll excuse me . . ."

Rusty, he didn't wait. He headed for the Ukrainian blondes, who were in their own special wagon, awaiting the next show. Lots of people from Doubtful were wandering the midway now, trying games of chance, and flocking to see Little Egypt. Some of the town ladies, they were a little put off, but curiosity got the best of them, and I watched them pay up, and slide into the show tent to see the famous belly dancer, and no doubt cluck their disapproval.

This was the first carny show I'd been to, and I wanted to see the whole works. But Rusty, he stalked through the place like a torpedo, and knocked on the door of those blondes, and pretty soon they opened. Together, of course. They had to do it all together.

Rusty, he actually removed his sweat-stained hat and held it to his chest. "I'm looking for Anna and Nastasha," he said. "I'm Rusty."

"Rusteeeee," squealed one of them. "Rusteee," squawked the other. They motioned us in to a tiny dark bunk room.

"This here's Sheriff Cotton Pickens," he said, dutifully.

"Pleased to meet ya," I said, thinking I'd marry whichever one was left over.

"Who's my bride?" Rusty asked.

They laughed. "Bride, what's dat?"

"Who did I send for?"

One of them sighed. "You don't send for one. You send for two. That was the trouble."

"Who are you?" he asked.

"I am Natasha. Too bad, Rusteee. We were coming to marry you, but the bosses got to us first."

"The bosses?"

"Ah, Rusty, Pike. He sends men to chase us when we were going to marry you."

"He kidnapped you?"

"Oh, no, Rusteee. We tried to sneak away so we could marry you."

"So his men made you get off the stagecoach?"

"Oh, no, Rusteee, we thought it was good, he sends a wagon to get us, and we joined the carnival. We laughed all the way to the show."

Rusty, he didn't know what to make of it. Me, I thought maybe Pike's story was probably the right one. Rusty had gotten milked for a ship's passage.

Rusty, he wasn't buying it. "Hey, you read this in English," he said, and handed her the contract, written in some foreign language.

"Oh, Rusteee, this is a letter from our mother. She is saying that he should take good care of us, and not send us back to Lvov, and pay us promptly, and send her a tenth of it. She says we'll be in Cheyenne soon."

"This is your mother's letter? Not a contract?"

"Oh, Rustee, you are such a simpleton."

Rusty, he was starting to deflate. I could see the hot air leaking out of him. I was about to tell him he should be content with Riley, but I kept my trap shut for a change. Rusty was hurting. A lot of dreams were sliding into the outhouse vault. A man needs his dreams, and Rusty had been alive with this one for many months. And now it was gone. Two blonde twins had taken him for a ride.

"Hey, Rustee," Nastasha said. "We'll marry you, but you gotta join the show. We'll both marry you, and you join the carny, and we'll have a lot of good times, right, Rustee?"

Rusty, he wheeled out of there into the night. I shrugged, nodded, and followed him out the door. The next act was about to begin, but Rusty wasn't going to stick around to see it.

Chapter Twenty

Rusty, he was so busted up that I tried to rally him some.

"Rusty, my ma always said, sometimes opportunity's staring you in the face and you're not seeing it."

"I'm tired of you and your ma," he said. "Leave me alone."

We were hiking along the midway, watching the last of the visitors as the evening wore on. If Doubtful wasn't earning much, the carnival would soon pull up stakes and head for the next town. Doubtful wasn't much of a place, and I wondered if the carny show would stay more than two or three days.

"While this outfit's here, you got a fine chance to woo the blonde twins," I said. "You got a real good chance to change their minds. You fetch Riley, and you go back to their wagon, and tell them that you want to be a family, and live right here."

Rusty sure was quiet.

"You're on your own," I said. "I'm looking into this outfit. Some of the things Heliotrope Pike said, they don't add up. Like buying the blonde bombshell act from a booking agent in the Ukraine, and then showing us a letter from the gals' ma that was supposed to be a contract. Like taking them gals off the stage at gunpoint, when they could have just as easy left the stagecoach at any stop and joined the show. There's something not fitting together here, and I'm going to be finding out what it is. I'll do that tomorrow, and you go visit the ladies, and get to know them."

Rusty grinned suddenly. "Sure, sheriff," he said.

He'd never called me that before. I sure was wondering what was cooking in his noggin.

He picked up Riley from Belle, who wakened the boy, and wrapped him in a blanket, and sent him into the evening. Me, I should have climbed up the stairs, but I was restless.

There was a show in town, and a lot of folks in Doubtful who depended on me for their safety. Shows could make me itchy; this one did. I hiked over to courthouse square, and the jail, collected a sawed-off scattergun, and headed into Wyoming Street, if only to rattle doors and make sure folks were locked up tight for the night. The carnival had quit, too, and was real quiet and dark down on the creek.

There was no one on duty at nights. The Puma

County supervisors told me there was no money to give me a night man. So anyone who wanted the law, they had to come fetch me at Belle's. Late at night, that was burglar time; evenings, that was bar brawl time. Days, a little of anything. I started patrolling the business places, rattling doors, peering through windows, but it was real quiet. I thought of all them people safe in their beds, pretty certain nothing real bad would visit them in the night. I was all there was that stood between them and trouble. That's what I was paid to do, and what I was sworn to do. Upholding the law was mostly keeping folks safe and keeping their property safe.

It sure was quiet around town. I drifted over to Saloon Row, but most of the joints had folded up. They didn't like shows coming in; they wanted the cowboys and ranchers to unload their pay right there, at their big bars. The ladies of the night felt the same way. Road shows were competition. Outfits with a Little Egypt rolling her belly, well, the cowboys could get all that locally, and didn't have to shell out dimes to see it on a midway.

But most of those places were sleeping, too. One place, Denver Sally's, still had a red lantern bobbing on the breeze. That's how it was. Cowboys, they got tired, and didn't get laid after midnight. The girls got tired, too, all that hard work, and wanted their beauty sleep.

I didn't see anyone busting windows or prying open doors, so I figured it was pretty peaceful over in the sporting precincts. But I still felt itchy, like something was bound to happen. My ma, she always said that the biggest things happened behind closed doors, and no one ever knew about them. Like a marriage that was outwardly real nice, and the folks seemed happy, might really be a brawl, or cruel, or rotten, behind closed doors, and no one would ever know how two people were doing their best to wreck each other.

Me, I didn't have enough of a life to put behind closed doors. The only time I ever closed a door entire, was the outhouse. When I was doing my business, and studying the Monkey Ward catalogue before tearing off a page for use, that wasn't public. The rest of me, I didn't care one way or other. I thought to give one last look at the carny. Truth was, those folks were under my protection, too. They might be strangers, maybe crooks themselves, but I was sworn to look after the safety and property of anyone in my county, and that included every person in the carnival, and everything the carnival owned. If someone stole a horse from the carnival, it was my job to find that horse and throw the rustler in the pokey.

The carny people were asleep. Most of their wagons had roll-up canvas sides, and some slept in those, some slept outside. It sure was quiet. I worked along the midway, until a couple of big dogs circled me and growled. Carny dogs. They stopped a few feet away and waited. They seemed to be sending me a message: steer clear of the camp. They'd either set up a racket, or come at me with a lot of big white teeth shining in the moonlight. I eased away, and they let me go. They were the sentries, and that's all the carny folk needed to keep an eye on things. They didn't need some country boy like me keeping an eye on them, or the camp.

Tough people, carny folk.

I itched to go on in there, wake up Heliotrope Pike, and get some answers about them Siamese twins from the Ukraine. His story didn't make sense. But tomorrow was another day, so I eased back from the camp, turned toward the creek, and wandered into their herd, which was artfully contained in a rope corral that employed wagons where there weren't trees to hold up the rope. Not that a rope would hold anything, but these mules and horses weren't going anywhere. They eyed me, ears up, as I drifted in. It was quiet there, too. All I heard was the purl of Doubtful Creek. The animals stirred slightly, and began a gentle rotation. They looked pretty thin; Pike used them hard. But at least they got vacations between each haul.

Some were eyeing me, and some were staring down the creek some, and that always is a sign. So I watched, too. A quarter moon didn't shed much light, and the bottoms were blurred and bleak, but finally I saw what them horses did. Something was moving along the creek. That's about all I could make out. Maybe it was a critter, like a catamount or a coyote, or maybe not so big. But I just stood in the quiet and studied on it, letting nature take its course.

Whatever it was, it edged forward slowly, half afraid. I studied on it, not making sense of what I saw until it was closer, and then I realized it was a person, and he was carrying a bindle stick, and he was a bindle stiff. A tramp. A small tramp, this time. Them hoboes, they put all their possessions into a bandanna or sometimes a piece of canvas, and tied it up and hung it from a pole, or stick, and carried the stick over their shoulder. That was a hobo suitcase: a stick over the shoulder with a bag hanging from it. It was the easiest way to carry a few things. And the cheapest.

This here puny hobo, he seemed a little itchy, sort of walking ahead some, quitting to look around, and then walking some more. He got to the rope corral, edged under the rope, but kept to the creek bank, as if all them mules and broncs weren't there, and he simply headed up the creek.

That's about when I got the oddest feeling. I knew that walk. That was a boy's walk, both cocky and scared at the same time. I'd seen that walk.

"Going somewhere?" I asked.

The boy, he turned, stared hard, knew I could catch him, and seemed to deflate there.

"Nice night for a hike, Riley. Mind if I walk along?"

"Leave me alone," he said.

"Heading out, are you?"

"I don't like it here."

"I'll walk with you, boy. We'll go where you're going."

"You'd let me?"

"Unless you want to go sit on that cottonwood log yonder."

The boy headed for the log, propped his bindle stick on it, and sat. "You gonna take me back?"

"I don't know. You want to quit us?"

"Yeah. I don't have anyone."

"You got a little food?"

"Cookies."

"Guess I'll have to rustle up more than that. You got some extra shoes?"

Riley shook his head.

"Peaceful night," I said. "Summer's always fine, except when it rains. Trees are all leafed out, there's berries on the bushes, at least in July and August, and lots of hills and valleys to look at. Wild animals, too. Used to be buffalo through here, but they got shot away. Now it's mostly ranches, lots of steers, and a few horses."

"It was better wild," Riley said.

"Some ways, yes, but it took a good shot to keep one's belly full."

"No, it was nicer when there wasn't anyone. That's what I think."

"Lot of people think that, too. I don't. I like a place where I'm safe and I can earn a living."

"You gonna let me go now?"

"How'd you get that name, Riley?"

"My pa, he was a sergeant."

"But the name. Where did it come from?"

"At Fort Riley. But he quit my ma, and I never seen him. Then she went East, and couldn't take care of me, and I got put on the orphan train."

"You named after a soldier post? I like that."

"It's a bad name. No one else is named Riley."

"That's what's good about it. Gives you the edge in life."

"Can I go now?"

"You unhappy with Rusty and Belle and me?"

"I don't belong to anyone."

"Maybe you got it backwards, Riley. Do we belong to you?"

The boy was puzzled. "Why should you belong to me?"

"You got to want us, Riley. All along, we've been hoping you'd adopt us. But you ain't done it yet, and we're pretty blue."

"Adopt you?"

"Yeah, Belle, she's just hoping you'll adopt her; Rusty, he'd like nothing better than to be adopted. Me, I'll be an uncle if you'll adopt me."

He sat quietly on that log, and I let him. Me, I don't know nothing about boys, not having been one in years, but I figured if he sat there on the log long enough, he might adopt all three of us. And I wasn't far off the mark.

I pulled out my jackknife and started whittling a stick.

"I'm tired, Cotton," he said. He picked up his bindle stick and started home.

Chapter Twenty-one

The next morning I headed over to the Pike Brothers Carnival to see the boss. I was tired of pussyfooting around, and this time Heliotrope Pike would give me some answers or face the music. My music.

I wondered what carny people do in mornings, and soon found out. They had plenty to do. Horses to feed and water and doctor, clothing to mend, games of chance to polish up, and food to cook. On a nice summer's day, it was easy, but I could see how some tough weather could make things real bad. But this was a sunny, lazy June day.

The Ukrainian twins were sitting in a specially made wide chair, sunning themselves. If Rusty had brains, he'd do something about it instead of whining about being robbed of his wife, or wives, or whatever. I never could get it straight whether he was marrying one or two.

The show wouldn't get going until noon or so;

then people could buy a lunch, play the games of chance, see the hootchy-kootchy girls, and disapprove of everything while shelling out their dimes. If nothing else, the show offered something new to people off the ranches of Puma County.

Sure enough, Pike was breakfasting with his raven-haired sweetie Little Egypt when I got there. He had his own wagon with a roll-out canvas shade, which made an outdoor arbor. They were sipping some sort of black coffee made in a brass pot when I barged in. She was in a silky red kimono, with nothing else, and he was in his underdrawers and that was all.

"Well, if it isn't the sheriff," he said. "Want some java?"

"No, but I want some answers," I said. I wasn't going to drown myself in a social call.

"At your service, sheriff."

Pike's tone had changed to coolness. Little Egypt decided to vamoose, and rose, revealing a lot of creped flesh. She wasn't as young as she looked in the lantern light at night. I chose to remain standing.

"We got a problem, and it's not solved, and it's gonna be," I said. "You got these Ukrainian twins in your show, the same as got taken off a stagecoach in my county, at gunpoint, stuffed into a red-and-gold chariot, and hauled away. There were a few laws got broke, and we're going to find out right now what happened, and why."

"What a bizarre story," Pike said, blandly.

"Yeah, well, there's a mess of witnesses, including passengers and the jehu, and if we don't get some answers, this show's not going anywhere until we do."

That sure perked him up some. "You have no right to stop the show from going anywhere."

"Just try me," I said. "We got abducted women in your outfit, and that's all I need."

"Who says they were abducted?"

"The people that saw them removed at gunpoint and stuffed into the chariot, which was the only way to move Siamese twins away fast."

"Fantasy," Pike said. "People have vivid imaginations."

"Yeah, and so do I. You go ahead and think about the twenty carny people, stuck in Doubtful, Wyoming, because no one's talking about how those ladies got took off the stage, and why, and who done it."

"You wouldn't hold innocent people, would you?"

"All you got to do is tell the story."

Pike eyed me levelly. "I haven't the faintest idea who abducted the women."

"You bought the act, you say. You got the women. So, talk. Where'd you get them?"

"On the road somewhere."

"Who sold them to you?"

"Sold the act, sir; we're not talking about slavery."

"Well, maybe I'm talking about slavery. Men with guns took them off the stage."

Pike looked annoyed. "So Pike Brothers is to blame for this?"

"You got brothers?"

"No, I own the carnival alone. The name suggests a larger show. Pike Brothers sounds like a big outfit."

"So someone in a circus chariot, seems like, made off with the Ukrainian women. And tried to cover the tracks. My deputy and me, we had to hunt hard to pick them up."

"Look, sheriff, that has nothing to do with us."

"I'm thinking maybe you got wind of the Siamese twins and wanted them in your outfit and kidnapped them. Somehow or other, they went from the stagecoach into your outfit, and until we get some answers, you ain't going anywhere."

Pike eyed me, carefully. "We'll post bail. This is rather commonplace. Pick on the carny show. How much? Twenty-five dollars? Forfeit the bail?"

He wasn't fooling me none. "If there's bail, it's set by Hanging Judge Earwig," I said.

Pike paused, looking perplexed.

"I'll check through my records and see if I can find the names of the people who offered me the act," he said. "You don't seem to grasp the business. Everything is a handshake deal."

"You better come squeaky clean," I said. "Or you'll be hanging around Doubtful for a long time."

Well, he didn't like that none. His next step was to try to sneak out, no doubt at night, and hope I'd forget about going after them. But he would be a little surprised. I had a few plans of my own, including tying up his livestock.

"And don't try sneaking out," I said. "Not by night, not by day. Not on a Sunday, and not on your mother's birthday. Your outfit's no match for a posse of Puma County cowboys."

He plainly agreed, even if he didn't say a word.

I had a hunch he'd come around. Carny box office in my little burg wasn't going to last long. My guess was that he'd come clean, and probably lose the act, if that's what staring at Siamese twins amounted to.

I headed down the empty midway. For some reason, no one goes to carny shows in the morning. Sin doesn't start until afternoon, and carny shows were all sin. My ma, she always used to say wedlock's no good mornings when the breakfast dishes need scrubbing; it only heats up at night, in the dark. Well, that's true of show business, too.

I headed for the Ukrainian sisters, who were camped behind their show tent, and in their chair enjoying the good Wyoming sunshine. And sure enough, Rusty had gotten smart and had settled in across from them, and had even taken his sweaty Stetson off and was rotating it in his hands while admiring his ladies. They were all sipping something that looked white.

"Slivovitz," said Rusty.

"What's that?"

"It's almost as good as marriage."

I smelled his glass and pretty near passed out. "You're on duty," I said.

"Cotton, you're a peckerhead sometimes."

"You could always quit," I said, "and drink slivovitz the rest of your life."

"This here's Anna, and this here's Natasha," he said.

"Is real damn nice, good piss water," Natasha said. Not bad English, I thought.

"I told them I wanted to marry, and they laughed, and then said which? I said, either way, I'd flip a coin. So we flipped a coin. Heads, Natasha, tails, Anna. Natasha won, so I proposed. I said, Natasha, let's get married, and then Anna got mad. Anna said that's not right, I've got to marry her, or both. I said I can't marry both, and they said go to hell, skunk head, and I said maybe I'll marry both. And now they're both mad at me."

"I gotta talk to them. Help me," I said.

I turned to Natasha. "You were coming here on the stagecoach and some men stopped the coach and made you get out, right?"

She dimpled up. "What a wedding invitation," she said.

But Anna elbowed her. "Every day, crossing the sea, people look at us. On the boat, on the rail-road, people look at us. We're used to it. Some days, men give us cards. One man said he wanted to put us in a show; we'd be happy. But Natasha, she always said no; she's getting married. Me, no one asks."

"So you got to Laramie and caught the Laramie and Overland coach here? Then what?"

"They are watching us. We get into the coach, and then we start to come here, yes? And then they stop the coach, out on the grasses, and make us get out. Three men, wearing masks, waving guns. And there is this cart, stand-up room. And there's a driver, also masked, and we get carried away, and go to some place I don't know, and we are told we are in a carnival, and that's better than one getting married and one not. We both get paid, yes?"

"Did the masked men who took you off the coach meet your boss here, Pike?"

Anna shrugged.

"They gave us this wagon," Natasha said.

"Didn't you protest?'

Natasha giggled. "We got a house!"

"Did anyone call it an act? Were you an act?"

Anna giggled.

"Did you sign a contract for an act? A show performance?"

They both looked puzzled.

"They like it because they're taken care of," Rusty said. "They can't care for themselves, so they like this carnival. They get fed."

Both the ladies were smiling at me.

"This sure makes Pike look like the one who planned this little deal. Is there a two-wheel cart around?"

"You mean the gold-and-red chariot?" Rusty asked.

"I mean any cart. A coat of paint, that makes a difference. Witnesses, they see a red chariot. My ma, she always used to say a little war paint on a woman hides the real McCoy. So I want to see if this outfit's got a two-wheel cart, and maybe, any color."

"You and your ma," Rusty said.

The women, they followed little of that.

"You got put here in the carnival? Did you say no to Pike?"

Natasha, she figured out that one. "I wanted to get married; this is my lover boy. Anna, she don't want that. So she's stuck. And I'm stuck. She won. She got us here. Me, I'd like to go to bed with Rusty. Wooee! Hot pajamas! Anna, she don't care."

This here was getting more and more tangled up, I thought. But one thing was clear: Pike abducted the twins and stuffed them into his show, one way or another. And I was going to get the facts, and figure what laws got busted, and no one was leaving Doubtful until justice got done.

"Make your deputy leave," Anna said. "He comes in here like he owns us."

"Make him stay," Natasha said. "He's my man."

"He's not my man," Anna said. "Make him go away; we got a good wagon, and a good act."

"Rusty, you wanna marry me, like in the letters?" Natasha asked.

"Maybe I could marry you both," Rusty said.

"You get her, not me," Anna said. "Go to hell."

"You're robbing me," Natasha said. "You're keeping bride from groom."

"I ought to kill you," Anna said. "And maybe someday I will."

Me, I stared at them two, stuck together for life, and felt real sad. When Rusty got loose, I planned to tell him to forget it. He was torturing them two ladies in ways we couldn't even imagine.

But Rusty, he just sat there and kept on wooing.

Chapter Twenty-two

No sooner did I get back to my office then I tangled with the Puma County supervisors. Reggie Thimble, the chairman, required my presence in the courthouse, so I grumbled my way over there, knowing what was coming.

Sure enough, he was laying for me. He sat behind a monster oak desk on an elevated platform, giving him an extra foot or so to look down at supplicants. He had a pouty little mouth, and now it was pursed with disapproval.

"I've had a little visit from Heliotrope Pike, who is the chairman of the board and chief executive officer of the Pike Brothers Carnival," he announced. "Is it true you are threatening to keep them in Doubtful until such a time as you choose to spring them?"

"No, they can leave whenever they fess up, hand over the masked men who abducted the Ukrainian

Siamese twins, and whoever else perpetrated the crime."

"I see," said Thimble, peering at me from over his wire-rimmed spectacles, which were perched delicately on his pulpy nose, with its red besotted veins.

"Do you suppose you are doing something entirely illicit, immoral, scandalous, and barbaric?"

"All of them, Reggie."

"Mr. Thimble, if you please. Now then, do you have the slightest evidence, I mean actual, hard, court-worthy evidence, that any such crime was committed? And by people in the carnival?"

"Nope. I've got witnesses who saw four masked men, three on horse and one in a chariot, order the blondes off the stagecoach, which they forcibly stopped at gunpoint. And I've got a lot of hot air from Pike, who first said he bought the 'act,' as he called it, in Laramie, but could supply no contract, and indeed, had more or less admitted there had been no vaudeville or carny act involving these ladies, and he had created one."

Thimble rapped his fingers on the beeswaxed desk, which he polished daily. "So there's nothing."

"There's four men in that company that snatched the women, or woman, off that stagecoach, in Puma County, where I am charged with keeping the law, and when Pike turns them over, and himself, if he was the one giving the command, then I'll let the carny show loose. But not until then."

"I don't suppose you'd imagine you have no right to do so."

"It'll get the job done."

"And what if these supposed abductors aren't associated with the Pike Brothers Carnival? What then, Mr. Sheriff?"

"Then I keep this outfit around until they tell me who did the job. They got those twins somewhere, so they know who done it."

Thimble stared his most withering stare, but I was used to it. Mostly when he stared like that I noticed his right eye, which was slightly crossed.

"You'll not impede the carnival when it chooses to go. That is an order, subject to termination of your job if you should disobey."

I'd heard that about fifty times. "I ain't budging," I said. "The law got broke, I got the perpetrators right here, and as soon as I can get them tried and sentenced, the show's free to go to Los Angeles or any other hell."

Thimble stared at a passing puffball cloud, through the grimy window. "Has it occurred to you that the merchants of Doubtful are suffering? Already this summer, they've had to weather a medicine show, a doomsday preacher, and now a carnival. Doubtful survives on the trade of the five hundred cowboys and ranchers surrounding us, but this year the cowboys have invested in quack medicine, donated their last cent to the Doomsday crook, and have opened their purses and pitched out dimes and dollars to play games of chance on the midway, gawk at a freak, watch Little Egypt's belly roll in syncopation with Memphis blues, and pitch rings at little posts, to win some sort of furry stuffed monkey or two. And our shops suffer. Mayor Waller tells me his trade is down. Leonard Silver says his is cut in half; even the blacksmith, One-Eyed Jack, has lost trade. Cowboys would rather gawk at freaks than see their horses shod."

"Sorry, but I got laws to uphold, and this show doesn't leave here until it coughs up the bandits."

"Come now, bandits? They didn't steal a nickel."

"They stole two lives, Reggie."

"Mr. Thimble, please. The ladies seem quite content. You seem to be inventing a crime and a tragedy out of whole cloth."

"I got laws to enforce, and if you fire me, the law of Wyoming and this county won't get enforced."

"That's the idea, sheriff, exactly the idea. You will not impede the carny. We want them out as fast as they can harness up and go. I wish they had left yesterday, but no such luck." He eyed me real severe. "You've been warned. This is the second offense on your ticket this week. The first being appointing a little boy a deputy, putting the whole county at risk. Have you taken the badge back?"

"Nope. He's pleased as punch. There ain't another kid in the county gets to be a deputy sheriff."

Reggie sighed. He had a way of sighing that was plumb theatrical. He sighed slowly, sadly, shaking his head, lowering his chin in sorrow, his eyes mournful. He used it at every board meeting, and every political rally. There wasn't nobody in Wyoming with a sigh like Reggie Thimble's.

"That was a good one," I said.

"I haven't the faintest idea what you are talking about," he said, sighing once again.

"That's how you got elected," I said, and walked out.

My ma always said I was stubborn, and I'd get myself in trouble because of it. And now I was being stubborn all over again, and pretty soon I'd be looking for another job. But as long as I was sheriff, I'd be the best one I knew how.

I found Rusty in the office, mopping up the jail. We'd had a couple of drunks in there, and they missed the piss pot, and puked in the bunk, so after Hanging Judge Earwig fined them two dollars each, we had to clean up. That's how it is for sheriffs. Mostly, we get to be chambermaids.

"How are your lady friends?" I asked, when Rusty emerged from the iron cage with a bucket of slop.

"They're getting into a catfight," he said. "Natasha wants to marry me and quit the show, but Anna, she don't want nothing to do with me, and they're really steaming. It sure ain't easy, being stuck so close to someone you're fighting with all the time."

"They talk to you about getting took off the stagecoach?"

"Oh, yeah, Natasha does. She wishes I'd come rescue her. These here masked bandits, they stopped the stagecoach, opened the door, and told the twins to get out. So the twins get into the cart, and bandits get their luggage, and away they go. They went direct to Heliotrope Pike. There wasn't any buying or selling of theater acts. Pike got the gals and put 'em in the show, and that was that."

"You think they'd testify?"

Rusty scratched his head. "Natasha, she would if you asked her questions real slow so she could understand. But everything she'd say, Anna would say different, and the testimony would nullify."

"I guess I hadn't thought of that. Who's telling the truth?"

"You need to ask?" Rusty asked.

No, I didn't. Natasha was. Anna was playing the spoiler. But maybe if they were both sworn in to tell the truth and nothing but, maybe she'd come around. But it sure made a mess of things.

"They know who abducted them?"

"Maybe one, but the gunmen wore masks, and they plain don't know for sure. No one was talking."

"You still want to marry them, the two fighting like that?"

Rusty, he grinned real crooked. "Both at once, that'd do it fine."

I told him about my talk with Reggie Thimble, and how the merchants wanted the outfit to leave town.

Rusty grinned. "The cowboys, they've hardly walked into a saloon since the carny show came, and before that, they were buying tonic from the medicine man."

"Let's do a little walk down the midway. If that outfit's going to slide out of Doubtful tonight, there should be a few clues."

"How you gonna stop them? If they go, they go."

"I got ways," I said. I was afraid if I told Rusty, he'd tell Natasha, and my little plan wouldn't work.

"You're gonna round up the draft horses, that it?"

"Nope, they'll be tight guarded tonight, and someone will get hurt. I got better ideas."

"That's what your ma always used to say, right?"

Rusty, he didn't believe I had any wits about me, just the same as no one else did, either. I never quite got used to it. But sometimes it came in handy, and it would tonight if the show was gonna pull up stakes after the midway died down.

We meandered along, watching the afternoon trade. It was mostly women and children, trying their luck on the games. Scalawag Marvel, the little punk, was trying to win a doll by throwing a baseball at a row of bottles. He didn't know them bottles were loaded with concrete.

I slid past the midway, into the camp, where the wagons were sitting willy-nilly. It didn't look like an orderly place at all, but in some ways it was. There were cooking areas, and bunking areas. The harness for each wagon rested in front of it, ready to be hooked up. Harness comes in all shapes and descriptions, but most of these rigs had breast collars, big straps that fit over the draft horse's chest. A draft horse really pushed into the chest collars, even though it looked like he was pulling the load. These were heavy-duty harnesses, intended to tie a draft horse to a big load. There were surcingles and bridles and reins and all the rest, but what I wanted most to look at was the collars. Without them collars, this outfit wasn't going anywhere at all.

"You satisfied?" Rusty said.

"You know harness?" I asked.

"Some."

"You pick out collars in the dark, maybe?"

He studied the piles of harness resting next to each wagon.

"I imagine. You think the dogs'll stop us?"

"We've been hanging around long enough. What we're going to do, Rusty, is fetch us those collars and lock up the whole bunch in the jail. We don't even need to get them all. Get enough harness collars, and this outfit isn't going anywhere at all, and we got Pike right where we want him."

"I suppose your ma gave you this idea," Rusty said.

"No, I thunk it up all by myself," I said. "You just study on where the collars are put, and how they'll look in the dark."

Rusty was grinning. "I guess I get another day or two to woo my wives."

Chapter Twenty-three

Me and Rusty, we done the job. That old carny show was roaring away on the midway; everyone in the show was over there, gulling the last dimes out of cowboys and suckers. The camp area, it was plenty dark, and no one was around except once when one of the old gals in the outfit came back to smoke her corncob pipe a while.

Finding the breast collars and unbuckling them and carting them out was a big job. Those things were hard to separate from all the rest of the harness. The breast collars run across the chest of the horse or mule, below the neck and windpipe, and are wider than most of the rest of the stuff. But neither Rusty or me was as good as Turk when it came to harness, so it took some doing.

There were fourteen wagons, each drawn by a pair of draft horses or big mules, and that meant finding twenty-eight collars. It was no ten-minute job, in the dark. But bit by bit, both of us collected what we could, stocked it away from camp, and went back for the rest, always keeping an eye out. The company was pretty well packed up. All the loose stuff was stowed away, and the outfit was going to roll out of Doubtful, maybe around midnight, when the rest of us were deep asleep. They planned to be far down one of the roads; they didn't let us know where they were going next. But they'd come up from Laramie, and I was guessing they would be heading for Douglas.

After we got all the collars we could find, unbuckled and in a heap, we carted them two at a time over to the jail, and stuffed them all in a cell. That was heavy going, too, all those trips hauling forty or fifty pounds of leather and buckles. But about the time the carny show was winding down, and people were quitting, we got them collars all locked up in a cell, and got the jail all locked up, so there wasn't going to be any busting in or out.

Rusty, he just grinned. "I get to visit my Ukrainians for a while more, seems like," he said.

I figured that was good for Rusty, but not for the Siamese twins, who were in a big spat over him and his designs. It sure must be hell to be locked into the same body as your twin, especially if one of you got favored, and not the other. But that was the way things were, and they'd have to figure out living, because no one could help them.

"We gonna sit here with scatterguns and guard the fort, or are we going to bed?" Rusty asked.

"Go to bed. You go look after Riley. Me, I'm going to Belle's. If they come knocking, I'll just let 'em hammer on doors."

I watched him go to his cabin, which was not far away, and near Doubtful Creek, where all them draft horses were, and I drifted toward Belle's Boarding House, where I'd roomed ever since I came to town. It was a quiet night, with a soft breeze, and not much of a moon so it was plenty dark, and I stumbled my way up the stairs and into my room. My guess was I wouldn't get through the night before all hell busted loose.

Well, I was right, but it wasn't an hour into the night before there was a racket in the hall, and then some thundering on my door.

I yawned, lit a lamp, and padded to the door. I sleep buck-ass naked in the summer, and thought maybe I'd better get into something, so I hiked up my britches, and then opened up. Sure enough, there was Heliotrope Pike, beet red, breathing fumes, and looking ready to kill. A man behind him held a kerosene lamp.

"Where is it?" he asked.

"You got some trouble?"

"The harness. You've got it."

"The harness?"

"Cut the crap, Pickens. Where is it?"

"Locked up tight, and it stays there until I cut it loose."

Pike was backed by a pair of bruisers, roustabouts for his show, maybe the very men I was looking for. They were big, and they all simply pushed into my room.

"You'll unlock, or we'll unlock," Pike said. "Your choice."

"You threatening a law officer?" I asked.

"You going to unlock or not?"

"You owe me the names of four abductors, and whoever cranked up that abduction. Did you do it?"

"The keys, Pickens."

"You do it, Pike? You put these roustabouts on horses, and got a cart to carry the twins, and went and grabbed them for your show, knowing you could get away with it?"

"The keys. Or do we have to force the issue?"

I heard a commotion in the hall, and pretty soon Belle was floating up the stairs in her robe, a light in hand.

"You're disturbing my boarders," she said. "You git."

They ignored her.

I thought I saw some opportunity in it. With a little luck, I'd put these three in the other cell, but it'd take some doing.

"It's all right, Belle. This here's Mr. Pike, and he

says someone's made off with his harness. So I'll get dressed and we'll see."

"You in trouble, Cotton?" she asked. I knew she sometimes carried her little .32-caliber five-shot lady revolver in her robe pocket, and I didn't want her messing with these bruisers.

"These here are nice carny folks, Belle. They're fixing to leave town, and mislaid some harness somewheres. I'm going to get my shirt and boots, and we'll go see what needs doing. Someone doesn't want them pulling out."

She eyed me skeptically. "Horse pucky," she said, but didn't pull her peashooter out.

Pike, he just glared. He sure was looking pouty. He was up a tree. He got caught trying to duck out at midnight, and probably didn't suppose I could tell a breast collar from a surcingle. Or that I'd go after his harness at all. Most people, they want to immobilize an outfit, they go after the livestock.

I got busy yanking pants up and stabbing toes in boots, all the while finding out what I could.

"When did you fellers come up missing?" I asked.

Pike just stared. "Pickens, cut the baloney," he said. "You got it and you're going to deliver it."

"Well, I'll trade it for the names of them fellers broke the law around here."

I collected my ancient Stetson and started to collect my scattergun, but Pike, he just shakes his head slowly. "I think not," he said.

Both of them roustabouts had their hands hidden, and I didn't want to mess with that.

So we rattled down the wooden stairs, waking up boarders, and Belle let us pass. Pretty quick we were in a quiet night, and walking toward the jail. I was surprised to find Rusty waiting at the door. He sure had a sense of trouble, and was quietly waiting for trouble to come, mainly in the form of Pike and two big roustabouts.

Rusty, he didn't say a thing, and I knew what we were about to do, and so did he. He opened the office door, and we pushed in, and he headed for a kerosene lamp, scratched a lucifer, and lit the place.

"Now, Pike, what is it you're looking for?" Rusty asked.

There was no harness visible in there. The dark, barred jail door loomed, and behind it two cells, and the farther one had the goods in it. There were a couple of shotguns and rifles in a wall rack, and a mess of papers, and some dodgers, and a few chairs, and my battered desk, all in shifting shadow as the flame wavered.

"You satisfied, Pike?" I asked.

It became a moment of calculation. Rusty was armed. The roustabouts no doubt had some weapons. Pike, he wore his midway clothing, a suit, collarless shirt, and bowler. His hands were not in his pockets. He eyed the room, all its shadowy corners, eyed the barred jail door, and eyed the blackness beyond, knowing where the collars were, but also knowing there would be big trouble if he pushed. Someone had to open the jail door, and open the cell door, and not get trapped in there. And Pike didn't want to shoot a sheriff and deputy if he could help it. Or get shot by me and Rusty.

I watched the gas leak from him.

"We bought that act from a medicine show in Laramie," he said. "I wish I had a receipt but I don't. It's all handshake in the business. That was the Zimmer outfit, that came through ahead of us. These gals, they were pleased to join a real carny, not a medicine show. Those are hard shows. They wear people out and go broke. So we got two grateful women for our freak show tent."

I said nothing. He knew how to get his harness back.

"This company. We stick together," he said. "It's a hard life, being a carny, always on the road, no home to go to, and all we've got is each other. It's us against the world, sometimes. These fellows behind me, they'd give their life for me if I asked them. I'd do the same for them. So whatever we do, we're all together. You can't just throw a few of us in the jail; we're in on everything. You want that? Collect every one of us and put us in those cells, and maybe you'd have what you want. There's no such thing as a few of us taking the rap."

Me, I said nothing. I didn't budge. I wanted the

masked men who'd abducted them Ukrainian twins, and that's how it was going to end.

He eyed me and knew that, without my saying a word. Silence sometimes says ten times more than a lot of talk. His carny show was coming to an end, right then and there. He had no choice. It was doomed if he admitted he had abducted them Siamese twins to put into his show and it was doomed if I refused to give him his harness. I wasn't budging.

He stared glumly into the lamp that was throwing wavering light into the sheriff office.

"Wake up the judge," he said. "I want my harness back. You've stolen my property."

He was on to something. Earwig was the only man in Puma County who might get his harness returned to him—if he was lucky.

"His name is Hanging Judge Earwig," I said, "and he usually cranks up his justice court at ten in the morning, after everyone's sobered up proper."

"I want him now."

"He's likely to dismiss your complaint if you pester him. He sure likes his shut-eye."

"Now," Pike said. He plainly thought he had found a lever to pull. "In spite of his name," he added.

"His name ain't got anything to do with his behavior. He got that because of his equipment. He's got low-hanging fruit."

"Now," said Pike, and I nodded.

Chapter Twenty-four

Hanging Judge Earwig stood in the dark doorway, wearing a white nightshirt and a tasseled cap. A big Colt Dragoon revolver poked menacingly at us. We stood on his porch, a bull's-eye lantern lighting us as Earwig studied his visitors.

"Court's in session," he said.

"Not in the courtroom?" Pike asked.

"Right now. And whoever got me out of bed is going to lose."

"Your lordship, we both did," I said.

Earwig studied me, and studied Pike, a large smile building. "I like that," he said. "All right, you there, with the carnival, you start this circus."

"Heliotrope Pike at your service, sir."

"Where did you get a name like that?"

"My mother was a florist."

"You look purple enough to qualify. All right, what's the complaint?"

"The sheriff here has stolen our harness. He has the breast collars locked in his cell room and won't release them. We are done here and wish to leave."

"Is that true, sheriff?"

"You bet your ass, your majesty."

"You are holding this company of law-abiding and honorable carny folk hostage? May I inquire why?"

"They have stolen goods, sir. They abducted two Ukrainian women, Siamese twins, off a stagecoach in Puma County, and put them in the carnival as a freak show. I am detaining the show until they tell me who in their company stole the women, so I may bring them before your court on charges of abduction and involuntary servitude."

"That sure is a mouthful, Pickens. You just want to bust a few carny people, right?"

"Justice, sir. They have stolen people and put them in bondage."

"That sounds a lot like my wife, sheriff. She's got me hogtied and stuck. Do these Siamese twins object to being in the show?"

"One does and one doesn't."

Earwig's eyes lit up. I could see he was getting entertained, and rousting him out of his slumbers was proving to be a delight to him.

"So one wants to be in the show? And one objects? Then my solution is to slice them in two and let them go their separate ways."

Earwig, he was suddenly shifting around on his bare feet, enjoying this more than any decent man should. He turned to Pike:

"Where'd you get the women?"

"We bought the act in Laramie, handshake deal, don't remember who owned it."

"Bought the act, did you?"

Earwig's big dragoon revolver drifted around until it was pointed at Pike's heaving bosom.

"Well, sir, that's how it is in my business. Acts are bought and sold. I wanted the Siamese twins; a sensation in any freak show. So I didn't mind shelling out."

"Horse pucky, Pike. Pure baloney. You are incapable of telling the truth to save your life."

He waved the dragoon around, until it ended up pointing at Pike's moustache.

"We paid too much for the act; a hundred dollars, and haven't gotten it back," Pike said, wheezing slightly.

Earwig turned to me. "So you stole his harness. Does the office of sheriff give you the right to steal citizens' property?"

"Well, my ma used to say that people love property more than life."

Earwig looked pained. He lifted his tasseled cap and set it back down, frowning. "All right," he said, "I will render a verdict."

He eyed us, looking for signs of rebellion, but me and Pike, we smiled sweetly at His Honor.

Earwig turned suddenly on me, and stabbed a finger my way: "You, sheriff, have stolen this man's property and denied him his liberty. Upon conclusion of this session of court, you will promptly return the harness and will not impede his departure. And I am fining you ten dollars for theft, and five dollars for court costs."

Youch. That was a large piece of my monthly pay. But then Earwig turned to Pike, and stabbed a finger at him. "I'm fining you ten dollars for lying to the court. And you will leave the women here. You will not take them, not even if they wish to go with you. If they were abducted, whether by you or the fantasy abductors you claim to have paid, they will no longer be part of your show."

"But Your Honor, our profit depends on the freak show."

"Ten dollars fine for protesting my verdict. That's cheaper than hanging you. And five in court costs. Now bring the women here, and when I have them in my parlor, the sheriff will be instructed to release your harness."

Pike clapped a hand to his forehead, stricken by ill fortune. Even so, he instructed his two roustabouts to fetch the Ukrainian twins.

"And their baggage," Earwig added.

It took a while. The night breezes toyed with

Earwig's nightshirt. Pike stood there, in his bowler, looking solemn and staring at the moon.

The dragoon Colt never wavered. It rested in Earwig's hand, a handy bailiff, imposing the majesty of the court on the litigants.

A woman's voice rose out of the dark bowels of the house.

"Judge? Where are you? You come keep me warm."

"I'm doing justice, Mabel."

"Well, when you're done, you come do justice to me, my snookum-diddler."

"I will rise to the occasion, my little dill pickle," Earwig said. "Just wait there, and don't pant like a dog."

"I'm your tiddlywinks," she said.

In time, the roustabouts showed up with the women, caterwauling about being deprived of their beauty sleep, the two wrapped in a single white robe. Rusty, he lifted his Stetson in admiration. The roustabouts had two big duffel bags full of the women's stuff.

"This is an outrage," Pike said. "You're stealing my property."

"That's another five dollars," Earwig said. He turned to me. "All right; I have the contraband in hand. You shall go to the jail and release your contraband and return it to Mr. Pike forthwith. And leave the fines in my charity jar in my chamber."

"I sure hate to let them get away with abduction, Your Honor."

"Five dollars, Pickens. The court has spoken."

This here was turning into a depression, if not a recession. So I backed off. Me and Rusty and Pike and his roustabouts headed for the jail, and once inside that dark place, I unlocked the jail door by the light of the lamp, and then unlocked the cell with the harness heaped in it.

Pike, he just glowered. "I never forget," he said. "It's not over."

The roustabouts, they collected armfuls of harness and headed out, and when they returned they had half a dozen more carny people with them, and in short order they carted away every bit of harness we had dumped in there. They'd sort it out, harness the outfit, and ride away, probably before dawn. It sure ticked me off, them people not getting tried for abduction. But maybe there was a little good in Earwig's justice. The Siamese twins, they were still here and free to choose their future if they could ever agree. And Rusty, he was sort of smiling to beat the band.

We finally got them carny people out of the sheriff office, and it wasn't far from dawn. That's when the twins showed up, looking a little put out, each of them dragging a duffel bag full of her stuff. They came along on the street, like a wide ghost, looking real forlorn. They sure weren't welcome at Hanging Judge Earwig's home, not with his wife demanding immediate snooky-wooky, or whatever. So there they were.

"Well, Rusty, my ma always says when opportunity knocks, you got to open the door," I said.

"Ladies," he said, "come into my parlor."

They weren't taking it kindly, and dragged their duffel up the stone steps and into the sheriff office. In fact, Anna looked like she was about to collapse, if not cry her heart out. They were homeless.

"Maybe Belle could work out something," I said.

"Belle, hell," Rusty said. "They're mine now."

He helped them wrestle their duffel bags and got them into the office, where the single lamp still threw buttery light over the gloom.

Anna, she was crying. Natasha, she looked better for the wear, and kept eyeing Rusty as if he'd solve their problems.

"You got any ideas?" I asked Rusty.

"Yeah, you get out of here and let me talk to them," Rusty said.

"I gotta stay and protect their virtue," I said.

Rusty, he just rolled his eyes and glared. I'd stopped him in his tracks.

About then the carny show pulled out. We heard the clatter of a lot of hooves, and then a dark parade in the deep of the night, the roustabouts either walking beside the wagons, or driving them from seats up top. The Pike Brothers Carnival was leaving Doubtful, and maybe it was good riddance.

The Siamese twins, they rushed to the door and watched the moonlit parade, and heard the hollow clop of hooves muffled by night breezes. Anna was crying. Great tears slid down her cheeks. Natasha watched silently, and I knew that a terrible gulf now divided the two women locked into one body. I felt real sorry for them. I'd never given any thought to the pain and grief people called freaks endured, every moment of every day. It was not just that people gawked at them; it was that their lives, their hopes, their wills, were twisted and tied down. They lived lives without any hope, or hopes so small that they seemed pathetic compared to the hopes the rest of us have.

Maybe Anna didn't mind being stared at, being the center of attention on a tawdry little tent-stage. But Natasha, she had come to a different view of her fate, and was filled with the dream of marriage to Rusty—somehow, some way, some place. The carnival slid out of town, its clopping and clatter gone, and then both the Siamese twins began weeping, there in my office, their shared misery for once overwhelming the pain of having to cope with each other, when they each harbored a different dream.

And I had nothing to offer them but an empty jail cell with a cot so narrow they couldn't lie on it, joined as they were. It was a pretty sorry mess, I thought. We'd rescued them from a tawdry life in which thousands of strangers would gawk and jeer at them. But what could they do now? At least in the carny, they were fed and clothed and sheltered, and befriended, too.

"You haven't got much English, but maybe you'll follow me. I'm putting you in my room at Belle's Boarding House. The little bed in there, it's wide enough. Can you walk a couple of blocks?"

Natasha nodded.

"Rusty, you bring their duffel, and I'll help them. They got some stairs to work up."

We started slowly up Wyoming Street. I saw false dawn beginning to crack the darkness in the northeast. The gals, they weren't much for walking, trying to get four legs working together, but they'd had long practice. We got to Belle's about when there was a thin blue line of light riding the skin of the earth, and got them upstairs, into my little cubicle, a few minutes later. There was a little bed, a dresser, a window showing some light, a washbasin and pitcher, and a few hooks on the walls.

Rusty, he settled the duffel bags on a wooden chair.

There was a thunder mug under the cot, and I showed it to them. They stared away, not wanting to acknowledge it.

"Okay, ladies, this is your home for now. I'll get my stuff out in the morning."

Natasha, she was weeping again. I didn't know what to make of it, but then she explained. "First room since Ukraine," she said.

It was nothing to me, but a treasure for them. A long time since they'd had a room of their own

We left them there, Rusty and me. I'd spend my nights in the jail.

Chapter Twenty-five

I thought Doubtful, Wyoming, had finally got free of all those road shows, but I was wrong. In the dog days of August, what should roll in but Billy Bones' Wild West. I didn't know what that was all about, but I learned soon enough. It was about half rodeo, and half Buffalo Bill. There was a mess of stuff like trick shooting, and a couple of female sharpshooters, and some scenarios from the old Indian wars, but there was also a mess of rodeo competition. Bull riding, roping, bronc riding, and a final act involving catching a greased pig.

They set up shop over beyond Saloon Row— they sure knew where to get their cowboy audiences. That ground was pretty much trampled down by the previous shows, and the slightest rain turned it into a quagmire. But that didn't slow them. In fact, I learned that when things were real muddy, they ran a mud wrestling contest with some women, and it was hard to say whether the ladies wore anything at all, beneath all that slippery mud.

I braced for trouble. Rodeo competition was a rough game, and cowboys got into brawls, and I knew my two jail cells were going to be jammed and overflowing real quick. But me and Rusty were up to it. Both of us had done our share of cowboying, and we knew how to deal with all that excess enthusiasm, namely, knock them all senseless.

This outfit soon had big bills plastered on every stray wall around town, and they all were promoting one thing: Miss Quick, trick-shot artist, the surest shot in the female universe. That didn't seem like good advertising to me. Cowboys don't want to get shot at by a female. And they don't want to get beaten in shooting contests by a female. But there she was, in color, wearing fringed leather skirt, boots, a big creamy blouse, and a flat-brimmed hat. And she's hefting a revolver in one hand, and a rifle in the other, and smiling away, like she knew what everyone was thinking

"I think we've got trouble," I said to Rusty.

He didn't reply. He was busy courting the Siamese twins and couldn't be bothered with law enforcement.

"I might see if I can outshoot her," I said.

"If it was a thinking contest, you'd lose," he replied.

I don't suppose I'll ever get used to it.

That's when Billy Bones himself walked in to

the sheriff office. He was a skinny fellow, dressed in black. Black boots, black britches, black shirt, with cream embroidery on it. He was black-haired, too, and lantern-jawed, and I could see he would have a black beard if he didn't shave, because there was a five o'clock shadow at nine in the morning.

"Sheriff? Bones here. That's my outfit setting up."

"Looks like you got a mess of cowboys out there."

"Mostly jailbirds. I hire jailbirds straight out of the pen as roustabouts and livestock handlers. Once in a while, they turn into cowboys. Nobody ever bothers us."

"That sure gives me peace of mind," I said.

"Well, I always want to talk to the law when we come into a town. We like to open with a shooting contest."

"And I'm the bull's-eye?" I asked.

He smiled. "Sort of. Here's the cookie. We challenge any sheriff or deputy to a sharpshooting contest with our Miss Quick. She's quick, all right. She'll shoot the hair off your balls."

"I don't think—"

"That's what we heard. But you're fast with a gun. But we'll have a little sharpshooting contest, you against Miss Quick. Shotguns and clay pigeons, fast draws, trick shots, and action shots from horseback. If you win, you get a twenty-dollar prize. If we win, we get out of jail free."

"What would put you in jail?"

"Jailbirds always have a yearning to return to their happy lives in the pen. I have an awful time keeping them out and free."

"That sure is interesting."

"Good. We open at four, and the sharpshooting contest is at four-thirty, while there's plenty of light. Bring your own artillery."

Rusty, he was smart-ass grinning.

"But I ain't agreed to it."

"Don't be a sissy, Pickens. If you don't show up, after we've promoted it, your name's mud in Puma County. Likely you'll get fired."

"Well, I know all about that," I said. "Once a week."

Bones was gone as fast as he blew in. And I was in for a shooting contest. Not that Miss Quick had any chance against me. My ma, she always said I was good with my hands, which made up for being slow. I sure wondered what this Miss Quick looked like. I thought she might be a fake; women can't shoot worth a damn. Put some little guy, a real sharpshooter, in skirts and powder his face, and who'd know the difference? That was it. These here shows, they didn't mind stretching truth a little.

Well, they were good at publicity. Next I knew, Mayor George Waller dropped by with a word of encouragement.

"Hear you're up against some female sharpshooter, Cotton. The honor of Puma County's at stake, but you'll whip her handily?" Funny how he ended that with a sort of question mark in his voice.

"I'll whip her," I said. "No woman shoots as good as me."

Waller smiled. "Your job depends on it. We can't have losers in the sheriff office."

Before the afternoon was half done, Reggie Thimble had seconded that. The supervisors were unanimous: win or walk out of the job.

I wouldn't let myself get overconfident. Just because she was billed as Miss Quick didn't mean she was. I was the fastest draw in Wyoming, and a few people planted six feet down could attest to it. And I was real good on horseback. I could hit the ace of spades at a gallop.

I got out my revolver, cleaned it, worked the mechanism, and pulled it smoothly out of its holster a few times. I had the reputation for being fast with it, but in truth, I was careful. I figured one slower good shot was worth a bundle of worthless fast shots. Let people think I was fast: The only thing that mattered was accuracy.

"You'll win," Rusty said, as he eyed me putting my artillery into top shape.

"Of course, I'll win." I was testy. How could I not win? I didn't need his encouragement.

I cleaned my rifle, and polished up my shotgun, and made sure I had plenty of shells and cartridges. They might cost a little, but I'd soon have twenty dollars and that would replace them with cash left over.

I don't wear my holster much. Doubtful didn't need some fool gunslick of a sheriff, making a public display of his weapons. I usually carried a billy club, and I could poleaxe people with that. But if all them cowboys wanted a show from me, and the city fathers, too, they'd get it.

Rusty, he kept smirking, and I'd show him a thing or two.

Then Miss Quick walked in. I knew who it was before she introduced herself.

"Howdy," she said, and thrust a tiny white paw into my sun-baked one. "I'm Amanda Quick."

"Howdy, yourself. You come to look me over, did you?"

"Oh, just to make your acquaintance. You sure are a big galoot."

"And you're a little one. Five feet?"

"Add an inch."

"You're real purty," I said. I thought that might disarm her. If I told her she was real purty, out there on the firing line, she'd melt like wax in a candle.

She eyed me. "Big and strong and manly," she said.

I sort of blushed. "My ma never called me that," I said.

"You'll want to prove that males can beat females."

"Oh, no, I want to prove that sheriffs are better shots than theater people."

She laughed. She sure was cute. She had little dimples on her cheeks when she smiled, and merry blue eyes, and was sort of strawberry blond, and was built with just the right curves. And she was dressed just like in the posters, with a fringed leather skirt, a loose blouse good for shooting, and a perky little western hat.

"If I win, you got to marry me," I said.

I don't know where that came. It just sort of bubbled up and erupted. It was like proposing in front of Old Faithful geyser.

"Well, usually they don't ask for that," she said. "They want all the benefits without the ring. And if I win, will you marry me?"

Holy cats, that caught me with my drawers around my ankles. "You bet," I said, "but the twenty dollars, it sounds more like what I'm after."

She laughed, a little twinkle in her eyes, and said, "I'll see you on the field."

She jounced away, leaving me lovestruck and bumble headed. I didn't want to marry her, but now I was stuck. I'd win easily, and then what? Hanging Judge Earwig would be reciting the vows, and I'd be a cooked goose. I don't know how I get into things like that.

Rusty, he was watching all this with a glint in his eye.

"Don't you say nothing," I said.

Time sure dragged. I was mad at Rusty, mad at Billy Bones and his show, mad at shooting contests, and mad at that perky little gal I didn't like one tiny bit. She was so small I didn't know how she could lift a rifle, or a shotgun. But according to all the publicity on them broadsheets pasted on every wall, she was a true marksman, and not just standing. Put her on a speeding horse and she was all the better.

It finally got late in the afternoon, so I strapped on my holster and revolver, collected my rifle and shotgun and a mess of shells and cartridges, and set out for the east side of Doubtful. People greeted me along the way, and it dawned on me they'd been waiting, lining the sidewalks, planning to cheer me along.

There were a few women, of course, wanted Miss Quick to whip me. I knew the type. They wore Amelia Bloomer's pantaloons, and devoted themselves to making life difficult for men. But I ignored them. Most of those nice folks were cheering me. Mayor Waller was even waving a Wyoming flag, and Sammy Upward motioned me to stop in for a drink, but I shook my head. I could whip her with six drinks in me, but decided not to take the chance, just in case she got some lucky shots in, when I was not paying attention. Leonard Silver waved from the door of his Emporium, and my landlady, Belle, in a vast pink tent of a dress, twirled her parasol by way of saluting me. Alphonse Smythe, the postmaster, smiled from in front of his log post office, and even Maxwell, from the funeral parlor, gave me a pale wave of his waxen hand.

It sure was a victory parade, right down Wyoming Avenue, me with my two long guns and the short one. Lawyer Stokes sidled up and volunteered to carry my boxes of shells, so I let him, and he considered it a great honor, and carried them as if they were a wedding ring resting on a lavender pillow. Turk, he was watching, but he wasn't properly worshipful, and was grinning like a hyena. I'd get even with him after I won my twenty dollars.

Well, by the time I got to the show grounds, there was a mess of people there, including most every cowboy that could escape the local ranches. Bones had set up a shooting area, and roped off the crowds, and there was Miss Quick, all dolled up and cute as a bug, waiting to sacrifice herself to me.

She smiled.

I tipped my hat. And then we were on.

Chapter Twenty-six

There sure was a nice crowd standing around the makeshift arena. Billy Bones, dressed in fringed and beaded buckskins, got the show on the road. With a wave, he ushered in a passel of riders, and a bugler and a flag-bearer, and these got into a smart trot, while the bugler bugled away, all sorts of stuff that sounded like the army—"Tattoo," "Boots and Saddles," "Charge,"—and the fellow with the flag broke into a trot, and ran the banner around the arena, while the cowboys cheered, except for the old Confederates, who stayed real silent.

But the noise of it all was real fine, and it got the show off to a bang-up start.

Then Billy Bones, on a white stallion, comes trotting to the center, and he lifts his megaphone, and begins bellowing at the mob.

"Ladies and gentlemen, may I introduce Miss Amanda Quick, ace sharpshooter, trick-shot artist, and bull's-eye champion."

She came sailing out, wearing a soft fringed buckskin skirt, boots, a generous silky blouse, and a flat-crowned hat with a bright pink hatband. All them cowboys, they whistled and lusted and some got real silent.

"And now, ladies and gentlemen, the local marksman and champion and lawman, the famous, the legendary, the invincible, Cotton Pickens!"

I guess that was me. So I trotted out there, lifted my old hat, bowed, and smiled. There was nothing to do but shake Miss Quick's dainty little hand, so I pumped it a few times, and we both smiled. I was going to clean her clock, so I smiled a heap.

Some gun bearers brought our stuff out. They would do the reloading, and all of that, so we could concentrate on the contest.

This was going to be good. This here lady, she was so small she could hardly lift a long gun, so I had all the advantage.

Billy lifted his megaphone and bawled, "All right, you fine citizens of Puma County, watch this. Our first event will be trap shooting, ten clay pigeons, and may the best, ah, person win."

Well, ladies first. Her man handed her a shiny little .410-gauge shotgun, a toy gun for a toy lady, and I smiled. That peashooter couldn't pop a pigeon. The fellow at the traps, about fifty feet away, was all set, so she nodded. The clay bird whizzed along a flat trajectory, maybe fifteen feet up, and she shattered it easily. She handed the gun to her batman, and he gave her another, loaded and ready.

The cowboys whistled. Some of them had gotten beers from the saloons, and were sucking hard, soaking up enough suds to begin making smart observations.

Well, the way this was set up, she would tackle all ten birds, and then it'd be my chance to beat her. She sure was cute. She wasn't paying attention to me, any, or the crowd, which was making anti-female remarks. She'd heard them all before, and they bounced off her back. Instead, she was all business. She blew away the second and third birds, took a corner out of the fourth, which counted as a kill, knocked the fifth to smithereens, almost missed the sixth from leading it too much, but nicked it and that counted as a kill. After each shot, she traded guns with her loader, one of the show's roustabouts, and smiled. It sure didn't take long to finish the job: She'd knocked down every bird, and with that toy gun, too.

She smiled sweetly, and I was thinking I wouldn't mind marrying her, but only if I could shoot better than her. Who'd want to be married to a sharpshooting woman? It sure was something to ponder.

So, she waited quietly for the applause to wither away, and then it was my turn.

Rusty, he had a nice sheriff-office twelve-gauge ready for me, and I took it. I didn't need anyone reloading, so I waved him away. I always do a job myself. I hefted the twelve-gauge, and nodded. They sent a bird sailing across the field, and I blew it to smithereens, with a good, satisfying boom. I stuffed another shell in, and blew the next one to bits. The boys watching all this, they started whistling and laughing. I sure was having a fine time. And Miss Quick, she forced a smile on her pretty lips, and clapped as I knocked each bird down. It was so easy I was almost feeling embarrassed. It didn't take long before I had permanently ruined ten clay pigeons, and then the local crowd, they were huzzahing the local sheriff, and I was feeling just fine.

Billy Bones, he was yelling into his megaphone. "Excellent shooting, a tie, both contestants not missing a trick."

I bowed to the crowd. Miss Quick, she just smiled.

"And now, we'll have some handgun competition," Billy Bones said. "Knock a hole through the ace of spades at twenty feet. Best of six attempts."

In other words, empty one loaded six-gun. Well, that would be a piece of cake.

They rigged up a pole with the ace of spades sticking out of it. I'd heard that in the show, Bones himself would hold the card in his fingers and let her blow the spade away. But not this fine August afternoon, with heat rising from the parched clay, and a mess of boozy cowboys watching. And Bones might trust Miss Quick not to shoot his fingers off, but he sure didn't trust me.

She punctured the spade, a little high, and Billy Bones paraded the card around the perimeter, where everyone could see it. She had a way of lifting the revolver, sighting down its barrel, and shooting in one graceful movement. Her second shot was dead center; her third a little left, and her fourth and fifth right through the ace.

Not bad, I thought. I was beginning to respect her. She used a little .32-caliber revolver, and knew what she was doing. I would use my old .44, which was big and heavy, and put the bullet right where I intended. I punctured those aces of spades each time, and we were tied once again, and she was smiling, and I was waving my hat, and everyone was having a fine old time.

This sure was a fine old afternoon.

"And now, ladies and gentlemen, a true test of marksmanship. A contest that separates the gifted from the brilliant. I give you, shooting clay birds out of the sky—with rifles. The contestants will take turns, five in all."

The cowboys, they began clucking at that one. How could you shoot a clay disk sailing through space fifty feet away, with a single bullet? I confess, I didn't like the odds on that one, but maybe it would be a tough act for little Miss Quick, too. If she could do it, she was some sort of genius.

The spectators knew it, too, and there was a sort of buzzing as they whispered about it. But Miss Quick, she was smiling to beat the band, and her man handed her a nice rifle, of a caliber I could only guess at, but not too large. She was still working with smaller, ladylike weapons. She seemed to enjoy herself, though. She must have blown a few cartons of bullets away, practicing this one.

She nodded, the keepers tripped the trap, and a clay bird sailed out into the blue. She followed it for a moment, squeezed, absorbed the recoil, and the bird sailed on, unscathed.

The crowd erupted. She'd finally missed one.

Me, I studied my old, battered forty-four, which used the same cartridges as my revolver, and I suspected I was in for it, this time. It was a worthy old rifle, and I knew its quirks, but blowing a clay disk out of the sky would be pushing its limits.

I nodded, followed the gray little thing, led it, fired, and watched it sail to earth untouched.

"Even up!" yelled Billy Bones, making sure everyone at the show got it.

Miss Quick, she took a loaded rifle from her batman, smiled again, nodded, and watched the target sail. A shot racked the quiet, and the clay disk disintegrated.

Holy cats. She had done it with a single-shot rifle.

I missed that next shot, so I was one down, and now the cowboys were jeering. Even Mayor Waller was yelling.

"Turn in your badge, Pickens," yelled County Supervisor Reggie Thimble.

The amazing Miss Quick nailed the next bird, and the next, and the next, and I was blowing lead through thin air. That sure was an experience.

"Congratulations," I said to her. "I don't think I'll marry you."

She thought that was pretty fine humor. She didn't know I was plumb serious.

That mess of friends watching this show, they turned real silent.

Billy Bones lifted his megaphone. "Now, wasn't that outstanding? Let's give Miss Amanda Quick a good hand. Have you ever seen anything like it?"

There sure were a lot of whistles from the cowboys, and Miss Quick curtseyed in each direction, cheerfully acknowledging the cowboy cheers coming her way.

At least I didn't have to curtsey to any mess of cowboys, so there was some good in it. Winning isn't everything, you know. A feller has to stay dignified and stern.

Then old Billy Bones, looking real cheerful, announced the next one.

"And now, my good friends in Doubtful, Wyoming, we will have an exhibition of equestrian marksmanship. While we set up that bull's-eye target over there, and we ready a steed for each contestant, I'll tell you what we're about to see.

"Each contestant will take three passes at the target, while mounted on a galloping steed, which the contestant will control with knee commands. Miss Quick will shoot at the target using an upside-down rifle. We know that your fine sheriff has not had occasion to fire his weapon upside down, so he is free to compete using his rifle any way he wants to. The contestants will take turns, of course, ladies first."

Well, I thought I had a real good chance if they didn't put some trick horse under me that would ruin my shot.

Miss Quick swiftly mounted on a fine gray charger, and was handed her rifle by her batman. Using only her knees to control the horse, she circled around the arena, waving to the cowboys and merchants, blowing kisses to all of them, and finally she headed toward the far end, put the horse into a trajectory that would take her past the bull's-eye, and spurred the horse. It leapt ahead, and she leveled her upside-down rifle, her trigger finger on top, rather than underneath, and when she was opposite the target, she snapped a shot.

Dead center. A hole smack in the middle of the middle.

My turn. I climbed up on the nag they gave me, gave him a quick whirl, and was satisfied. It was an improvement on Critter. I cut loose, leveled my forty-four, and blasted away as I came even. I watched the paper disintegrate where I holed it.

It was a good shot, but a bit off center, an inch or two high left.

"Well, that was a fine exhibition, just fine, outstanding," Billy Bones announced.

But now the cowboys were hooting at me. And that's how it went the next two passes. I did fine; she did better, while holding a rifle that was upside down.

"Ladies and gentlemen, we'll now show you the targets," Bones said, as his roustabouts carried them around the edges of the arena. "Your man Cotton Pickens did just fine, outstanding shooting, but I'm proud to say our little Miss Quick bested him."

All them cowboys were sure applauding and yelling and hooting.

"Turn in your badge, Pickens," County Supervisor Reggie Thimble yelled.

"You'd have to pay her more than me," I replied. I had him there.

Chapter Twenty-seven

Rusty, he sure was smiling a lot. Maybe he thought he'd get my job. I thought maybe he'd get it, too. Them people in Puma County, they wanted their sheriff to be top dog, and I'd just gotten whipped by an itsy-bitsy trick shooter, cute as a button, but she didn't have to go hunt down bad men or shoot it out with real people.

It sure graveled me. I was thinking of proposing, back when it all started. She was real nice material for a wife, but not if she could outshoot me any time she felt like it. It got me all churned up. She was just the sort of woman I wanted. She sure was a looker, and she smiled sweetly, and was even more smart than my ma.

Speaking of which, my ma always said I might be slow, but I made up for it by being quick with my hands. But not quick enough to beat Miss Amanda Quick. It sure was making a mess in my head, all this feeling that was getting constipated and I couldn't get it out.

Rusty was spending a lot of time with the Ukrainian twins, but the twins weren't happy. Anna, she wanted no part of Rusty, and Natasha, she wanted to marry him right away, real bad. So the two were fighting, and getting mad, and feeling hopeless because they were connected. And no one could help them.

Rusty wandered over to that big field after the first Wild West show, and got to studying the clay pigeons that we'd shot up. I don't know what had started him doing that, but he did it, and he found some pigeons that weren't broken up, and that were peppered with little pits in them, especially where a part had broken off. He slid a couple of those in his britches, and came back to the sheriff office.

Things were bad around there. Some of those people, like Reggie Thimble, they really did want me to turn in my badge, and were saying they didn't feel protected in Puma County anymore because some pipsqueak girl had shown the whole world that I couldn't hit a barn side at ten feet.

The one that annoyed me the most was Delphinium Sanders, the banker's wife. She wanted me to ask Miss Quick to be the sheriff of Puma County. She thought the idea of a female sheriff was just fine, but I reminded her that Miss Quick might be a trick shot, but could she drag drunks to the lockup, and wrestle some bank robber to the ground?

They were all just salivating at the chance to get rid of me, but I wasn't going to be got rid of. I'd stay glued to my job until they got tired of getting rid of me. That's how it had been since I got hired to clean up Doubtful.

Rusty waited patiently for all those mean-spirited people to get out, and then he laid the three clay pigeons on my desk. Two had an edge nipped away, and one was intact.

"I waited until they got past the rodeo stuff, and thought I'd have a look," he said.

"What am I supposed to do? Put these up on the wall?' I asked.

Rusty, he just looked like he was tired of me. "You got eyes, dontcha?"

So I studied them, not making much of it.

"She's shooting sand from her rifle," he said. "Turned her rifle into a little shotgun."

Sure enough, the surfaces of the clay birds were pitted, especially along the edges where they had a piece blown off.

"Sand did that," Rusty said.

"She's a good shot."

"Sure she is. A fine shot, but she was giving herself an edge you didn't have."

That sort of relieved me. Maybe I'd ask her to marry me after all. I was a better shot than she was. If I was going to fall for a gal, she'd better not outdraw me.

"Sand. I'd heard about it. Someone was telling me once that's how Annie Oakley does it. She's so good, I don't believe it, but you never know. This little sweetheart, she's too good to be true, and I got the itch to look at the targets, those that weren't busted up."

I eyed the clay birds. Show these little pigeons around, and maybe the town would get off my back. But I decided that for now, I'd just let it be a secret. I was sweet on her, and didn't want to hurt her any. She had a way of dimpling up when she smiled that made me think of a little white cottage and rambling roses, and a big double bed.

The next day, I went to watch the show again, and sure took some ribbing.

"You gonna study how it's done?" Turk asked.

That's how he was. He was always asking if I was going to study how to get Critter tamed, and I always told him I didn't want Critter tamed. I wanted him ornery enough so no one would mess with him but me.

The show was just fine. Billy Bones could sure put on some star-spangled entertainment. The crowd was sparse that afternoon, mostly because it was threatening to rain, and not even weathered cowboys want to stand around through a mess of showers. Not even for Miss Amanda Quick, World's Finest Sharpshooter.

She was wearing those same embroidered buckskins and white boots, and a big loose blouse that wouldn't constrict her movement. There wasn't a contest this time; she just went through her stuff, adding some tricks to the display. She shot a playing card in half, aiming at its edge, not its flat side. She shot a cigar from Billy Bones's mouth. He wasn't even nervous. She had a few more equestrian tricks, too. She shot at targets from under the neck of a galloping horse, and did it bareback. I sure didn't know how she could lean forward along the neck of a racing nag, lean over one side without falling off, aim her revolver from somewhere under the nag's jaw, and hit a bull's-eye.

But she was doing it, and all them cowboys, they finally started clapping. Who'd ever seen the like?

Me, I was just getting more and more sweet on her. It was making me sort of grumpy. She'd pull out of town in a few days, and the show would go to the next town, and that would be the last I'd ever see of her.

The rodeo part of the show was pretty good, too. Calf roping, bull riding, bronc riding, stuff like that. But there were acts in between, including a mess of wild Indians chasing a stagecoach. We hadn't had anything like that around Doubtful for a few years, with all the tribes stuck on reservations, but it was fun to see all the roustabouts in the show painted up and wearing bonnets, and shooting blanks at the stagecoach.

Well, on my way back into town I passed Belle's, and there was Rusty, and stretched on the walk were the Siamese twins. Natasha was out cold, and Anna was stuck with waiting until Natasha woke up, so they could move again.

"Trouble?" I asked Rusty.

"Yeah, Anna got mad at Natasha again, and bonked her with a skillet. See that lump? She hit her sister so hard it knocked her out. But there's nothing she can do, since Natasha's got to wake up first."

That was assault, and I had laws to enforce, but I'd have to wait until Natasha came around. Belle, she was applying cold compresses to Natasha's blonde hair, while Anna stared enviously, not getting any attention at all. It sure was hell to be a Siamese twin, I thought.

Rusty wasn't very happy. He kept staring at me, knowing exactly what I was going to do. I was going to arrest Anna for assault.

Natasha finally shook her head, glared at Anna, said something in Ukrainian that sounded pretty tough, and then moaned and felt the lump on her head.

"All right, ladies, I got to haul you to Hanging Judge Earwig," I said.

"But you can't," Rusty said.

"There was an assault, and I'm sworn to uphold the law."

"Oh, Cotton, come to your senses," Belle said.

But I was feeling stubborn. I just got whupped by a button-sized sharpshooter, and I was ready to take it out on the nearest offender.

"Ladies, you get up and follow me."

"I'm sick," Natasha said. "I need to lie down."

"You just got assaulted. Come along now."

"If you do this to them, find some other place to board," Belle said. "You're a beast."

"I got the law to enforce," I said.

Rusty just shook his head and eyed me as if I belonged on some other planet.

We made our slow way to the courthouse, up the stairs, while Natasha groaned, and into the chamber, rank with Judge Earwig's underarm odor. Both Belle and Rusty tagged along. Belle was acting like a pregnant thunderstorm. And Rusty had gone silent.

"What have we here?" Earwig asked, licking his moustache.

"Assault, Your Honor. This here one, Anna, conked this here one, Natasha, with a frying pan, and I will show you her bump as evidence."

Earwig studied Natasha's bump, which bulged from her head, just above the forehead.

"You, the alleged victim, tell me what happened."

"I don't know the words," she said.

"Well, if you want justice, learn the words," Earwig said. He was in a testy mood. The courtroom was hot and he probably wanted to go home and soak his bunions in Epsom salts.

"I saw it, and I'll tell it," Belle said.

"Are you prejudiced on one side or the other?"

"You bet your ass, I am. These two have been at each other ever since they got moved in. The one on the right, Anna, didn't want to leave the carny show. The one on the left, Natasha, is being courted by the deputy, here, Rusty Irons, and wants to marry him. And now the fight has turned violent, and neither is going to win it."

"That so?" he asked Natasha.

She nodded.

"You have any means to make a living?" he asked Natasha.

She shook her head, but Anna said yes, with the carny show.

"Vagrants," he said. "I sentence you to two days in the county jail."

"But Your Honor, the cot in the jail is too narrow. And you can't put the victim in prison; Anna did it, not Natasha," Rusty said.

Hanging Judge Earwig glared, and for a moment I thought he'd throw Rusty in with the ladies. But he chose a more subdued approach.

"I'm punishing them for vagrancy. They'll both go in; sleep on the floor."

"You're a beast," said Belle.

Hanging Judge Earwig didn't object. In fact, he smiled, ear to ear, with the compliment.

"I'll suspend the sentence if someone puts ten dollars in the Charity Jar," he said.

He was looking at Rusty, who was beginning to acquire some understanding about the burdens of marriage.

Rusty sighed, dug into his britches, pulled out two fives, a fifth of his monthly wage, and stuffed them into the charity jar. Earwig was, of course, his own favorite charity.

"Say, where are they from?" he asked.

"Lvov, Ukraine, Your Honor," Rusty said.

"Ah! A Lvov triangle," he said, and leered.

Out on the street, Rusty lit into me. "You just cost me a fortune," he said.

"Well, propose to both. Maybe that's the problem."

"Fat chance any preacher would marry all of us," he replied.

"Men ruin women's lives," Belle said.

I was thinking the opposite. That little blonde sharpshooter sure had made my own life a lot meaner.

Chapter Twenty-eight

When I saw Big Nose George barreling in to my office, I knew there was trouble afoot. And I pretty well guessed what it was about.

"The hooligans have busted loose," he said. "Big Finn and Mickey, from the orphan train."

"Where'd they go?"

"They vanished. On two of our fastest broncs, with two more they took for their joyride."

"What's the deal?"

"They stole a hoof rasp. And bit by bit, they filed away at their irons, but not the chain. They worked on the irons around their calves under their pants where no one could see."

"I don't know how you can cut iron with a hoof rasp."

"Well, they done it, and got the irons off some-how. Maybe they had a few other tools. They got clear of the place at night, and were missing this morning."

"Armed?"

"Hell, yes. There's no lack of weapons around the Admiral Ranch."

"With what?"

"We're still sorting that out. But they have side arms and long guns and boxes of shells."

"Any food?"

"We don't know. They sure been planning it, so probably they do. Maybe both spare horses carry packs."

"They make any threats? Talk about going somewhere?"

"They kept to themselves, real quiet."

"What were they doing, mostly?"

"Ranch gardens. The Glads grow a lot of what we eat."

"You spot any trail?"

"In August? Bone-dry, hard clay?"

"Well, you got trackers, and they'll find green apples."

"They stayed on main trails; lots of apples, plenty still green."

"You got any hunch?"

Big Nose scratched his head, pondering it. "Those two were so sour, I think they're more interested in evening up some scores than leaving the country. They never made friends with anyone around there. It was them against the world."

"That's good. We'll start there," I said. "But you put your ranch hands out, and see if you can find a trail. You fellers hunt them out of town. I'll start around here. Evening up the score means me, Rusty, Earwig, mostly. Thanks, Big Nose. We'll be watching our backs."

"You gonna get up a posse?"

"You're the posse. I'm deputizing you. Raise your hand."

We went through that, and I handed him a badge.

George stared. "No damned good. Horse theft, saddles and tack, pack frames, weapons and shells, food, and who knows what?"

"Also escaping a sentence," I added. "Earwig sentenced them to a year in the chains."

"Yeah, that, too."

"All right. These orphans are armed and dangerous, have made threats, and probably plan to do them all. Watch your backs."

Big Nose left. He would leave his sweated horse at Turk's and borrow another. I buckled my revolver on, checked the loads, collected a short-barreled scattergun, and headed out. Rusty was off, spending time with Riley. That was one good orphan. Hanging Judge Earwig needed to be told, and protected. If I could guess at the motives of two bitter hooligans, who hated their chains,

I'd say they'd go straight for the judge, get him first, and finish him off. Boys, even smart boys, might prefer revenge to escape.

At least that's how I figured it. Not that I'm right very much. But a lawman's got to start somewhere, and that's where I went with it. I left a note for Rusty to watch out, and line up some help if we needed it, then I angled across the square to the courthouse, but Hanging Judge Earwig wasn't around, which made me uneasy. Well, he often lunched at Barney's Beanery, so I went over there, and didn't find him. Next I headed for Earwig's house on the north side, where all the fancier people lived.

The house looked quiet, but the front door was open, and things didn't seem right. I studied the windows, looking for faces or the glint of weapons, but I saw nothing at all. I yelled, and got only silence coming back. Mabel should have replied. I edged behind the big cottonwood, removed my old hat, waved it, but no one shot at it. I checked neighboring buildings. The hooligans were smart enough to set up a trap and watch me walk in. But there wasn't any real places close by; not revolver close. Rifle close. I couldn't see inside of them, but the windows were closed, and nothing was poking out of any of them.

The Earwigs had a buggy, and it was still in the

carriage barn back of the main house. They used a Turk Livery Barn nag when they wanted one.

Time to go in. I pulled my revolver, raced straight for the open front door, and threw myself sideways when I reached the porch. Nothing happened. I stood on the porch, beside the door, waved my hat, but no one shot it. I got down on all fours, peered low through the door, but no one put a bullet between my eyes.

"All right, Mickey, Big Finn, hands up, come on out; alive or dead, your choice."

No response.

The hooligans probably weren't there, but maybe a couple of bodies were.

I worked around the house, avoiding windows, darting up to look inside, and lowering my head. Nothing. What I dreaded was something like two dead people lying in one of those rooms.

I burst through the rear door, mostly used to reach the outhouse in back, and found no one in the kitchen or parlor or pantry. It sure was quiet in there. I had my .44 in hand, ready to use it, but it was a worthless piece of iron just then. There was a bedroom downstairs, empty, and an attic room, empty. I saw no sign of violence or trouble, except the open door, but I could nearly sniff it. This house had been invaded; Judge and Mabel Earwig had been hurried away, and I didn't have a clue where to find them. It made me sick to think about all that.

I stood there on that porch, trying to fathom where the hooligans went and what they had in mind. My ma, she always said it was hard to get inside someone else's head and know what's what. But I had to now. There was no time to waste. The Earwigs would soon be dead, if they weren't already dead.

The only thing that came to mind was that the little punks would choose some grandiose gesture; the itch to show off would trump the need to flee. They could have shot the Earwigs in their house and raced away, but they didn't. They were prodding the Earwigs to some destination, and my instinct was that the place would be plenty public, and what a couple of dreaming hooligans wanted most was to do something very public and very bad. They wouldn't take the Earwigs off to the woods and shoot them miles from anyone; they would do whatever they had in mind in front of as many people as they could, and then race away, laughing. That meant Doubtful, not some obscure corner of Puma County.

A distant shot yanked me from my guesswork. Then another. From down near the creek. And that meant the Hanging Tree, a big cottonwood with a stout horizontal limb near the creek bank, where the population of Doubtful had been reduced from time to time.

I didn't like the sound of all that. I raced in that direction, a handgun in one hand, my sawed-off scattergun in the other. A couple of men were racing that way, too. A few others were heading the opposite direction, getting out of harm's way.

Two more shots, rifle fire if I gauged it right, shattered the morning. I had no idea what was happening, but I intended to stop it. I got past the mercantile and cut through an alley, and then past a row of houses whose rear yards ended up in the creek bottoms, and there it all came clear, even as a rifle cracked and the bullet ripped through the branch of a cottonwood near me.

I ducked, studied the scene, and didn't like what was right there in front of my eyes.

The hooligans were there, all right. On the ground, under the tree, sat Judge and Mabel Earwig, their hands bound behind them. Mickey was the one using the rifle, and he was holding off half a dozen townspeople, none of whom were armed, unless someone had a revolver. Mickey had plenty of shells, seems like, and didn't hesitate to shoot anything that moved, even a hundred yards out. No way we could rush them, and none of us had a long gun.

They had strung lariats around the necks of the Earwigs, thrown the lines over the trees, and Big

Finn was tying the first of these lines to the saddle horn of one of their stolen horses. I saw a big carriage whip leaning against the cottonwood, and I knew what would happen the moment he got both lines tied to both saddle horns. The horses would bolt under the whip, the lines would yank the Earwigs up, up, and up, and probably pull their heads off. There's no good way to die, but this would be the worst.

"You, Finn, drop that line. Now!" I yelled.

Mickey replied with a shot that burned through my hat and knocked it off. I settled lower, hugging dirt. I had some quick decisions to make. Everyone else was scared off. Mickey was pumping lead at anything within a hundred yards. I was closer than that, maybe two hundred feet. My sawed-off shotgun wasn't worth spit.

"Let them go," I yelled. "Right now."

I edged left. Another shot burned close.

I could shoot the horses or shoot twelve-year-old Finn. Shooting the horses wouldn't work. It took only a whip crack to hang the Earwigs, whether or not the horses had a revolver bullet in them.

The boy, then, and there was no time to feel bad about it. I lay prone, leveled up my .44 as best I could, and targeted Finn. He'd finished tying the lines to the saddle horns, and was reaching for his whip.

I shot. Finn toppled. Blood bloomed on his chest. I felt like hell. The horses skittered, yanking the Earwigs to their feet. Mickey screamed, pumped three shots at me, and ran to fetch the whip. Finn writhed a few times and then lay still. I shot Mickey, who howled, a bullet in his arm. The horses skittered around again, yanking the Earwigs to and fro, but not lifting them up. It was as tough a deal as I'd ever seen.

I yelled at the townspeople. Waved them away. I had to get to those horses and keep them from bolting. Anything could do it, including the smell of blood. If they bolted, the Earwigs would die after all. Shaking, I circled clear around until I could approach them from the front. Mickey was holding his arm and howling.

I began talking gentle to those skittery nags, just trying to whoa up their instincts, and they let me come in. I got ahold of the bridles of both, and backed them up until the Earwigs were no longer on their tiptoes, and could stand, and then sit. Mabel was weeping. The Hanging Judge was looking mighty stern. He'd sentenced a few to their fate at this very tree.

There was still danger, but the town folks, George Waller leading the race, slipped in and began loosening the lariats around the Earwigs' necks, and then cut their hands loose. I held them horses tight until it was over.

Big Finn was dead, looking quiet and innocent on the clay, not a line in his face, as peaceful as some altar boy. Mickey, he howled and held his arm, and I found a handkerchief and tied off the wound that had torn a lot of flesh. He'd live if he didn't bleed to death.

The boys' horses were tied nearby, packed and ready to go. Revenge and run. But it hadn't worked out like that. One orphan boy was dead; the other might die, and faced a life pounding rock and enjoying the hospitality of the Territory of Wyoming.

Earwig, he just sat on the ground and stared, too shaken to talk. But then he looked up and offered me two words.

"Thank you," he said.

Chapter Twenty-nine

Doc Harrison saved the boy. The Admiral Ranch proudly claimed Big Finn, and put him in the Glad family plot out there. Having a notorious outlaw and the youngest criminal ever to be shot by a Wyoming lawman would help make the ranch a legend, so King Glad retrieved the corpse.

All that I got out of it was big trouble. Reggie Thimble led the parade. "What kind of sheriff have we got, shoots boys? Why don't you quit, Pickens? Or pick on someone your own age."

That sort of took me back a little, seeing as how the boy was a few seconds away from hanging two good citizens, and was then intent on escaping justice. But people didn't see it that way. Only a few days before, I had been soundly whipped by a little sharpshooter, and now they figured I was picking on boys, and no matter that he was a rotten little hooligan.

It sort of got me down. But there was a side of it no one was confessing to, namely, a mess of people would have been delighted to see Hanging Judge Earwig strung up and left to dangle for a week. As for Mabel, she was guilty simply by marriage to him. Earwig wasn't the most beloved critter in Doubtful. Sammy Upward, who ran the Last Chance Saloon, wanted to have a near-hanging celebration, and send the bill to Earwig, but I talked him out of it.

"Cotton, there's a joke going around the saloons. What does it take to put Sheriff Pickens out of office? Two boys and a girl! Just thought I'd let you know."

That sure steamed me up. The boys were about to kill two people, and the girl blew away clay pigeons with a load of sand. But that didn't matter. The damage was done. And the town was fixing to make me hand in my badge.

I sure didn't like shooting that boy, and I didn't like putting lead into Mickey, too. I kept chewing on it in my mind, and didn't see anything else I could have done. I asked a few people, like George Waller, what else I could have done, but all I got was a shrug. Anything but shoot a boy, is what they seemed to be telling me.

Reggie Thimble had me right where he wanted me, in the crosshairs, and I knew he was going to talk it over with the other Puma County supervisors and start looking for a new sheriff. At least the other boy, Mickey, was showing signs of recovering, but his left arm would always be useless. The bullet had severed some muscle, so he'd not only be in jail, he'd be about half fit to do anything. It was a bad ending for a kid who came out on the orphan train, an outfit that tried to give abandoned children a better life.

Rusty became my eyes and ears, since no one was talking to me. Rusty patrolled the town, stopped in at all the saloons, and visited with bankers and blacksmiths.

"You're in a bad way, Cotton. They think they have a joke for a sheriff."

Well, some things can't be changed. But then I remembered something my ma used to say, which was, you make your own luck. Maybe I should make my own luck. But how?

"Rusty," I said, "if I got me a rematch with Miss Quick, have we some way of keeping her from blowing away pigeons with sand?"

Rusty stared at me. He'd been so busy wooing the Siamese twins he had forgotten all about my troubles. "I'll think on it. We've either got to have her shoot some other rifle with real shells or we've got to have a target that sand won't even dent."

"Maybe I call a rematch with someone else calling the shots? So she doesn't use them cartridges of hers she's got loaded with sand?"

"I'd like to see her blast away with the sand, and nothing happens," Rusty said. "Make her crazy."

"Maybe she'll marry me," I said.

Rusty eyed me like I was some walrus. "You'll do better at Denver Sally's," he said.

"My ma, she always says, marry someone you can live with. I could spend the rest of my days side by side, shooting with Miss Quick."

"Can you afford the powder and ball?"

"Nope. I can't afford her, but faint heart never won fair woman. That's what they say."

"Tin cans," said Rusty. "Shoot at tin cans, and only ones with a hole in them count."

"I've been thinking, Rusty. That sand doesn't carry far. It's no good beyond fifty feet. So I'll challenge her to a match at fifty yards. Clay birds at a hundred fifty feet."

Rusty, he just grinned.

"I'll make a big deal out of it, too. Pick off moving targets with a rifle at a little distance. And I'll talk it up first. That way, she can't back out."

"Sand or no sand, she's a dandy shot, Cotton."

"We'll see," I said.

I started with Reggie Thimble, since he was the supervisor most interested in axing me.

I found him closeted in the outhouse behind the courthouse.

"Reggie, that you in there?"

"What do you want?"

"I want to preserve the honor of Puma County. I'm gonna challenge the little lady to a shoot meet, clay birds with rifles at a hundred fifty feet."

There was nothing but silence in there, so I left him to his business. There's nothing more important in life than tending to one's business. It beats everything, including women. If I could get through my entire life without one day of constipation, I'd count it a life well lived. But I could tell that Reggie was having a bad time of it.

I headed for George Waller, over in his store. The mayor should be informed.

"Hey, George, don't fire me just yet," I said. "I'm going to challenge the little lady to a real match, not some close-up shooting. Clay birds at a hundred fifty feet—with rifles."

"I hope you lose," Waller said. "We don't need an excuse to fire you anymore, but it would help matters along."

I tried Turk at his livery barn next. Turk just grinned. "You should challenge her to a Critter contest. Whoever doesn't get killed by Critter, wins the prize."

"Not a bad idea, Turk."

Pretty quickly, I let word out all over Doubtful. I was gonna take on Miss Amanda Quick and maybe show her a thing or two.

I hated to think what would happen if I lost. But my ma, she always said take one thing at a time, so I did.

I headed out to the show grounds beyond Saloon Row, and found Billy Bones easily enough.

"Hey, Billy, I've told all the good folks in town,

I'm ready for a rematch, and what's more, I'll make it tougher: clay pigeons with rifles at fifty yards. We're all raring to go."

Bones, for once, frowned. "You told them that, did you?"

"You bet. If that little shooter of yours can't beat the sheriff this time, why, ain't nobody gonna show up for the next show."

Billy Bones shook his head. "Any rematch has to be exactly like the one before."

"Oh, ho! Scared of some real shooting, is she?"

"I'll ask her, but she'll say no, sheriff."

"That's fine. That puts Puma County back on the map."

Bones, he just stared. I was whistling. I never whistle. It's what idiots do. But now I was trilling like a meadowlark. I headed for town, but Bones caught up with me.

"Wait!" he yelled. "I'll work something out with her."

"Nah, Billy, we'll do the match this afternoon, at the start of the show, or you might as well pack up and go."

He sure didn't like that.

The upshot was, I was at the show grounds promptly at two, and there sure were a mess of people come out to see it, and Bones was looking mighty bleak.

"She'd be pleased to match you at fifty feet, Pickens. Otherwise, she'll retire from the contest."

"You just tell this here crowd that I'm shooting alone; and it's at a hundred fifty."

Rusty was just so pleased he could hardly stand it. Bones, he gave in, and started the show.

"Ladies and gents, we'll begin this afternoon performance with a special exhibition of marksmanship by your sheriff, Cotton Pickens. The sheriff, assisted by his deputy, will attempt the impossible: shooting clay pigeons out of the sky at a hundred fifty feet with a rifle. My good friends in Doubtful, Wyoming, I welcome Sheriff Pickens."

Well, I took my bows, and Rusty set up the spring-loaded trap, and away we went.

Sad to say, I missed the first one, and that started some hooting. There wasn't a large crowd on hand; most of the cowboys were hard at work on the ranches. But plenty of folks had heard about the rematch, and were studying me.

The second bird sailed high, and I led it slightly, squeezed, and blew it to bits.

I saw Miss Quick eyeing me from her wagon, but mostly staying out of sight. Well, fine, I'd show her a thing or two.

I knocked the next bird right out of the sky, and nicked the next one. It counted as a hit. I was doing what I do best, boring in on the target swinging along with it and then firing at just the right moment. I was born to it.

Of the ten birds, I missed one more and knocked eight to smithereens. That sure pleased the crowd, but not Bones, and I suspected he'd pull up stakes the next day. His star shooter was sulking in her wagon, and everyone noticed.

I saw Reggie Thimble staring at me. His plans to shove me out the door had suddenly gone awry, and he was looking sour. He should have stayed in his outhouse and read the Monkey Ward catalogue in there.

Bones began the rest of the show, with cowboys roping calves, riding broncs and bulls, and all the rest. Then Miss Quick came out to do her sharpshooting stuff, but she wasn't all flouncy and perky this time. She looked a little down at the mouth. I watched, real interested, and was quick to note she didn't do any rifle stuff at all. Just trick shots from horseback, and blowing holes through the ace of spades with her revolver, stuff like that. It sure was an admission that she was no match for me with a rifle. And the crowd caught it, too. Still, she was one fine shot, and a dandy performer, and anyone who knew anything about shooting had to admire her.

After she was done, I headed her way, as she and her batman were picking up all her stuff, and I lifted my old sweat-stained hat off my head.

"That sure was pretty shooting, Miss Quick," I said. "Makes a man think of marriage."

She eyed me, the strangest look on her face, and then laughed.

"Me, I'd love a wife who's a shooter almost as good as me," I said.

"Sheriff, you're a card," she said, and walked off.

That sort of bothered me some. I was real earnest about it, but she just dismissed me in a wink of an eye.

"Cotton, you've done it again," Rusty said.

Chapter Thirty

George Waller caught me early in the morning.

"That little punk stole three licorice sticks. You owe me three cents, you or Rusty. I shook the brat until his teeth rattled, but it won't do any good. That orphan train, all it did was haul the punks out of the cities and spread them around here."

"You're talking about Riley?"

"Who else?"

"Has he done this before?"

"How'm I supposed to know? I got a store to tend, and customers to look after, and I can't be studying every little rug rat that comes sneaking in to swipe something."

"What did you say to him?"

"I told him he was no good, he'd never be good, and he'd spend his life behind prison walls. He starting crying, and I told him he wasn't man enough to take his medicine."

"How long ago was this?"

"Yesterday afternoon, and maybe a hundred times before that."

"But you don't know that."

"I know a rotten little crook when I see one."

"You ever swipe anything when you were a boy, George?"

"Not ever. I grew up straight and true, and well bred. Unlike that little turd."

"I dipped my fingers into the cookie jars a few times," I said. "Got caught, too. And got my knuckles rapped. I mean rapped, with a ruler. It didn't do any good."

"If you don't have the breeding, nothing does any good."

I dug into my britches. "Here's a nickel for the licorice. I'll talk to Riley, and also to Rusty and Belle. Maybe we can do something."

"It won't do a bit of good. Bad blood, it's going to show in that boy. And you got him in your sheriff office. I don't know how you ever got in, Pickens. You've got all the town's half-wits in there."

I'd heard all that before—bad blood, bad breeding, all of that. I sure didn't have any good blood or good breeding, but I wasn't sure what that stuff was. Mostly it was people who looked down their noses at everyone else.

I left word for Rusty that I was going to take the day off, and take Riley fishing. I supposed that would steam up everyone. But Rusty wouldn't need me. He'd cover the Wild West grounds in the afternoon, and deal with any trouble there. Those rodeo cowboys and all sometimes got a little unruly, especially in the saloons after the show.

I collected the boy; he was at Belle's getting some lessons. He'd had no schooling, running on the streets back East, so Belle was teaching him at home during the day, and maybe when Riley got caught up, he'd get put in the grade school in Doubtful.

I found Belle teaching him arithmetic. They were doing addition. I never could figure it out myself, but I got good enough to add things up. But I always had trouble with eight and seven. It seemed like thirteen to me, not fifteen. Belle eyed me standing there, but finished up her lesson.

"I thought I'd take Riley fishing, Belle," I said.

"But . . . he needs school."

"I'm taking some time off."

She eyed me. "There's something here I am being kept out of."

"For a few hours maybe."

She sighed. "It's a man's world. All right. Take him."

Riley peered up at me. "Fishing? There's fish around here?"

"There's a couple of holes in the creek, and maybe there's something in them."

"There's not a fish closer than fifty miles from here," Belle said.

"Maybe you're right," I said.

Belle just stared at me. She always knew when something was up.

I had some line and fishhooks. We'd have to hunt for worms or bugs or grubs for bait, and cut some sticks for fishing poles. Maybe we'd catch something. I didn't much care one way or the other.

"What kind of fish?" asked Riley.

"Maybe some whoppers, boy. Big as liars can make them."

Riley grinned. "We're really going to fish? I never been fishing."

"You sure are a pain in the butt, Pickens," Belle said. That was as tough as she ever got with me. She made a sour face when I kidnapped the kid.

It was a fine August day, too dry, but that was August in Wyoming for you. We headed for the creek, and then walked its banks upstream. It was slow and lazy in August. It got cold and swift in the spring, carrying off snowmelt from the Medicine Bow Mountains. In Doubtful, there were a lot of outhouses along its banks, so if a feller wanted to fish, he'd be well advised to head upstream.

We got to the big swimming hole a way upstream. A lot of stuff happened there that I carefully didn't look into very hard. Most of it happened at night. But now on a sleepy, sunny morning it was empty. The mountains in the distance looked somber and tired.

"Let's try here," I said. "Maybe there's some monsters in there."

"You mean real fish?"

I cut off some willow branches with my knife, and sliced off the little shoots until I had a couple of long sticks for fishing poles.

"Scrape around for bait, Riley. Bugs or worms."

He had a talent for that, and by the time I'd gotten the lines and hooks all tied to the poles, he had a mess of caterpillars, a few beetles, and some bugs I had no notion of. I made a couple of little floats from sticks, and tied them in, so the baited hook wouldn't just drop to the bottom. And then we were set.

"Let's sit here in the shade, so the fish don't see us," I said, sounding like I knew something. Actually, I didn't know nothing.

So we pitched the hooks in, each hook laden with some fish grub on it, and nothing much happened. The floats just drifted downstream until our lines checked them.

"Why don't they bite?" Riley asked.

"Beats me, boy. Tell me how you like it around here."

"Am I supposed to like it?"

"Well, there's a man, Rusty, who's spending some of his hard-earned salary as a deputy of mine, keeping you fed and clothed and all. And my landlady, Belle, who's trying to give you a good start on life."

"The fish ain't biting."

"You remember your ma?"

"I don't want to remember her."

"Miss her?"

He eyed me. "What is this? How come we're doing this? You taking me fishing or is this something else?"

He was one street-smart kid, I thought. "We're doing a lot of things here, Riley."

"This is because Waller caught me. He pretty near twisted my ear off, until I bit him."

"That's one of the things, yes."

"I knew it. My ass is in trouble. So give me the lecture."

"Well, I could, if you want it, but lectures don't do much good. If you want to dip into George Waller's licorice jar, you'll keep right on, no matter what I say, or Rusty says."

"You got that right, copper. You're gonna tell me I'm not a deputy anymore; deputies got to obey all the laws and all that, so you're kicking me out, is that it?"

"Well, you got me there, boy. I was thinking along those lines."

"Well, ship me off to somewhere else. I don't measure up."

Riley was staring straight ahead, and I knew he would land on anything I said.

"We'll fish, boy. You're still my deputy sheriff. You still get to wear the badge. You just keep that badge shiny for me, make it shine."

"You mean don't steal."

"Oh, let me put it this way. Give more than you take."

"I don't get it."

"Well, here's an example. You could go to George Waller, who owns that store, and you could say, sir, I'll sweep your floor for you. If you'll show me where the sawdust and the push broom are, I'd do it for you."

"You're just trying to turn me into a slave. That's what all the orphans end up as. They get us off the orphan train, and they got a slave."

"No, Riley, not a slave. Just someone who gives back."

"I don't feel like giving back. For what?"

I was tempted to say for the food and shelter and clothes and attention he got, but I didn't. Children had a right to those things, whether or not they gave anything back. A child needs those things, no matter who or what he is.

"For me, it's being a man," I said. "I get my pay in a brown envelope once a month. And I try to give the county and town some safety. If I took the money and didn't give the people around here some safety, I wouldn't feel very good."

Riley was watching the stick float bob a little in the creek.

"Someone worked real hard to harvest the plants that give that candy its flavor. And other people worked hard to cut sugarcane or harvest beets for the sugar. And someone made the sticks in the jar, and someone transported the licorice sticks to here, and George Waller hoped to sell them for more than he paid, so he could make something, too, putting them in front of the public. So a lot of folks did work that paid them back, and the licorice sticks got to here, and everyone put some labor and skill into it, and took some pay out of it."

"Yeah, and now they don't get paid."

"No, they got paid. All except George Waller."

"I'm gonna resign as deputy. I'll give you my badge when we get back. I'm tired of fishing."

I was tired of it, too. I thought maybe we could talk it out, but I didn't have whatever it took to do that.

Riley's bobber dipped. Then it began making a circle.

"I think you got a fish, Riley."

"Yeah? What do I do?"

"We haven't got a net, so we'll need to draw it in slow, and then beach it, over there where you can reach into the water."

The boy suddenly came alive. He tugged and pulled, and worked the fish to shore, and we saw its silvery body thrash as he drew it close. But then it spit out the hook, or maybe Riley tugged too hard, and it was gone.

"Got away," Riley said. "That's me for you. I haven't got anything."

I got ahold of the boy and sat him down on the

riverbank, and we just sat there for a while. There was some sort of big, hollow ache in him, an ache no one could ever banish.

"We know there's a big lunker in there, and you're going to catch it," I said.

Riley just shook his head. Catching a fish was too much for him to hope for.

"I'll get us a proper rod with a reel and a net, and you'll catch him," I said.

"How'm I gonna pay for that?"

"It'll be something I'll give you. But if you'd like to earn it, I think I can find a few people who'd pay you to sweep their stores."

"More of your crap," he said, and clammed up.

But he was thinking about it. And that was as much as I could hope for. We headed back to Doubtful, and somehow I thought the time had not been wasted.

Chapter Thirty-one

Well, I was expecting trouble while that Wild West was in Doubtful, and I'd told the barkeeps to call me fast when it broke out. You can't hardly expect a cowboy show without a string of fistfights or even shootouts. Cowboys are a little unruly, and that's the way they want it. So the barkeeps, like Sammy Upward, kept a sawed-off shotgun under the bar, and that usually did the job.

But after the show, when Doubtful was settling down for the short summer's night, I got a holler from Denver Sally. She sent her bouncer, Maginnis, over for me. She has a real good bouncer, and usually he can grab someone by the ear and throw him out if he starts abusing her girls, or he's too drunk, or he's getting into trouble. Once Maginnis even stopped an arsonist who was going to burn the place down and fry the girls.

"We got trouble, sheriff," Maginnis said.

"What kind of trouble?"

"We got a girl in a room with two people, and they's a mess of shots getting fired in there, and some screaming, and them walls are flimsy and don't hold lead, and no one's got nerve enough to bust in and stop it all."

That sure didn't sound good. I strapped on my gun belt, and hurried over there to Denver Sally's, with Maginnis, whose short legs worked twice as hard as mine.

"Who's in there?" I asked.

"Lily the French Bombshell, that's Sally's highest priced girl, and two from the show. A big lunker named Rinkydink, and that shooter, Amanda Quick."

"The sharpshooter? In there?"

"That's who. They came together, rented Lily, and now all hell's broke loose."

"What's Miss Quick doing in there?"

"Don't ask me, and I won't tell you."

"I gotta know."

"Well, when I was checking through the peephole, the three of them were all having a fine old time."

My idea of Amanda Quick was changing fast, but I'd wait and see about this. People sure had strange ideas of what they want from life.

"Who's Rinkydink?" I asked.

"Mostly a roustabout, all muscle and no brain. He puts up tents, does grunt work, stuff like that.

He's been at Sally's every night, after the show's done, and stays the night."

"Is he in the show?"

"They're all in the show. That stagecoach scene, wild Injuns chasing the coach, he's driving it, or sometimes he's painted up and wearing a breech-clout, or something, and firing blanks at the stagecoach."

When we got to Denver Sally's, I found all her gals huddled in the parlor, except for Lily, who was caught in the back. Sally rushed up to me in her robe. She'd been busy with the trade herself, until the trouble started.

Just then I heard another shot, and a scream, and the girls all clutched one another and a couple were crying. Then another shot, more screams, and some whimpering from the back somewhere. Sally's had two floors, but all this was unfolding straight down the main hall.

"Sally, what's the story?" I asked.

"They're torturing Lily. They shoot, she screams."

"You're talking about the show people? Rinky-dink and Miss Quick? What are they doing in there?"

Sally sighed. "It's their idea of a threesome, only it's all bullets and whips and pain. If they mark Lily, I'll mark both of them in a way they won't forget."

I was feeling real dumb, so I fessed up. "You mean they're doing stuff that hurts?"

"Cotton, you're a child in some ways."

"You let 'em do that?"

"Long as they pay, and don't get rough. But this is rough. They'll likely kill Lily. You gotta stop it."

So I had to stop it, and not catch lead sailing through that flimsy door.

"All right," I said. "You keep clear."

I clumped real hard down that hallway. "This is the sheriff. Open up, with your hands up," I yelled.

"Go to hell," Amanda Quick yelled, and she punctuated it with a shot. The bullet busted through the door and smacked the hall wall.

"Miss Quick, you put that shooter down," I yelled.

"Which one? His or mine?"

"You come out of there, or I'll come in there, and it won't be peaceful."

"Just try it," she said, and fired again.

Every shot sure jolted me some. She couldn't finish a sentence without a bullet for a period.

Truth to tell, I didn't know how to stop this. I could hear the girls whimpering and yelping back in the parlor. I could hear a crowd gathering in the dark outside.

"Miss Quick, you send the girl, Lily, out the door now," I said.

"We paid for her, and we're not done with her."

"What do you do to her?"

"Sheriff, you're such a card."

"All right, send out the guy, Rinkydink."

"He's just getting heated up and ready to roar."

"You send him out the door."

She shot another hole in it. I could smell burnt powder in the hallway. Back in the parlor, Denver Sally was trying to quiet the sobbing women.

"All right, Miss Quick. If you won't come out, then nothing's going in. No food, no water, not a thing until you call it quits."

"Call it quits! We're just getting ready for a hoe-down!"

A man's voice followed. "Sheriff, you just bust your bum butt out."

"Rinkydink, you come out of there now."

He just laughed, hoarsely. I heard a crack and a scream.

"You hurt, Lily?" I asked.

"Help me! They'll kill me!"

I heard another slap and a scream.

That did it. I got opposite the door, which was badly splintered now, reared up, and smacked it with my shoulder. It caved in, and I fell into the room, staggered, and got a glimpse of things before Rinkydink threw the kerosene lamp out the window.

The three didn't have a stitch on between them. Miss Quick wore nothing but a gun belt, and she sure looked cute in it. Made me think of proposing, but she was also waving her revolver at me, and I decided not to propose.

There was just enough light so I could see Lily dive onto the bed, followed by Rinkydink. But Miss Quick just waved her revolver at me.

"So, join the party," she said.

It wasn't a bad idea, but my ma always used to say finish what you started, so I decided on that. "You two from the show, you get yourselves dressed and out, because if you don't, I'll haul your bare butts to my jail and you can sit in there and think about things."

The sharpshooter eyed me. "You're a turd, Pickens."

But she grabbed her stuff, and began to get dressed. By then the dollies down the hall were all creeping toward Lily's room. Rinkydink stuffed his shirt into his pants, yanked his boots on, and pushed through the crowd. Miss Quick was sure looking grumpy, like she had been deprived of a cookie. She got into her fringed buckskins and pushed her way out, and vanished into the night. I wondered how many times she had pulled her trigger that evening.

"Don't come back," Sally yelled.

Lily was a trouper. She was not only smiling, but enjoying all the fuss her pals were making.

"Man, did he have a gun," she said.

I managed to hold back the crowd that was swarming in, but Sally saw her chance.

"We'll open in five minutes, half price," she said. There were about fifty males jammed into the parlor and the hallway. "Even Lily the French Bombshell. Half price for the next hour."

You sort of had to admire Sally. There are people who know how to take advantage of events, and turn everything into cash, and she topped the list. All those gents, they were digging into their britches to see if they could come up with a dollar instead of two, and pretty quickly there were greenbacks floating into Denver Sally's hand.

"We should stage one of these every night," she said. "I could retire."

It was the strangest thing. All I could think of was Amanda Quick, wearing nothing but a smile and a gun belt. I thought I'd like to put her in a little cottage with rambling roses, and we could shoot at tin cans on fence posts for our entertainment, when we weren't heating up the bedroom. But that's just me. Some men, they'd be better off leaving her alone. I like guns and I like women who like guns, and there aren't very many of those.

I like to compare women to guns. Now, Amanda Quick, she was like a fine Navy Colt. Other women, they're like a blunderbuss. A few are like derringers. I've hardly ever met a woman who reminds me of a shotgun, though. But I'd like to meet one.

Belle reminds me of a Dragoon, big and hearty and makes a lot of noise. The ones to watch out for, though, remind me of a dueling pistol, a big caliber, smooth, and mean.

About then, Billy Bones showed up.

"Trouble?" he asked.

"Nothing to it," I said.

"She does that, you know. She likes little parties of three."

"I'm hoping you'll leave town. We've had enough trouble around here."

"Thanks, sheriff. You're really welcoming."

"It's her," I said. "She's trouble. I don't know a thing about women."

"She's our big draw. Without her, we'd not have enough gate to pay our freight."

I didn't know what all that meant, but it didn't matter.

"You're lucky she's not sitting in the jail bare-ass naked, along with that stud of hers."

"No luck at all. I wish she was there. We'd have a sell-out crowd tomorrow."

I might be a slow learner, but I was beginning to understand road shows, and show business. Those people sure were strange.

I headed back to the jail. I was sleeping in Cell Number Two, because I'd given my boarding-house room to the Siamese twins. Doubtful had finally quieted down, after the excitement in the sporting district. I unlocked, didn't light a lamp, washed up, got out of my shirt and britches and boots, and headed for the cell cot in my under-drawers. It had been a long day, wrestling with Riley and his little thefts, and fishing with him, and not getting anywhere with him, and then trying to prevent a cathouse bloodbath.

No sooner did I lie down on that hard bunk, mostly just sheet iron with a pad on it, than some-one was tapping at the door. It wasn't real loud, just persistent. I grabbed my shooter, and decided not to light a lamp. I'd open the door a little, and see who was there without being seen.

I creaked the door open some, and saw herself, Quick, standing there alone. The moonlight caught her locks and caught the smile on her face.

"Mind if I come in, sheriff?"

"Well, I mind. Unless you got something to report. It's late and I'm ready for a sleep."

She ignored me, and drifted in, and I thought I'd let her talk a minute and then push her out. I lit a lamp. She studied the office, with its gun racks, my desk, the open door to the jail, and the dark-ness beyond the wavering yellow light of the lamp.

She was smiling. "I sure like guns," she said. "You got guns on every wall, and they just make me happy. Put me in the middle of a lot of big long guns, and I'm a happy woman."

"Well, I like guns, too, ma'am. I got a mess of

them, and I'm always a sucker for the next one. But I like the older ones better than the new. I like 'em when the shine's gone, the blueing is worn off, and I know what way off-center the shot'll go."

"Sounds like you're talking about me, Cotton Pickens. I thought maybe you'd like to pull my trigger."

Chapter Thirty-two

There she was, cute as a button, famous across the whole country, a woman like no other. I peered around the sheriff office, with all its deadly force, and made up my mind.

"Ma'am, I'm not a big-game hunter. I'm a meat hunter. I go out hunting, I want to put elk steaks or antelope on the table, for myself and family and my friends. I never was one to shoot an elk because of its big rack, or shoot an elephant just to say I did, or kill a Bengal tiger so I could have a taxidermist mount the head, with all those feline teeth bared."

She studied me for a moment, and I was expecting some smart reply, but instead she turned real soft, there in the dim lamplight.

"I like you, Cotton Pickens," she said. "You know what the trouble is with road shows, and show people? We're all lonely. We're not making friends. We're all as alone as people get. The show's going to change every week, people come and go, and nothing's the same. No homes, no neighborhoods, just ourselves, all bottled up. I've a favor to ask you."

I couldn't imagine what she wanted, but I nodded.

"Could you sit beside me somewhere and just hold me? That's all. Just hold me gently. You're the only person I've seen in years who cares about me."

"I could do that, ma'am, but all I've got is the bench in the cell there."

"Then we'll make the cell our alpine meadow, full of sunshine and breezes," she said.

We walked back there, in the dark, and sat down, and she surrendered herself to my arm, and we sat like that almost forever. She didn't kiss me; she didn't mess around. She just cozied up, and I felt her relax. She held my hand. Peace overtook her, and it was the thing she needed more than anything in the world. So I sat with her, even while my arm ached, and along about dawn, she straightened up, smiled, and whispered two words that meant something to me.

"Thank you," she said.

She straightened her doeskin skirt, touched my stubbled cheek once, and walked away.

I hadn't slept much, but I'd be fine. She would return to her world, and I to mine, and we would remember a few hours when we were each in another world. Maybe some other time and place, or on some other planet, we might have found each other, and lived a life of companionship. But not in this world.

I slept some, and was awakened when Rusty wandered in, looking like hell.

"Bad night? Riley trouble?"

"No, twin trouble," he said, pouring some ancient java from a pot on the woodstove.

"Woman trouble," I said. "No man escapes it."

"I suppose your ma told you that."

"No, I got that idea myself."

"The twins are fighting," he said. "There they are, locked to each other for life, sharing bodies, and they're fighting. It tears me to pieces. They're miserable."

"Still about marriage?"

"Anna's insisting they go back to the carnival and earn money. No one's taking care of them here; I keep them in food, and that's about it. There's nothing for them. But Natasha's just as determined to marry me, since I proposed to her, and she won't go back, and the whole thing's at a stalemate."

"And the territory won't let you marry both. It's a problem," I said.

"There's no solution. It'll just get worse. It's tragedy."

"There's common-law marriage," I said. "Just marry Natasha and live with Anna and call her your wife."

"Cotton, you're a card. You don't know women."

"Where have I heard that before?" I asked. "Blame it on my ma and pa. I don't have any sisters. Let's go talk to Hanging Judge Earwig. He owes us a favor."

Rusty looked morose. "He'll find some way to make it worse. I'll end up shipping them back to the Ukraine."

But he came along with me. We angled across the courthouse square on a fine August morning, and found Earwig snoring on a couch in his chambers.

"Oh, eh, not much business this morning. Have you something to put in my Charity Jar?"

"Well, if you would do two weddings, you'd get double the donation," I said.

He eyed me, and Rusty. "More Ukrainian crises?"

"I think you already know the trouble," Rusty said. "We were wondering if you have any ideas."

Earwig stared owlishly at Rusty. "You sure got a doozer, my boy. Two poor women, locked together for all their days, each with a different dream, a different will. And one wants to be your bride, and the other wants to put herself and sister on display again. As miserable as that sounds, it's a life and an income. Am I right?"

"You're right, sir."

"Have you tried proposing to both?"

"This isn't Utah, sir. No, no one will let me marry them both."

Earwig pursed his lips and stared into space. "Irons, you go propose to Anna and tell her you'll find a way to marry both twins at once. And come back and report to me whether she accepts."

"How you gonna do that, sir, if I may ask?"

"Desperate problems require desperate remedies," Earwig said. "I have one in mind that should satisfy the law, satisfy moralists, satisfy religionists, and make your lives happy."

"All that?"

"I thought to hang one and you could marry the other," Earwig said, a tiny smile erecting on his bushy face.

Rusty, he just looked peeved, but I winked at the judge, and then Rusty and me, we went to Belle's Boarding House to have a go with the Ukrainians.

"How's he gonna do that?" Rusty asked.

"Beats me," I said. "Do you want me to sit in on the proposal, or should I go visit the outhouse?"

"You sit in on her. Maybe you should propose to Anna, and we'll make everyone happy."

"That's a little too intimate for comfort, Rusty. No, the twins are yours alone."

At Belle's, we clumped up the stairs, knocked, and found Natasha and Anna glaring at each other, as usual. Natasha didn't even seem happy to see Rusty. The dilemma had exhausted any goodwill anyone possessed.

Rusty, he got right down on one knee, and took

Anna's hand. "My dear Anna, will you marry me, now and forever?" he asked.

"What's this? You are a madman."

"No, my dear, I am a man overflowing with the love of both of you in my bosom."

I thought Rusty was laying it on thick. Natasha, she was studying him like he was a toad. Her biggest joy in life had been Rusty's proposal, which hadn't extended to Anna, but now Rusty was robbing her of all her prestige, and turning this into a three-way deal.

"I don't know if I want you. Natasha can have you. No, I don't think so."

"My dear Anna, Judge Earwig says he'll find a way to marry us," Rusty said. "Please change your mind."

Anna turned grouchy. "My only pleasure in life has been to frustrate you and Natasha in your cruel plans to wed without me. Now you are robbing me of my sole pleasure in this miserable existence."

"I'll take that for a yes," Rusty said. "Congratulations, Anna. You've accepted. Now wash up, and we'll see what Hanging Judge Earwig can do for us."

The twins stared at him, and at each other, and rose. Anna poured water from the pitcher into the washbasin, and took a washcloth and washed Natasha's face. And then Natasha washed Anna's face. And then they combed each other's hair, and straightened their dress.

First Natasha smiled, and then Anna.

"Take us," Anna said.

I took Natasha's arm, and Rusty took Anna's, and we helped the twins down the creaking stairs, and made our slow majestic way to the courthouse as the midday sun smiled warmly on us. People stared and smiled, and a brat boy tried to look under the twins' skirt, but I snarled at him. He thumbed his nose at me and skittered away.

Somehow, Riley got wind of it, and caught up with us, walking next to Rusty.

We made our slow and stately way up the courthouse stairs to Judge Earwig's courtroom, and found no one in it. That was either because I kept law and order so well that there were no cases before him, or I kept law and order so poorly that I brought no cases to him. I never could figure out which. But Earwig had a good job, in which he only rarely had to work.

He emerged at once from his chambers, eyed us, and retreated. When he returned, he was wearing his black robe, and carrying some marigolds, which he divided and gave to each bride.

Natasha looked at them, and at him, and began oozing tears. Rusty, he was kicking himself for not stopping to get some flowers beforehand.

"I take it this is a bridal party?" Earwig asked.

"It is, sir."

"And you wish me to wed both of these lovelies to you, Mr. Irons?"

"I do, Your Honor."

Earwig, he seemed ready to burst. "I've been meditating on this, and I have found a solution."

I sure was itching to learn it, but I kept my yap shut.

He seemed uncommonly pleased with himself. The courtroom was starting to fill up; word buzzed around Doubtful, and not a few citizens wanted to see the show.

Natasha, she was smiling to beat the band. Anna, she was eyeing the crowds, a little uncertain.

Earwig eyed the crowd, which gave him a captive audience, which pleased him all the more, because he was about to put his natural brilliance on display. I could see it in his face. He was fairly bursting with whatever was percolating inside of his cranium.

"Now, I welcome you all to this joyous occasion," he said. "I shall be marrying Natasha and Anna to Mr. Rusty Irons, and I will be doing it with all legality, morality, and propriety."

I saw Delphinium Sanders, the town's certified prude, whispering heatedly at the rear of the room. Judge Earwig saw her, too.

"We shall have silence here, among those who have come to share this joyous moment," he said.

Delphinium whispered for a few moments more, long enough to let him know she wasn't taking orders.

"Now, then, unusual circumstances require

unusual remedies," he said. "These lovely ladies are bonded by nature for life, and each desires in her most secret bosom to share her life with her husband. Which poses difficulties with the law of the land, but not difficulties that are insurmountable. Given the nature of this matter, I concluded that each couple will have to divide its time with the other couple. That is to say, each couple can be married only half the time, instead of all the time. It is unavoidable, given that each bride is attached all her life to the other bride. Therefore, if it suits my petitioners, now standing before me, I shall marry Rusty Irons to Natasha on odd months of the year, and to Anna on even months of the year. Since your vows and marriage contract will embrace only half of each year, there is no need for divorce. Since Natasha will marry Rusty during January and March and May, there is no need for her to divorce Rusty during the intervening months of February and April. Each marriage is for half a year only, alternating months."

The audience listened, mesmerized.

"What about February? Short month!" Anna asked.

"Ah, my dear, we live in an imperfect world, and the fact is, you will have slightly less time with your husband, but bear in mind that you alone will enjoy leap years. You will have leap year Februaries with your beloved, and Natasha won't. Is that fair enough?"

She nodded.

It went fast. Within ten minutes, Rusty was married to Natasha on January, March, May, July, September, and November. And to Anna February, April, June, August, October, and December.

And the crowd watched, some with pursed lips. Riley was the first to kiss his moms.

Chapter Thirty-three

Billy Bones told me his Wild West would pull out the next morning. That was a good sign. It wouldn't be sneaking out at night, leaving unpaid debts around Doubtful. That meant I wouldn't have to yank Rusty from his honeymoon and put him to work.

The Wild West had drawn good crowds off the ranches. The drovers liked the rodeo stuff and the town liked the shooting exhibits and western stuff.

"There'll be a farewell party at the Last Chance Saloon after the show, sheriff. Come join us," Bones said.

That sounded fine to me. The Last Chance, and its barkeep, Sammy Upward, was my favorite saloon. It was big and generous with its drinks, and Sammy kept good order with a billy club and sawed-off shotgun. He'd never had to use the scattergun, but it had a way of subduing trouble fast.

It sure was a pleasant August evening. The crickets were chirping, and bugs committing suicide in the kerosene lamps, and the town dogs were peeing on every post. Bones had told me he did fairly well, for a small town like Doubtful, and he was leaving a few bucks ahead. Some places, he said, he was lucky to get out with the show intact. The outfit was heading for Casper next, and he was worried because Casper had the reputation of being the roughest town in Wyoming, full of rural hooligans. Not that the show couldn't defend itself. Bones had some roustabouts who were really soldiers, ready to spring into action any time. Rinkydink was one of those.

Well, it was a dandy show. Word got out that this would be the last performance, so all the town came out to the grounds to enjoy the sights. There was no grandstand seating. People just came and stood, or threw a blanket on the ground and sat. Belle was there with Riley. She was caring for Riley while Rusty was making whoopee with his Siamese twins.

Miss Quick, she did just fine, knocking clay birds out of the sky. She went on first, while the light was good. By the end of the show, light was fading, and they did their grand march just in time, finishing up at dusk. People had a fine old time, and then they drifted into Doubtful, full of inspiration. That final drum and bugle parade was just right.

I watched Bones's crew dismantle things, and they did it so fast I could hardly believe that for a few days, they had conducted a big Wild West show there. In the morning, they'd hitch up their teams and ride away.

It sure gave me a good feeling. I drifted over to Sammy Upward's saloon, and it was already filling up. There were a mess of cowboys from the Admiral Ranch, and I spotted Big Nose George and Spitting Sam, belly to the bar, sipping the first red-eye of the evening. There were boys from all the ranches in there, sucking beer, laying out coin for a shot of rye, or a glass of sarsaparilla if they weren't the drinking sort. Plug Parsons and Carter Bell were in from the T Bar, along with Rudy Beaver. That outfit was far out, and they'd come a piece to see the show and rub shoulders with the crowd. Those cowboys were slicked up, in high-heeled boots and bandannas, and some had even washed up for the occasion. But there wasn't a sidearm among them, and I liked that, because sometimes one of them got a little frisky and began perforating the ceiling. But this here was a social occasion, wall-to-wall smiles, and that would make for a fine evening.

The Wild West boys began drifting in, looked around, and settled on a corner table. They were mostly drinking rye whiskey. Maybe that was the preferred booze for the outfit. They were a muscular bunch. Cowboys were mostly thin and wiry and short; these show people were muscled up. Cowboys mostly sat on a horse; these show people were wrestling teams and tents and furniture and livestock all the time, and were all bruisers. The cowboys were more colorful, all spangled up in bright colors and gold and silver, while the roustabouts were wearing brown britches, old boots, and tight, knit shirts. I saw Rinkydink among them, and wondered what Miss Quick saw in him. Maybe it was none of my business, I thought. He was no bigger than the other roustabouts, but his shoulders were axe-handle wide, and he had hands the size of hams.

Everyone was sure having a fine time, and Sammy Upward was dishing out the booze faster than I'd ever seen him, coining money as he went along. It got crowded in there, and Sammy lit a couple more kerosene lamps in the wagon wheel chandelier, so there was good light even in the far corners. The T Bar boys and Admiral Ranch boys were old enemies, so they stayed at opposite sides of the place, and mostly sat there in the heat, looking dreamy. It sure was a fine August evening, even if the place needed a little more air.

Amanda Quick and Billy Bones showed up, still in their show outfits, she in her fringed buckskins, he in a giant sombrero topping a black suit of clothes. They sure looked fine. I waved, and they both saluted me from across the room, and next I knew, someone had lifted her to the bar, and she stood up on it, and was lifting a glass with something green in it.

"Here's to Doubtful, Wyoming," she said, and all the good folks in there cheered.

"And here's to Sheriff Cotton Pickens," she said.

That evoked a hoot and a holler, and Smiley Thistlethwaite emptied a beer mug over me, and then Rinkydink beaned Smiley with a whiskey bottle, and then Plug Parsons kicked Big Nose George in the crotch, and then Sammy Upward yanked out his shotgun and fired at the ceiling, which was an awful racket, and then no one paid the slightest attention to Sammy. A mighty howl rose up and swamped the Last Chance Saloon, and drinking was forgotten for the moment because everyone had some new entertainments to keep him busy.

I felt a crack on my shoulder, and I saw Carter Bell's fist whiz by my nose. I thought that this could be an enjoyable evening, but I had a duty to maintain the peace, and also preserve the Last Chance Saloon before it was torn to pieces. So I leapt over the bar, looking for Sammy's billy club, grabbed it, and climbed up on the bar, planning to rap hard for attention.

Well, my ma used to say that good intentions aren't enough. Miss Amanda Quick kneed me where it hurt, and as I folded over, Spitting Sam shoved me off the bar and into Sammy Upward's prone carcass. Big Nose George had knocked him cockeyed, and he was nursing himself under the beer spouts.

I heard wild laughter, whoops, howls, and a rumble of anger in there, too, as all them rowdies began to get serious about the whole business. A bottle of booze landed on my head, but my hat softened the blow.

"You all right?" I asked Sammy.

"You're an idiot," he replied.

"You got any bright ideas?" I asked.

"Arrest them all," he said.

"I'll give her a try." I clambered up, dodged a tumbler that shattered on the back bar, and yelled, "Stop! You're all under arrest!"

A beer bottle conked me on the forehead. A fist caromed off my shoulder. That hurt.

"I'm ruined," Sammy said.

"This place is about to burn. One spilled lamp, and it's all over," I said.

Some roustabout leaned over the bar and puked on my boot.

By then things were beyond human restraint. I heard the roar and squeal, the shatter of glass, the cackles, the thump of fist on flesh, the snap of glass underfoot, the whoosh of air exploding from a gut, and shadows danced on the walls as the chandeliers careened this way and that. There was less laughter now and more rage. I heard glass shatter. Something busted the mirror of the back bar, and shards of glass landed on Sammy and me.

"You want the revolver?" Sammy asked. "Shoot out the lights?"

"And burn down the town," I said. "I'm gonna haul the bodies out."

I edged around the bar, worked my way outside, saw that Amanda Quick and Billy Bones had escaped, and saw a crowd collecting there.

"We'll haul out the bodies," I said.

A reveler came flying through the door, dripping red. He had been rolling around in shattered glass. He sat on some horse manure, laughing.

I edged in and dodged a flying chair, spotted a bloody cowboy who was being stepped on, got him by the ankles, and dragged him out. He howled as he scraped over glass, but in a moment he was lying on the street, leaking blood.

"Fix him," I yelled, and plunged back in. A beer mug hit me on the head, and I started after the roustabout, but thought better of it. I found another cowboy slumped against a wall, out cold, his mouth pulverized and leaking blood. I lifted him up, dragged him by his belt, and dropped him next to the rest in the manure outside.

"Hey, sheriff, why don't you just let them kill each other?" George Waller asked.

"Help me. We got people getting killed in there," I said.

Waller laughed.

I ducked a flying fist—this time it was Rinky-dink's ham hand—and got ahold of Spitting Sam, who had been no match for the roustabouts, and lolled stupidly against the bar.

"Come on, Sam," I said.

I got an arm around him, and was about to get him out, when someone shoved me from behind, and I tumbled into the glass, taking Sam with me. All that glass cut me up, but I got up and hauled Sam outside. A bandaging crew was at work out there.

The brawl was winding down, and it quit as suddenly as it started. Some were laughing, and some were sobbing. Sammy Upward was surveying his saloon, or what was left of it, moaning and groaning.

The townspeople outside suddenly got brave, and helped me drag the casualties out to the clay road, stanch the blood, and line them all up like corpses.

One roustabout sat there laughing. He was unharmed. The cowboys got the worst of it. Show people did hard work every day; cowboys only occasionally, and now it showed. There were twice as many cowboys on the injured list.

"All right, I'm taking you all in," I said.

"But we're leaving at dawn," Billy Bones said.

"After Hanging Judge Earwig has his say," I replied.

"What are you charging them with?"

"Well, let's see. Disturbing the peace, assault and battery, destroying the saloon—I'll need to look that up—you name it, I'll include it."

"Hey, suppose I just donate a hundred dollars and you let them go."

"I don't take gifts," I said.

Waller stepped in. "Just get them outta town, Pickens. Tell them to vamoose."

"Nope, I've got twelve roustabouts and twenty cowboys moaning and groaning around here, and they're going to stand before the judge."

"I don't know how you ever got appointed," Waller said.

"You shouldn't have appointed me," I replied. "Now help me move these galoots."

But the jail was a long way off, and we'd have to drag about twenty of these wrecks.

"I'll help you," Sammy said. "I want my saloon paid for."

But it was Bones himself who came to the rescue with a two-horse freight wagon. We piled in the bodies, moaning and groaning, and I took the first load over, and locked them in Cell One. Then we loaded up the wagon again, and herded those who could walk, and we filled up Cell Two. By the middle of the night, I had over thirty revelers crammed into two cells, thanked Billy for the wagon, and told him I'd get the judge up early so the show could be on the road.

"They ain't fit to travel, sheriff. So there's no rush," Bones said. "You can treat me to breakfast."

Miss Quick eyed the sorry humanity in the cells. "I'm glad I'm not a man," she said.

Chapter Thirty-four

That was Hanging Judge Earwig's finest hour, and he knew it. He convened court at six in the morning, making sure that everyone was grouchy and no one had dosed himself with coffee yet. I marched the criminals into court, thirty-three in all, and they were a surly lot, stained brown from all that dried blood. They shed a lot of it, wrestling on the floor with all those broken bottles.

Billy Bones came along with a bag of money; he was reconciled to what was coming, and wanted to bail out of Doubtful as well as he could manage, which would mean forking over.

Earwig leered at the assembled miscreants, cowboys off the ranches, roustabouts, and show cowboys from the Wild West.

"What a beautiful morning, gentlemen," he said. "At least I think you're all gentlemen, aren't you? What a lovely, sweet dawn welcoming a glorious day in Puma County. Do you wish to plead guilty to whatever charges we can think up? It will save time. If not, why, I will set the trial for two weeks hence, and you may post bail for a thousand dollars apiece, or enjoy the hospitality of Sheriff Pickens. I understand the piss pots are overflowing, and there's a lack of bunks, but you'll have no trouble accommodating yourselves to minor discomforts."

All those miscreants stared up at Earwig, not yet fathoming his opening sally, since half of them were still drunk, and the rest were hurting, or leaking liquids from every pore and orifice. Still, they listened.

Earwig was enjoying himself. "There is the small matter of Mr. Upward's saloon, which is now suffering from the recent and memorable joust in which you participated. He has yet to give me an estimate, but he lost every bottle of spirits in his possession, most of his glassware, most of his furniture, and sundry other items. Even the Montgomery Ward catalog in his outhouse, he tells me."

He peered owlishly at the silent and surly crowd of miscreants. "There is the matter of disturbing the peace. The matter of assault to do great bodily harm, if not exterminate anyone in your way. There is public drunkenness. I believe there were threats and foul language. There was the matter of defying the sheriff, who ordered you to cease and desist. And I suppose I can think up a few more, and court testimony will enlarge and embellish the list of infractions against the good order and peacefulness of Doubtful, Wyoming Territory. How do you plead?"

No one said a thing. So Earwig pointed at each man and asked him to plead, guilty or innocent. But they were all clamming up.

"Very well, I will remand the prisoners to the sheriff, and direct them to appear at their combined trial in a fortnight," he said.

"Ah, Your Honor," Billy Bones said. "May I be heard?"

"Step forward, sir."

"I am the employer of twelve of these gents, and I will enter a guilty plea for those in my company."

"A guilty plea, is it?"

"If it can result in a fair settlement, Your Honor, guilty it will be."

"And what would a fair settlement be?"

"Ah, let us say, no more than forty percent of the cost of rehabilitating Mr. Upward's business establishment, if you determine that my group was at fault. However, since they didn't initiate this difficulty, but sat peacefully until set upon by drovers, the true amount should be less, no more than ten percent, because they were merely defending themselves."

Earwig leaned over, and jabbed a finger at Rinkydink. "You there, how did you defend yourself?" he asked.

"We were sitting peacefully at our table, Your Honor, when we were set upon by local rowdies. We remained seated until it was plain that we needed to protect our persons, and guard our private parts against the unruly mob."

"Good, good, sir. Now how did you protect yourself against the drovers from the ranches, may I ask?"

"Well, sir, we invited them to join us for a drink, and we expressed our friendship and best wishes, for we had just competed in certain rodeo events in our show, and we offered to buy them a round of drinks, but they chose to hit us."

"Hit you?"

Rinkydink sighed. "We did our best to keep the peace, sir, but it came time to defend ourselves, and so we did, it being a principle of justice that we have the right to defend our persons against harm."

"Ah!" said Earwig, his eyes aglow.

"Your Honor," said another roustabout, "it was a matter of honor and decency. The star, the glory, of our show is our shooter, Miss Quick. She came to have a friendly drink with all parties, being of a generous nature, but the locals began to abuse her, threaten her, mock her honor and skills, and needless to say, we were ready and willing to defend her against these calumnies, canards, and gross perversions of the truth."

That fellow sounded real practiced at this, I thought. Maybe he had some experience. I thought I'd ask Bones if this sort of departure was ordinary.

Earwig leaned forward. "And so you defended

her honor against the local drovers? Who were demeaning her? Is that it?"

"Yessir."

"What are calumnies? Tell me about canards."

"Those are real evils, sir, right out of *Webster's*."

"And what truth was perverted by these drovers?"

"They said she couldn't shoot worth a damn. If she didn't load her rifle with sand, she couldn't hit the broad side of a barn."

"Ah! Now we are getting somewhere," Earwig said. "And does she use sand?"

"Never, sir, she shoots nothing but lead. And anyone who says otherwise is a rotter, a cad, and a bounder."

"Those are from *Webster's*, too?"

"That's what Billy Bones taught me to say."

"Your boss is a fine, upstanding gent," Earwig said. "A lady's virtue is at stake."

He turned to the rest of the miscreants, familiar faces from the assorted ranches around Doubtful. "Ah, it's always a joy to spot old friends and acquaintances," he said. "Now, then, my curiosity has got the best of me. I shall point, and you shall tell me how many times you have been before this court. If you wish to repeat your name, that is fine; if not, it won't matter."

He pointed a crooked index finger at Big Nose George. "Tell me truly, sir, how many times you have stood before me in this court of law."

Big Nose scratched his nose, dipping into assorted memories. "I believe it was four, sir."

"Ah! And you, fella?" he asked, pointing at a T-Bar cowboy.

"Five, sir."

He pointed at Alvin Ream, from the Admiral Ranch. "And you?"

Ream puffed up some. "I don't rightly remember, sir. So many times I can't quite say, but it's in the double digits."

"Ah, more than the fingers on my hands," Earwig said, spreading out all his fingers.

"Yep."

Several cowboys whistled. A little brag was good.

"How about you, sir?" Earwig asked, pointing at a cowboy unfamiliar to me.

"Well, sir, five or six times, before you, and eight or ten before the previous judge, best as I can recollect."

Earwig nodded. "A true reprobate, and proud of it."

He aimed his finger at Smiley Thistlethwaite.

"Beyond counting, Your Honor. Simply taxes my mind to remember them all," Smiley said.

"Good, good. And you, Spitting Sam?"

"I've never had the honor, sir, but only because I've dodged the law. But I've been before a dozen judges throughout the territory, and have survived twenty or thirty good fights."

"Good, good, good," the judge said.

The motley crowd looked plumb worn out after a night of uproar and blood, and then a few hours packed into cells intended to hold one or two. The culprits weren't bleeding now, but they looked pale and drawn, as if they were on their last legs. All of which delighted Judge Earwig.

One by one, he had the locals fess up. And most of them put the best face possible on it, and confessed to far more infractions than they had to their credit. I thought most of them had been before the judge once or twice, at most, but this lot was confessing to five or seven or a dozen arrests for brawling. There was something really satisfying about it, and it did my heart good to see so much manhood confessing to so much public disturbance in Doubtful. There was not a town in the territory that could match or beat Doubtful when it came to public disturbance. And I must say, those roustabouts with the show were really impressed. They hadn't the faintest idea, until last evening, what they were facing in Doubtful, Wyoming.

But now they knew. Judge Earwig finished his questioning, with a vast smile building under his rough beard. A gleam lit his eyes. I knew this would be a decision for the ages. I could see it coming, like a burst of sunshine in that courtroom.

"Well now," he said. "We have a bunch of splendid confessions here. We've listened to more confession this fine morning than I've ever heard in one session of this court. We have confessions upon confessions, admissions upon admissions, crime upon crime, duly noted and officially accounted for. When it comes to confessions, this is a truly manly crowd, except for the show people over there, who were swift to blame anyone other than themselves. They're a shameful crew, but the locals who have paraded before this court dozens of times, they're as fine an example of Puma County manhood as ever came here."

I was getting antsy, seeing as how Earwig was going on and on. I was plumb wore out, and wanted some shut-eye, but this was Earwig's moment of glory, with the sun and moon and stars all shining on him, and he wouldn't let go.

Some of those fellows needed some medical attention, I thought. Or at least their pals needed to put them on a horse and carry them back to their ranches. But Earwig ignored that, or if he saw it, he thought there was divine justice in it.

He rapped his gavel sharply, awakening the dead and dying, and alerting the crowd.

"The Wild West scoundrels are herewith fined twenty dollars or two weeks in our iron cages, their choice. If they choose to pay, they must leave town before sundown."

They sighed. Billy Bones would pay, and extract the fines from their pay down the road. They settled morosely while Earwig grinned at them, enjoying every moment.

He rapped again. "Now, then, the locals, who have intently confessed to crimes beyond number, crimes exceeding the stars in heaven, must endure a harsher fate. I herewith sentence them all to hang by the neck until dead, one week from today."

That sort of stopped the show. That was it. Sentence imposed. The cowboys looked at one another, amazed. I sure was going to have a mess of hangings on my hand, and the only way I could do it was with a scaffold wide enough to drop them all at the same time. I'd get the carpenters busy on that. I'd have to order a mess of rope just to put nooses over the heads of twenty or so culprits.

Big Nose George sat down on the floor and rubbed his eyes.

"Stand up, you. You're in a court of law," Earwig snapped.

Big Nose slowly unfolded and stood erect.

Earwig rapped again. "Now, then, it would impose a great hardship on our esteemed sheriff if he were to keep all twenty-some of the condemned in his two cells, feeding them, changing diapers, hosing them down, and all. Therefore, I am remanding you to your ranches for one week, provided you put a dollar each in the Charity Jar, and you will report here one week hence for your choking party."

The mob stared, absorbing all that.

"I'll be there, your lordship," said Smiley, who

dropped a greenback into the Charity Jar and walked out. A certain amount of greenback exchanging went on, but pretty soon, the jar was laden with bills, and the last of the culprits had staggered into the morning sun.

"Now, then," Earwig said to the show people, "you may take your leave, providing the fine is paid."

Billy Bones sighed, dug into a black leather purse, spread out some greenery before His Honor, and then marched his charges out the door into the glaring light of day.

Earwig turned to me. "Should be enough to put Sammy back in business," he said.

Chapter Thirty-five

The hanging judge and I watched the culprits stream into the day and vanish. He was looking self-satisfied, and I could well understand it. Sammy Upward's famous saloon would be restored. The Wild West show would depart without taking a lot of Doubtful's cash with it.

"Your Honor, the county has a gallows stored away, but it won't drop twenty-one at a crack. You mind if I hang them in shifts?"

"That's not really fair, you know. Some fellows have the honor of croaking a few minutes before the next lot."

"I could have them draw straws to see who goes first," I said. "I can hang six at a time."

"Well, not all of them'll show up, you know. Then I'll have to issue warrants for their arrest. You'll have a stack of warrants in your office, to use at will. They might be pretty handy for keeping the peace around Puma County," he said.

I was beginning to see the genius in his sentencing.

"That's pretty fine, Your Honor. Maybe we'll only hang a few in a week."

"Well, set up the gallows, and we'll see."

That sounded fine to me. "I'll get a crew busy," I said. "We'll get some fresh hemp. I never could tie those blasted nooses, but I know a few who can. I'll get Rusty to do it, if I can unloose him from his honeymoon."

"Or honeymoons," Earwig said, winking away.

Earwig was nobody's fool, I thought.

I got a couple of fellows from the Puma County Tax Collection Office to put up the gallows on the village square. Collecting taxes was about the same as hanging people, so I figured they knew what they were up to. And they did. They got the frame in place with the trapdoors on it, and little stairway up there, and then the uprights, and the beam, and I had Rusty build six nooses and let them hang there in the August breezes. It made a nice addition to the town's sights, and lots of visitors off the ranches paused to admire it. The tax boys did a good job of it, getting the upright posts going straight up, and bolting down the crossbeam, which I had used a few times before this.

The joke was that the county was going to hang anyone who didn't pay his taxes, which was not a bad idea, because I sometimes wasn't paid regularly. But Reggie Thimble let it be known that

I'd be hanging a mess of unruly cowboys who were advised to show up for their demise or face a warrant.

I ran a few test runs, using sandbags, and the whole deal worked handsomely. When I pulled the lever, the hinged trap dropped, and the sandbags plunged downward and then dangled in the wind. I thought that maybe Spitting Sam and Big Nose George would die with a smile, but some of those other dudes would whine and struggle. But you never knew what a man was made of until he was about to croak.

Rusty was feeling mighty fine, full of joy. He had two wives and a boy, and how could you beat that? The Siamese twins had settled down and were no longer trying to throttle each other, so there was peace at last in Doubtful. As long as there was bad blood between the twins, I knew trouble was not far away. Rusty and his family would sometimes parade up and down Wyoming Street, just to show off a little. The town ladies quit gossiping, and greeted the twins like long lost sisters. Everyone in Doubtful admired Hanging Judge Earwig's fine solution to an impossible dilemma.

I thought summer was about over, and life would be peaceful again, except for hanging twenty-one cowboys, but then a slicker rode in with some fancy horses and challenged everyone to a match race, with a few side bets for spice. His name was Algernon Limp, but I think he invented it to give him some advantage. Anyone in Wyoming knows that Algernon is a sissy name, and Limp is worse. It's as if his horses limped, and that was what he was trying to convey with a name like that. I studied him some, and went back to my office to paw through the wanted dodgers and posters, but I didn't find anyone matching Algernon Limp's description. Actually, he was a pint-sized dandy, with pinstripe black suit, a red paisley vest and bowler hat and waxed mustachios and patent-leather shoes so shiny that they pretty near reflected starlight.

But Limp was more than a dandy dresser. He brought with him three of the finest horses I'd ever seen, full of thoroughbred blood, I thought, almost dainty in their stepping. There was a black, a bay with white stockings, and a palomino.

He began by parking them at the hitch rails of the saloons, and it was plain he was letting people take a gander at them. A few cowboys had filtered back in, but the hanging was still a couple of days away, so Limp didn't have the usual bunch of drovers around to talk to. He eyed the gallows, inquired when the big day would be, and offered to run races to celebrate the event, but mostly he was waiting for the hangings to go away so he could get down to the business of staging match races between his steeds and any local talent the cowboys came up with.

He stopped by the sheriff office to inquire about a good place to run the match races he had in mind.

"I have here, some of the finest horseflesh not only in the territory, but in all of the United States and all of the world," he said. "Have with me a trainer, jockey, and an oddsmaker, Boston Bill, who will take wagers laid on one nag or the other, and fleece the cowboys out of their hard-earned monthly salaries."

"I imagine your ponies lose a few," I said.

"I like to give that impression," he said. "In fact, I always understate the virtues of my running horses, so that people are willing to test their own nags against mine. That's how I make a dandy living, and I expect to retire soon because I have husbanded my winnings and built them up."

"How do you do it?"

"I have a quarter-miler, a half-miler, and a miler, all southern bred," he said. "And Egbert Engstrom, the demon Swede jockey who squeezes juice out of my turnips, I lay out the game to the local talent, and they can decide whether or not to run a match race with my plugs. If there are no takers, I move on to the next town, and see who'll swallow the bait."

"What if you lose?"

"Oh, I pay my stakes cheerfully, and my bookie coughs up, and we accept our licking. I have excellent credit with the Greengrocers and Bail

Bond Stock Bank of Manhattan, and I draw a certified check, and head for the next burg."

"You have stakes?"

"Of course. We each put up a stake, and the winner walks away with it."

"What if there's a false start?"

"We always have independent judges, drawn from the community. One at the starting line, and one at the finish."

He sure seemed to have all the answers. And he may have run a square game, but I'd reserve judgment on that. There had been so many road shows coming through Doubtful that I figured there weren't two nickels left to rub together, but horse racers are a different breed, and half of them are mad, and they can get all heated up faster than a virgin in a cathouse.

"Well, the best day for a match race would be the day of the hangings," I said. "We've got twenty-one cowboys lined up, and we'll hang them in shifts, and maybe you could run a match race between each shift."

"Oh, boy," he said. "Doubtful will have a glorious day."

"How do you promote the event? The hanging's only two days away."

"The saloons, my friend. They are regular gossip machines. Put out the word, and next thing, there's a dozen calculating strangers eyeing my livestock."

"Do you exercise them so they folks can watch?"

"Absolutely. We train first thing every morning. As soon as we measure up the track, we'll do light runs for the edification of the locals. We've got the finest horseflesh west of Kalamazoo, and we'll put it all on display."

"We got some fine horseflesh around here. Over at the Admiral Ranch, Smiley Thistlethwaite's been working some quarter-milers that can't be beat, at least locally. Trouble is, he's scheduled to be hanged. You might want to get him to race his tomorrow, before he expires."

"Well, that's a thought, but ideally, he should match my nag on the day of the hanging, so if he wins, he can go to the noose happily, and the crowd can cheer him."

"Well, we can schedule a little time between each shift. My deputy's got to cut down the bodies anyway, and build fresh nooses. I imagine a good match race would occupy people until we're ready to hang the next lot."

"Capital, just capital," he said. "Well, I'm off to the saloons, to troll a little. Wish me happy days."

After that, things sort of picked up steam on their own. Maxwell, the funeral parlor man, ordered in some ice so he could keep all them corpses cold and run the funerals by rotation with the criminals well preserved and looking prime.

The women of the Methodist persuasion planned to sell fried chicken and potato salad box lunches to the crowd. But the Episcopalians, not to be outdone, offered to set up a whole lunch counter, hams, steaks, green snapper beans, strawberry tarts, and frosty fizzes, all donations going to the widows, if any—cowboys were not known for getting into holy wedlock uninspired by a shotgun—and the Lutherans decided to hold a Sons of Norway lutefisk supper following the hangings, right next to Maxwell's Funeral Parlor, so folks could eat and view the stiffs in one tour.

I toured Saloon Row that eve. It sure was entertaining. Sammy had got his saloon back in business. He bought booze from the Lizard Lounge and Mrs. Gladstone's Sampling Room so he didn't have to wait for a shipment from Denver. He didn't have much variety, but that didn't matter. Who cares about taste?

There were cowboys in town from all the ranches, but none of the condemned. They were smart enough to steer clear until the last. And sure enough, there was Algernon Limp, the center of attention, boasting up his nags. He chose Mrs. Gladstone's Sampling Room, mostly because Cronk ran a faro game there, and betting was what the place was all about.

"Now, friend," Limp was saying to a certain cowboy named Bark, "my quarter-mile runner is unbeatable. His name is Booth, after John Wilkes Booth, and he is the Terror of the West. He was born and bred in the South. If you'll put up a hundred dollars as a stake, winner take all, I will match you, and we will race tomorrow."

"A hunnert? Where am I gonna get a hunnert?" Bark asked.

"You form a pool with your pals from your ranch," Limp said.

"Well, I got a quarter stallion, it can't be beat, and it's mean enough to take a piece of hide off yours," Bark said. "Ain't that the truth?"

Some of his friends allowed that it was.

"Well, then, you've got an easy hundred," Limp said. "You got ten friends? Have them put in ten, and win ten. Or they can make side bets, too, with my bookie. He'll post the odds, and you can bet or not as you choose. You want to lay two dollars on my nag, or his nag? See the bookie."

Bark eyed his pals, who nodded, and agreed. "We'll match you, and race tomorrow," he said.

I had a hunch that Bark and his pals were about to lose their asses, but my ma told me never to bet on hunches.

And Algernon Limp was smiling like he owned Doubtful.

Chapter Thirty-six

Hanging Day would be hot and sunny, I thought, eyeing the cloudless sky. That's fine; better to hang twenty-one in sunshine rather than rain or overcast. Everybody would see well if there was plenty of sun.

The first hanging was scheduled for ten in the morning. After lunch, and the first match race, the second hanging would be held at two, followed by another match race, and the third hanging would be at four, and any leftovers would be hanged at six.

There wasn't much shade at the gallows, but some nice cottonwoods lined the square and people could collect there in good shade, for the big events.

Rusty and I were all set. I'd tie the wrists of the hangee, put a noose over his head, and pull the lever whenever we got one bunch ready. Rusty, he would cut the noose free and cart the corpse to Maxwell's wagon. Then Rusty would build another noose and we'd dangle it from the crossbar. We didn't know how many would show up for their croaking, but we'd be prepared. I'd gotten plenty of rope from the Mercantile, and some thong to tie up wrists. Enough to hang all twenty-one, if need be.

There were a couple of preachers around, just in case the condemned wanted a last rite, and these fellows lounged in canvas chairs, waiting to be called upon.

Hanging Judge Earwig would be on hand to conduct the ceremonies.

By the time I got to the town square, crowds were already collecting. Many brought blankets to sit on, and wicker baskets filled with chilled sandwiches and iced tea. The ladies were all in summery white gauze, and their daughters wore white pinafores or cream-colored little dresses. The town's gents tended to stand, and waited solemnly for the day's events to roll.

It was a noisy crowd, with little boys and dogs circling in packs through the mob, and a few horses shying from all the ruckus. But finally ten o'clock did roll around, chimed by the courthouse clock, and Judge Earwig, wearing his judicial robes and a silk stovepipe hat, promptly emerged from his chambers, stepped up on the gallows with a borrowed megaphone, and began the show.

"Ladies and gentlemen, we will now hang the malefactors who trashed Sammy Upward's Last Chance Saloon a few days ago, a crime unspeakable, and unequaled in the history of Wyoming. Will the following criminals please step forward to meet your moment of destiny with the noose.

"Silvan Boot, Max Dell, Parson McCullough, Wagner Wick, Delbert Battles, and Jocko Mortensen."

I waited for the culprits, but no one emerged from the crowd.

"I repeat, yonder villains, step forward and take your medicine like men."

But blamed if anyone stepped up.

Earwig pulled his giant timepiece from somewhere in the interior of his cloth tent, eyed the hands, and stuffed it under his robes again.

"All right. Since no one among them is man enough to take his medicine, I will require that they be hanged in absentia. The sheriff will drop the trap, in token of which the criminals will be dispatched in absentia, and the first lot of criminals will be carted off to the undertaker, in absentia."

It sure was entertaining. I had the attention of the mob, all right. I climbed the little wooden stair, stood at the lever until Earwig dropped his arm, and I pulled the lever. The floor underneath the row of nooses suddenly swung down, and the crowd stared, and then cheered.

"A shameful lot," Earwig said. "Not a real man among them. But they can restore their tarnished reputations by contributing to the Charity Jar, the proceeds to go to Sammy Upward."

Maxwell drove the bodies, removed in absentia, to the funeral parlor, where they would be on display, in absentia.

"All right," Judge Earwig said. "Eat your lunches. The next recreation is at two. And there is a match race scheduled at one."

The Charity Jar rested prominently on the gallows, and pretty soon I saw some of those miscreants slide up and drop some greenery into it. They were all ruined men, marked forever by their cowardice. They sure were smiling a lot. Max Dell, he had pulled a cheroot and was firing up. Lots of fellas were patting his back.

A few wandered off to the funeral parlor, where Maxwell had arranged for the absentees to lie in state, a block-printed name at the head of each bier. A few folks studied the list of the shamed, and a few tossed pennies onto the bier, which Maxwell snapped up as his rightful fee.

By the time lunch rolled around, some youthful entrepreneurs had set up a lemonade stand, and I debated arresting them because they didn't have a city business license. But my ma used to say, there's a proper time and place, and maybe I'd arrest them late in the afternoon, so I could confiscate their profits and put the cash in the Charity Jar.

"Hey, sheriff," Reggie Thimble said. "This sure is fine."

"Maybe I should hang you," I said. "You want to volunteer? Confess to countless crimes in office first?"

"I'll see you fired one of these days," he said.

It sure was a fine August day, even if hot. A mess of people were digging into their box lunches. Children were playing hangman on the gallows, and I had to chase off a little squirt who got his neck into a noose. Then a mess of ten-year-old boys tried to hang a red-haired girl, and I got to roaring, and for the moment, I scared them off. Trouble was, the girl was egging them on, and I finally had to take her by the hand and lead her back to her ma. But her ma got mad at me for being a bully.

A little after noon, the crowd drifted along Wyoming Street to the improvised race course that Limp had set up there. The horsemen in town had all drifted that way earlier, and were standing around, gauging the nags, making sage comments about how one or another was built for racing, and muscled up in the chest and flanks, and had a wild look in the eye, and all that. I'd heard it all before, mostly from a lot of males who thought they knew more about horses than anyone else. These sages had all acquired their followers out there as they preached their message one way or another.

There were a mess of them who thought that Limp's quarter gelding, Booth, would triumph. But there were plenty of others who'd gathered around Bark's ranch horse, named Sherman, and eyeing his hooves and flanks and the look in his eye.

Limp knew what he was doing, naming his nag after Lincoln's assassin, just to stir up some passions, and some heavy betting. Wyoming was northern turf, even if most of those cowboys on the ranches had drifted up from the old Confederacy. Limp, he just stood quietly, letting nature take its course, but his bookmaker had a little blackboard and chalk that he was using to take bets. Every time he made a bet, he put the bills in a little black bag that he tucked into his pocket.

He wasn't bleating, either. Limp's outfit was simply standing around, taking money from bettors, while shrewd observers studied the two nags. Limp's other horses were on display, but in rope corrals a bit away. There was his bay half-miler Robert E. Lee, and his black one-mile thoroughbred, Jefferson Davis, both of them prime horseflesh, lean, nervous, wild of eye, and restless. There were plenty of cowboys studying those two, professing to know their bloodlines, plumbing their ancestry, citing hoary records and victories to make their case.

Limp had run a chalk starting line along the path, and a quarter mile down a chalk finish line. The match race would begin when the starter fired a shot. If either horse broke early, the judge would blow a whistle and the horses would return to start once again. Bark had got a crazy ranch kid to jockey for him, but Limp had put his mad Swede in purple silks, so that the Limp horse looked like a serious racer and the ranch horse, Sherman, and his jean-clad rider, looked like something cobbled up locally.

I watched the good citizens of Doubtful lay bets with the bookie. I watched Mayor Waller squander three dollars on Bark's horse, Sherman. But then I watched Turk, the liveryman, who knew a thing or two about nags, push a ten-spot to Boston Bill, that bought him an additional eleven if Booth won.

"You like the looks of that palomino, do you?" I asked.

"It's no contest," Turk said. "That quarter gelding's got heat in him, and I'd guess he'll cop it by a length and a half."

"You're the man who should know," I said.

For once, he didn't take it as an insult.

Hubert Sanders, our banker, was hesitating, and finally came to me. "You got any idea how this'll play out?"

"Nope, I hardly know a horse's molars from his incisors."

"Well, I'm leaning slightly toward Limp's fine steed, but his name puts me off. I am a devotee of Abraham Lincoln, and naming a horse after Booth is scurrilous. Which is why I'm inclined to bet on him."

I wasn't quite following the logic, but I let her lay.

I sure as the dickens didn't know which nag would win, so I focused on keeping the peace. With all them nooses dangling back there, some loser might take the notion to hang a winner, or maybe hang Limp or his bookie or Swede jockey. I hoped Rusty was keeping an eye on the nooses back on the square, so a bunch of bratty boys wouldn't hang a dog or something like that.

Denver Sally, my favorite madam, slid up. She was wearing gauzy scarlet, as befitted her station.

"You got one picked?" I asked her.

"It won't be Booth," she said. "He's rank. I can tell. He'll throw his jockey and lose. A horse needs to be ridden hard."

"I guess you know a thing or two about that," I said.

She laughed and patted me on the thigh. I've been thinking about marrying her ever since she came to town, but I keep getting diverted. One of these days I'll get around to trying it out. My ma, she always said we should try the fit before we buy.

It was getting along toward one, time to run the

match race on the Hanging Day, and the rest of Doubtful drifted out. I wondered who was manning the stores. Some unlucky clerk, I supposed. Even Maxwell was out, maybe hoping a horse would drop dead or break a leg, and he could offer a horse funeral for its bereaved master.

Well, that crowd knew where to go. Pretty near everyone in town kept going past the starting line, and began collecting around the finish, where the finish-line judges were eyeing the chalk, and studying the course. The judges for this race were King Glad, off his ranch, and Cronk, the faro dealer at Mrs. Gladstone's Sampling Room. Doc Harrison was appointed tie-breaker in case the two judges couldn't agree. And now the three were making learned examinations of the track, the noon light, the wind, the sun, and the condition of the heavens.

The calmest man around was Limp, who seemed a little bored by it all, He stood around, wearing his morning coat, silk stovepipe hat, and white gloves. He carried a small riding crop, and I thought that was to beat off angry people if their bets failed.

"Who you betting on?" I asked, shrewdly. There were always some owners who bet against their own nag.

"I don't bet," he said. "If I win, my profit's the purse."

He pulled out his turnip watch, eyed it, and sighed.

"Race time," he said.

Just about then, a shot fired a quarter mile distant echoed, and a hoarse cry lifted into the blue sky. The horses were running.

Chapter Thirty-seven

It wasn't even close. Bark's nag, Sherman, sailed in half a length ahead of Booth, with the kid riding it flapping around like he couldn't hang on. Booth, ridden by that Swede in purple silks, seemed half awake, even though the Swede was popping his butt with the crop. The judges hardly needed to debate it. The match race man, Limp, was out the stake. Now we'd see if he paid up.

The jockeys slowed their mounts, turned them, and trotted them back to the finish line. Bark's horse looked like it had barely worked up a sweat, while the matchmaker's nag was lathered through the flanks.

"Well," said Limp, "you've some fine, fine horse-flesh here, Bark, and my fine little gelding's been properly whomped." He pulled out his little black bag, slowly extracted a mess of twenties, and paid them out, one at a time, to Bark, who watched the bills collect in his horny hand. Bark allowed himself a little smile.

The bookie, Boston Bill, was paying off some wagers, too, less cheerfully but, even so, it got done. Lot of fellers from Puma County walked off with a few more greenbacks in their britches than they started with, and the day was uncommonly cheerful for them. A good Hanging Day and winning a bet on some nags, that made a memorable day if one was in from the ranches, where life was dull and no one could think of anything to do except target practice and practical jokes.

There were a mess of people around the nags, eyeing them, gaining knowledge, turning themselves into racing experts, and priming themselves for the next match race, scheduled at four that afternoon after another hanging. I sure knew the feeling. I could see how Bark's horse was better built, had more chest and lung, than Limp's horse, and I could see how Bark had trained it up real fine, so that it could run a short race better than anyone else's nag, at least in Puma County. Maybe it'd not be so fine down in Laramie, where there were fancy horsemen calculating how to win races.

People sure were having a fine day. Bark collected his friends and headed for the Last Chance Saloon to have a lick at the bar before going to the next hanging. The matchmaker and the judges were laying out a half-mile racetrack, this time a big oval with the four corners marked, so people wouldn't have to walk far out of town to see the finish. I didn't know who was running against Limp and his Robert E. Lee, which was one sleek bay that looked like it could whip anything in three states.

It got along toward the hanging time, and all the town collected at the gallows. Rusty had chased off the brats who were playing hangman, and he was operating the trapdoor so it dropped proper. Old Whiskers himself, Hanging Judge Earwig, was impatiently waiting to condemn anyone who showed up. The crowd slowly gathered. I saw the Ukrainian twins, rosy and fresh from their honeymoon, watching the proceedings along with Riley, who was bug-eyed at the thought of hanging anyone, and kept feeling his neck to see if it was still there. Belle was there, too, itching to see some criminal croak.

It had gotten pretty hot, and the businessmen had doffed their suit coats, and the cowboys had big black stains under their armpits. If it wasn't for Hanging Day, most everyone would be having a siesta. My ma used to say that a nap in the middle of the day made the evenings better, but I never saw it. Evenings were one and the same, usually cooler and welcome in the summer.

Earwig pulled out his giant timepiece, decided

the moment had come, and climbed up onto the gallows with a megaphone.

"All right, step right up, see justice done. We'll hang the next batch. When I call your name, step forward and take your medicine, or forever be branded as a craven coward." He eyed the growing crowd. "It's five minutes ahead of the hour, but I've elected to get on with it. What's five minutes to the condemned? A blink of the eye. All, right, all right. Here are the deceased:

"Randy Packer, Mulligan Meyers, Dinty Stepovich, Walker Wayne, Joe Popper, and Big Nose George."

There were little gasps of pleasure as the crowd took the measure of the condemned. Most of them were Flying D men, but a couple were Admiral Ranch men, including Big Nose.

"Packer, step forward," the judge called, but there was no Packer anywhere around.

"Meyers, take your medicine," he bawled, but no Meyers threaded through the crowd.

"Stepovich, step up!" But that didn't yield a hangee.

"Wayne, you lily-livered coward, step into the noose." But the lily-livered didn't.

"Popper, you come up here and face the music." Earwig peered around, seeing no cowhand of that description.

"And you, Big Nose, you come forward and pay for your crimes."

Big Nose George moved slowly through the crowd, headed for the gallows, while the crowd watched, electrified. He seemed somehow alone, separated from the hundreds of people surrounding him.

It suddenly occurred to me that Big Nose was going to be hanged, and I was going to do the hanging.

Big Nose, formidable and heavy, walked slowly to the front of the gallows.

"All right, hang me," he said. "Hang me for a little brawling in a saloon. That's a hanging offense."

Hanging Judge Earwig seemed to expand. His wattles ballooned. His bosom grew. His ears reddened. "Hanged by the neck until dead," he snarled.

The crowd of merrymakers suddenly turned silent. The game was over. Big Nose was calling Earwig's bluff. Earwig could not call Big Nose a coward or a craven criminal, not now, not ever again.

"Go ahead, hang me, you little fart," Big Nose said softly.

The crowd stirred. This was new and unexpected. This might ruin Hanging Day. This might turn Hanging Judge Earwig into a monster. It had all been fun, fun to call all the condemned cowards for not showing up for their appointment with the noose. But now the fun stopped cold.

I saw a few of those mothers suddenly send their daughters home, and I watched the girls retreat, scared, in their bright summer whites, into the crowd, and off the square.

Judge Earwig began to redden. He bloated up like a bullfrog, staring at Big Nose, licking his lips, pinking up until I thought he'd burst a blood vessel.

"Hang him, hang him right now," Earwig said.

Big Nose, he calmly stepped onto the trap and fitted a noose over his neck, and even drew it up, and twisted the knot so it would snap his neck. He held out his hands to me to tie behind his back. I stared at him. He was calling the game, and he held the aces and twos.

The mob down there, they turned so silent that the breeze seemed noisy. I watched George Waller, the mayor, looking rapt and discomfited. And Reggie Thimble, swallowing hard. And Delphinium Sanders, the banker's wife who approved of hanging everyone, on principle, looking mighty solemn.

And I was looking into my own heart, knowing the act of killing a man would be mine alone, and that there was no justice in it, and that Big Nose didn't even deserve an hour in my jail, much less a grave in the little cemetery just outside the city limits.

"Do it," Earwig said, jamming his finger at me.

"Tell me the law," I said. Let him show me book and verse that said that the Territory of Wyoming had the lawful right to hang a man for getting into a saloon fight.

"You'll be next if you don't get busy," Earwig said, all bloated up and glaring at me, the instrument of the will of the court.

That mob down there, it sure was quiet. All the ladies at the sandwich stand, they were crying. Time had stopped. That's the only way I could put it. The clocks all quit.

"Hang him," yelled Cronk, the faro dealer.

"Hang him," yelled Manilla Twining, the grand dame of Doubtful.

Lawyer Stokes stepped forward. "You must do as the court directs, young man. Do it promptly, as required."

But Denver Sally had a different view. "Cotton, don't be a jerk," she said.

Big Nose, he was staring at me, his eyes mocking. He was the winner, in a way. No one would ever call him a coward.

I scratched my ear, which is what I do when my brain quits on me. Riley was watching me; so were the Siamese twins. Rusty was quietly waiting. The judge's glare was so fierce it bored right through me. He stood there, a rock of wrath, waiting to hang me, too if I didn't comply.

I knew pretty much what I had to do, and wondered what it might mean for me. I had to do what was right. And damn the consequences. There were a lot of people down there, their gazes riveted on me, and on my old friend Big Nose George, and even as they watched me, I made up my mind.

I unpinned the brass badge I wore on my shirt. It came loose easily, slid out of the gray fabric of my shirt, and into my hand.

I dropped the badge into Earwig's hand. He seemed to bloat up, and then he started laughing. I couldn't believe it. There he was, laughing like some old geezer who'd just told a knee-slapper.

I am not bright, everyone likes to tell me, and I was even less bright trying to figure this one out. There he was, wheezing away, and pretty soon the crowd, they were hooting and cackling, and there was Big Nose, still solemn, but he had won, and no bullying judge would ever call a cowboy a coward or a craven criminal again. Me, I didn't mind the laughter. Let them call me a coward, or slow, or whatever they wanted. I'd done what I thought was the right thing.

Big Nose, he came up to me, and threw an arm around my shoulder, and smiled.

"Here's a man," he said. "A real man."

I confess, I didn't know the difference between a man and any other male, but if he wanted to jabber at me, that was fine.

Earwig, he slapped the badge into my hand, and laughed, and wandered away, leaving an odd hole in the crowd, because no one wanted to come close to him.

I didn't know whether to pin the badge back on, and decided that if I'd resigned, maybe the supervisors needed to appoint me. But then the blamedest thing happened. Reggie Thimble himself, he made his way through the throng, took that brass star out of my hand, and poked the needle part of it through my gray shirt, stabbing me only twice before he got it hooked in proper. So I was sheriff again, but I couldn't figure why. A feller always has to do what's right, and that was clear. I never did argue in my head about whether the hanging was right; it wasn't. Not for that. All I worried about was whether I'd lose the job. I don't mind being sheriff, but there are times I'd just as soon climb onto Critter and go work cattle somewhere as far from people as I could get. California or some awful place like that.

But no one was coming up to me. I had a little space around me, same as Judge Earwig, and I felt real alone in the midst of all those people who were staring at me like I was a two-headed calf.

Hanging Day was rescued, seems like. Pretty soon the ladies were peddling sarsaparilla and fried chicken, and the brats were up on the gallows, playing hangman again.

"Rusty, cut them nooses off," I said, pointing to a dozen little devils who were running the nooses around necks.

He hollered at the brats, and pretty quick he sawed through all that rope, and then pulled the handle of the trap, which fell down on its hinge. I'd get the county workmen to take the thing down and store it once again. Maybe someday I'd need it for a real hanging of a real bad man. But not this August day.

Chapter Thirty-eight

The rest of the hangees seemed to crawl out of the woodwork, their reputations unblemished, and a few of them climbed the little stair to the gallows, and peered around, looking into the trap, and studying the dangling ropes. They were a smiley lot.

But there were another event scheduled for Hanging Day, namely a half-mile match race, so folks were drifting across town, stopping in the saloons along the way to fortify themselves for the great event. Hanging Day sure was big business in Doubtful, and I thought maybe we should schedule some regular hangings so the shopkeepers could profit. A hanging cost the county some, but the sales made up for it.

People didn't know what to make of me. One old cob off the ranches told me I should've hanged the sonofabitch.

"You ever been in a good bar fight?" I asked.

"More times than I got fingers."

He had eight left, so I thought he'd brawled maybe ten times.

"Well, how come you ain't hanged yet?" I asked.

"Because I'm smarter than Big Nose," he said.

"Well, if you need hanging, just drop in and I'll arrange it," I said.

"I don't know how you got to be sheriff," he said.

What a fine day. The hangings had put everyone in a festive mood. The ladies wore straw hats loaded with silk flowers. The gents broke out the arm garters and brushed their derbies. The crowd had shifted back and forth from courthouse square to the racetrack, and now the good people of Doubtful were standing around the track, which consisted of four red flags on poles, forming a rectangle. A breeze flapped the flags, and lifted the oppressive heat away. That was the track. The match race would be run outside of the poles. I supposed it was half a mile; someone with a better brain than mine had figured it out.

The start and finish line were one and the same, a white chalk strip on the clay.

There was Limp, duded up in a silk stovepipe and tails, his handsome nag, Robert E. Lee, groomed until he shone, with the mane done up in small braids. The Swede jockey stood impassively in his royal purple silks, chewing Bull Durham and watching the crowd. The horse sure had gathered a lot of attention; there were cowboys, businessmen, a few ladies, some children who had to be shooed away. The horse yawned, baring green-stained incisors, and settled into its usual boredom. Some of the bettors found clues in it. The horse lacked fire, and would lose.

The bookie had a big chalkboard, and was offering bets on both nags, with Robert E. Lee the slight favorite. Bet a dollar, make a dollar and a half if the horse won. Pretty slim pickings, but the bookie was collecting cash and handing out chits. I had the feeling that the bookmaker didn't care which nag won; he had his butt covered.

There was a smaller crowd around Ulysses Grant, the other horse, a dappled gray that had a little Arab in him, if I was any judge. He had the dished Arab head, anyway. He was lighter and leaner than Robert E. Lee, and his owner, Milo Drogovich, was holding him quietly. The man had a small ranch on the far edge of the county, almost in high country, on a mountain creek, and no one knew much about him. I sure didn't. I had no idea he raised running horses. This nag, a gelding, stood quietly, while the jockey, Drogovich's son Piers, stood nervously. The boy wasn't wearing silks, but did have a loose white shirt of coarse cotton and carried a small black riding crop.

"I didn't know you raised runners," I said to Drogovich.

"I didn't, either. It's just an accident. The boy

was running him one day, and I was watching, and I thought, this is a runner. So we worked him. He's the only runner I've ever owned."

A lot of people were listening, and some were even taking notes. What Drogovich was saying, that this was his first attempt to run a horse, immediately cooled a lot of people. I could almost sense the switch to Limp's nag, even though Grant was the local challenger.

"Mind if I look at his hooves?" a rancher named Garvey asked.

"Have a look," the owner said.

Garvey expertly lifted each hoof, looked at the shoe and the frog, and set it down. He said nothing, simply wandered off. I thought the horse was well shod, but I'm not in the racing racket, and if Critter can walk without a limp, I'm usually satisfied that the blacksmith shoed him well enough. Racehorses they shoe special, and I don't know a thing about it.

It got to be race time, hot and dry, and the same judges, Doc Harrison, King Glad, and Cronk, got lined up, one either side of the line, and one on a stool, looking down in. The jockeys walked and trotted their nags once around the loop, and then lined up at the chalk line. It got real intense there, with half the people in Puma County crowded close. The starter, Bo Windy, got his revolver ready and waited for them jockeys to get lined up, and this time he didn't delay. He squeezed off a shot, and away they went. It was a good start, no one broke too soon, and that pair of nags, bay and dappled gray, hunkered low and clattered down the track, turned at the first pole, the gray wider and faster, the bay slower for a moment and cutting sharp, and then they were running the next piece, and curving around for the third, with the gray edging half a length ahead, and gaining ground.

The crowd was real quiet, and even the clatter of hooves was muffled.

Sweat was foaming around the flanks of the bay, and along the stifle, but I didn't see any stress in the Drogovich horse. They thundered around the final turn, the jockeys low and using their crops, and the dappled gray pulled ahead and crossed the chalk a length out front. The crowd hooted, this time at Limp, whose first two horses had lost to locals, and it sure pleased the winners to collect from the bookmaker. Limp headed over to Drogovich, shook his hand, and the rancher was a hundred dollars ahead, collecting the match money.

The horses trotted in, while the crowds collected around the gray, admiring it, appreciating its sleek body, barely sweated up compared the wet, heaving bay.

"That fella Limp, he thinks he knows nags, but he don't," said one cowboy, a little loudly.

This sure was a fine moment for Doubtful. A professional match horseman had gotten whipped twice. It was the perfect end of the Hanging Day, and the whole town was celebrating.

"Now wait, gents, is anyone going to match my miler, Jefferson Davis?" Limp asked.

A lot of folks stared at one another. Ranch horses weren't known for long-distance running, and were largely bred to maneuver cattle. Still, there was Limp, with some losers in his string, and another day of racing if anyone wanted to challenge him.

That's when the stranger stepped up. Young feller, with down at the heels boots, raggedy shirt, skinny, a big Adam's apple, and a stubble of blond beard on him.

"I guess I got here just in time," he said.

I suddenly was aware that he was leading a sorrel horse, with no markings on him, plain as horses get but long and built on thoroughbred lines. They wouldn't call him sorrel back East; that was a local way to describe a chestnut. It sure was a common color.

"You looking for a match?" the lad asked.

"Well," said Limp, "I'm looking, but I'm not sure you'd want to match that horse against mine. I've got to tell you, my horse has walked away with more match meets than I can count."

"I got a nice runner here," the youth said. "He's proved out. I've got a pasture with some stumps in it, and I run him around a big circle in there. My friends all say this boy's a runner for sure. And he likes a long run, too."

"Has he ever been in competition?" Limp asked.

"Well, I matched him up with other horses on the ranch, and around there. And he done real good."

"Where you from, fella?" Limp asked.

"Medicine Bow County, next to here," he said. "I'm Elmer Skruggs."

"Well, Elmer, I don't think you'd want to risk a hundred dollars of match money. That's a lot for a cowboy."

"Well, me and my friends, we got a hundred together."

"You'll just lose it, boy. This horse, Jefferson Davis, is the fastest streak of lightning in the West, and he's good for a lot more than a mile, too. I can run him one and a half or two, and he's just getting warmed up. You better think on it, boy. I wouldn't want to take a hundred out of your hands like this. You bring me an experienced nag, with a record, and a reputation, and we'll talk business. A hundred's a lot of money."

Skruggs looked disappointed. "I come a long way to race this pup here. Across one county and half across another. All on foot, too."

By now the two were collecting a crowd. There were plenty of local boys eyeing the new horse they'd never seen, and shaking their heads. These cowboys knew horseflesh and knew a runner when they saw one. And this nag wasn't making a dent in their thinking.

The rube from the next county just swallowed hard, making his Adam's apple bobble, and he looked about ready to shed a tear. "I come a long way," he said. "I come to race."

"I don't like easy pickings, boy. You season him, and bring him around next year, and I'll meet you here and we'll have a regular run for the money."

"You mind if I just give him a little run around this here track you got set up? I'd sure like to show you how this sorrel runs."

"What's his name?"

"His name is Jones. You get a plain horse, you want to give him a regular name. You wouldn't want to call this sorrel horse Lord Fauntleroy," Skruggs said.

"Sure, we'll all watch Jones," Limp said. "That'll cap the day, all right."

Skruggs brightened. "Oh, this is what we wanted," he said. "I'll just put a regular saddle on him, not a racing pad, and we'll do a loop."

What was it about that hayseed? He seemed to glow. It didn't make sense, some fair-haired kid off some ranch, with light shining out of him. I'm a regular man, and don't have any mystical notions, but this boy just seemed to be a sun all to himself, and there was no explaining it, least not by me. Why are a few people like that?

He brushed down his sorrel, tossed an old saddle

blanket on, and tightened up the beat-up old saddle, and climbed on. The only thing I noticed was that the sorrel shivered, like it was awaiting something, its flesh twitching and jerking. He led the horse to the makeshift track, while a lot of people studied him, and walked the horse, then trotted him, and finally settled the sorrel into a rocking chair lope, the easiest gait for most horses, and that old sorrel kind of settled into a run, and did the oval twice, and somehow even at that relaxed lope, gave the impression nothing could pass him by.

That was all. Elmer Skruggs reined Jones to a halt, and sat there, waiting. Limp looked him over, and made a decision:

"Boy, you want a match race, you got one. Put up a hundred, and we'll run tomorrow."

Chapter Thirty-nine

I'd never seen anything like it. The whole town was getting heated up about it. At the Last Chance Saloon, that was all they talked about along the bar. The town swiftly divided into two camps. Some were supporting the stranger, Elmer Skruggs, and his horse Jones. That sorrel, they said, had all the mysterious powers of a great horse, and the lope around the track proved it. They were going to lay money on Jones, and walk away with plenty, because Jones was the underdog and he'd go off at high odds.

But the rest of the town, including all the fellers who thought they knew horseflesh, they were ready to lay cash on Jefferson Davis. The oracle for that crowd was Turk himself, the liveryman with a lot of experience in gauging horses. Turk was opining that Limp's classy bay would run several lengths ahead when the finish line loomed up, and that only suckers and innocents saw anything to like in Jones.

I don't know what set off the debates. Skruggs wasn't even a hometown boy, coming from the next county, but he was a good substitute for one, and a lot of people in Doubtful wanted Jones to whip that Confederate horse being put up by that slick operator named Limp, who probably was a man with a checkered past, though no one could prove it, and I couldn't find any wanted dodgers on him. I did look through the pile, wondering if he was a crook, but he seemed clean as a whistle. He seemed square enough, if you didn't look real close.

I made a bar tour that eve, stopping at the Lizard Lounge and McGivers' Saloon and Mrs. Gladstone's Sampling Room, and I swear that's all I heard. There were arguments along every bar rail. The savvy ones, the ones who claimed to know horseflesh, they were solidly for Jefferson Davis, but the others, the local boys who thought the territory produced the best horseflesh in the country, they were all for Jones, the mystery horse out of Medicine Bow.

It was sort of turning into the experts against the sentimental, the fellers who knew nags against the wishful thinkers. It was as if the reputation of Puma County was really at stake. No outside nag was going to walk away with the stakes if they could help it.

Well, all this struck me as odd, since no one

could point to a record by either horse, and no one could say they'd seen either horse in a race. The best anyone could say was that he'd watched a workout, some easy loping, a brief gallop, intended to keep the nags in shape. So there they were, arguing feverishly about nags whose racing records they didn't know, and who had never viewed the nags running flat out, even against a stopwatch. It sure got me to scratching my head some.

Turk, he was the kingpin of the Jefferson Davis crowd, and people listened because he knew more about horseflesh than any twenty other citizens of Doubtful. That crowd was going to lay cash on Limp's thoroughbred, a lot of cash if I was hearing right. That horse was the favorite, and probably wouldn't pay well, but it was a sure thing, and a feller could lay down two dollars and get a sure two-fifty out of it a few minutes later, or a feller could put a hundred on Jeff Davis and collect a hundred twenty-five in minutes. And people who laid money on Jones, liking the high payout, well, they were suckers, born and bred.

That's how the evening went in the smoky saloons. Elmer Skruggs showed up briefly in the Last Chance, said he wouldn't discuss it, just drink his pilsner, and leave. Lots of people tried to get him to open up, but he just stood at the rail, light falling from him, and smiled and sipped and kept silent, and walked out. Limp didn't show up at all, but the bookie did, quietly taking bets as the evening wore on.

The bookie, Boston Bill, acted like he didn't much care who won; it was all mathematical science for him. But he'd get his thirty percent cut no matter which horse won. He didn't even announce his presence, but he took bets, and wrote out chits, and I got to wondering how much cash that feller was taking in, and where it went. The way things were going, he'd stand to make a lot of money, the way the whole town was laying bets on him. I wasn't quite sure how his game worked, but I knew he would calculate the odds in a way that gave him thirty percent of the take, no matter what, and it looked now like Boston Bill would get thirty percent of ten or twenty thousand dollars of wagering. A lot of money, at least to me, in my forty-seven-a-month sheriff job.

Rusty wasn't paying attention. He was keeping his two Ukrainian Siamese twins happy, and his boy, Riley, in socks and shirts, so it was all the same to him. He was happy to sit in the jailhouse and feed prisoners and swamp out the floors.

Hubert Sanders showed up in the saloons, and said he'd open the bank at eight, instead of ten, since so many people wanted to get some cash. It was looking like this match race would have about half the loose cash in Doubtful riding on it, and no one could tell me why, since no one could say for sure what horse was a good runner. It finally dawned on me that the reason everyone was so heated was that no one knew the horses. You could settle an argument pretty quick if you could pull out a record, and say this or that horse won seven races, ran in so much time, and so on. That would settle it. But no one knew these here nags, and the guesses of the experts were just as good as the guesses of the rest of us.

Boston Bill had come into town with Limp, but always hovered a little out of the way, just acting like he barely knew Limp and was along to make a few greenbacks if he could. I wondered some about Boston Bill, but I could find nothing about him in the wanted dodgers. He was dapper, wearing a black bowler and a collarless shirt, and a spray of lilies of the valley tucked into his lapel. Maybe that was his mark, lilies in the lapel. He was easy to find, even if he seemed to keep a little distance from the crowd.

He was staying at the High Plains Hotel, over near the Sporting District, which was a favorite of whiskey drummers and barbed-wire salesmen. It was next door to the Laramie Overland stage stop, which is how it got a lot of its trade. I happened to notice Boston Bill in the lobby, and wondered where Algernon Limp was hanging his stovepipe hat. The kid, Elmer Skruggs, was camping out at the race course, with his horse on a picket line and a bedroll for a place to spend the night. Limp was probably the sort who'd stay at the Wyoming

Hotel, which catered to people with a few dollars in their britches.

Well, I went to bed at Belle's boardinghouse— I'd gotten my room back now that the Ukrainians were bedded down at Rusty's cabin—and slept fitfully, knowing I'd have a tough time of it the next day if a riot started. This here match race might end up killing a few people if I didn't keep the peace.

By dawn I was up and prowling. When a town like Doubtful gets heated up, full of cowboys, and brimming with people in from every neighboring town, I get itchy. I ate at Barney's Beanery and headed for the sheriff office to feed the drunks, and found Rusty asleep in a cell. He smiled and bobbed up when I growled at him.

"I'm wore out," he said. "Two wives is one too many."

"That's what drunks say," I replied.

"I'm gonna hide in here for a while," he said. "I'm half ruined."

"You could divorce one," I said.

He smiled.

By the time I reached the streets for my morning rounds, a crowd had gathered at the Merchant Bank. Hubert Sanders opened the door, and the mob flooded in, forming a line at the one open wicket.

Sanders slipped over to me. "They're all taking out cash to bet on the race," he said.

"You got enough?"

"I hope so. Maybe I'll have to borrow from Boston Bill. It's all going into his pocket."

"And the morning's hardly begun. It's a long time until the race," I said.

Sanders looked a little frayed. "I don't like it, sheriff. This deal bothers me."

"I've been wondering about a crooked race," I said. "Them jockeys could throw it, make some money that way."

Sanders stared, pondering it. "I just don't like it," he said.

I watched the line move through the bank, with all sorts of strangers withdrawing cash, or changing twenties and fifties into fives and ones. I'd never seen the like.

I headed over to Turk, who was holding court in his livery barn. "You got a minute?" I asked. Turk looked annoyed. He was telling a dozen drovers why the Confederate nag would clean up.

But he followed me into his cubbyhole office.

"You got any way of seeing whether this race gets throwed?" I asked.

Turk looked at me as if I was in first grade. "If that's your worry, forget it. I'll be watching. I know every game, from hamstringing to putting a burr under the saddle. You worrying about that? I'll be there, and I'll guarantee you a clean race. If I see some hanky-panky, you'll be the first to know it."

"Well, that's mighty fine, mighty fine," I said. "I'm gonna ask you to keep this race square."

"It's that cowboy, Skruggs, worries me," he said. "He's a little too smiley. I'll be studying on him. Nothing gets by me. There isn't a trick I haven't seen."

That made me feel better, and I let him go back to lecturing all the dudes on why Jefferson Davis was the nag to beat.

I found Algernon Limp eating grits and cornbread in the little dining room of the hotel. He sure looked dapper, dressed up for race day with a red paisley cravat, fresh-ironed shirt with a new collar, newly brushed black suit, and patent-leather shoes, wiped clean for the great day.

"Well, Algernon, who's going to win?" I asked.

"Funny that you should ask, sheriff. When I first saw that rube and his red nag, I thought it's a joke. But now I'm thinking it'll be a tight race. Just instinct, you know. I can't say. But I'm guessing it'll be my horse by a neck."

"What changed your mind, sir?"

"That boy, he's a horse whisperer. He senses what's going on in a horse's walnut-sized brain, and he tells that horse to run, and the horse takes orders."

"Horses got a walnut-sized brain?"

"If that. Half as smart as a mule, you know."

"That's what they say about me," I said. "That's why I'm sheriff. You got the judges lined out?"

"Same as before, and I'm putting observers at the far flags, so no one cuts a corner."

"Sounds dandy, Mr. Limp. What'll you do after this one?"

"Pack up and go to the next town, my jockey and me."

"You travel with Boston Bill?"

"Oh, no, he just shows up wherever he thinks he can run a game."

"He's taking heavy bets this morning."

"I'm sure he is. I've never seen a match race that generated so much interest as this one. It's one for the record books, wouldn't you say?"

"Beats me," I said.

He returned to his grits, spreading butter over them, and I drifted out to the street, watching the crowds that were already milling around Doubtful. Given the amount of cash changing hands, I thought maybe I'd better head out to the racetrack and keep an eye on Boston Bill. The man needed protecting.

Chapter Forty

I'd never seen such a mob. Most of Puma County was there, and plenty from the surrounding counties, too. I guess word got out, and there were people came a hundred miles just for this race. They were setting up to stay a while at the track, putting down blankets to sit on, and carrying picnic baskets. The ladies had got up in their best finery, lots of big straw hats against the August sun. I sure enjoy seeing women who are dolled up and looking flirty.

The heat was building, and I knew we'd all get burnt and roasted this race day, and I hoped people had sense enough to stay under big hats. By noon, the crowd had swelled to a couple thousand, which was more than we had in the county, so they were sure pouring in.

Boston Bill had a chalkboard on a tripod, where he posted the latest odds. The sorrel was the longshot, and if he won, he would pay out five for one. A feller could make a sawbuck on a two-dollar bet. Most of the smart money was on the Confederate horse, as he was being called, and the winners wouldn't collect much. But they were calling it a sure thing, so it didn't matter. A man could bet two simoleons and two minutes later have two and a half. But there were a lot of Union men who wouldn't put a plugged nickel on a Reb horse, and a lot more who itched for a local horse, like Jones, to cop the race.

Much to my surprise, Walt Zablonski, sheriff of Medicine Bow County, showed up. He didn't say much, just eyed me, eyed the track, eyed the bookmaker, Boston Bill, and eyed the competitors, Algernon Limp and Elmer Skruggs. It sure made me curious. Maybe there was more to it, but Zablonski wasn't talking.

Boston Bill sure was doing a business. Folks were lined up to lay some greenbacks on him, and he received each bettor courteously, making sure people got the exact change, and a printed yellow ticket with the words "Davis" or "Jones" carefully written into a blank on the ticket.

"Winners, redeem your tickets ten minutes after the race, and after the judges have declared the results final," he kept saying. "I'll post the results on the chalkboard."

The judges were all on hand early, all dressed in black suits for the occasion, in spite of the hot sun.

King Glad at least doffed his suit coat until race time. But Cronk, the faro dealer, seemed impervious to the heat and just sat in a folding chair, smoking cigarillos and watching the mob. Doc Harrison was busy treating heatstroke, so he didn't have a chance to stand around and look important.

By one-thirty, the place was half crazy. People were still in line, buying chits from Boston Bill, but now Bill was saying that he'd quit selling ten minutes ahead of the race. Sure enough, at ten minutes to two, he shut down.

"Sorry, fella, it's race time now," he said. "Betting's closed. Hear that? Closed now."

The crowd got the word, and drifted away, and Boston Bill asked me where the nearest outhouse might be.

"Behind the Last Chance," I said.

"Watch over my deal here," he said.

I kept an eye on his seat and chalkboard and a small black bag, glad to be of assistance.

Well, race time rolled around. The crowds milled around the two nags, studying them. Skruggs had got a racing pad on his sorrel, and would ride the critter himself. No fancy silks for him. In fact, he left his stained cowboy hat at his campsite. But Limp's Swede jockey, Egbert Engstrom, was all duded up in purple silks and looked ready to run for the money.

The owners shook hands, the jocks mounted, and began exercising their nags, walk, trot, easy lope for a bit, while the judges stationed themselves.

The nags would go twice around the track, and the chalk line was both the starting and finish line. So that's where the big crowd collected, as many in the infield as outside the loop.

At the stroke of two, King Glad bawled into a megaphone. "Jockeys, line up your mounts."

The jockeys lined up the horses at the line, with the Swede having a little trouble holding in the bay. Limp, dressed to the nines, watched blandly, puffing on a fat Havana. He'd been through all this lots of times.

I sure got fascinated. Skruggs sat easily on his red horse, but Engstrom looked twitchy.

A sudden silence swept the crowd.

Glad fired his shot; the horses broke away, a fair start, and the race was on.

They ran neck and neck through the first loop, with the Confederate nag on the outside and taking broader sweeps around the corners, but as they raced into the second loop, Jefferson Davis pulled ahead, running easily, and pretty soon it was a length, then two, then three, and finally four lengths ahead at the finish. It was a clear victory, and beyond dispute. The crowd watched silently. There hadn't been enough drama to stir up much feeling. I thought that Turk had it right; he'd picked that horse and touted it, and now he must be crowing.

The horses slowed, their flanks heaving, their

stifles sweat-soaked in the heat, and the jocks turned them back to the finish line, where the crowd waited.

The horses stood at last before the crowd, their jockeys relaxed.

King Glad consulted briefly with the other judges.

"The winner of this match race is Jefferson Davis, by four lengths. The judges are unanimous," he said. "This race is over. The stakes go to Algernon Limp, owner of the bay."

King Glad handed the match race cash to Limp.

There was a little weak cheering, but the drama was already over at the three-quarter mark.

The crowd examined its race tickets, and the ones who'd put cash on Jones were pitching their tickets away, while the larger crowd that put money on Davis began lining up at the bookmaker's stand, where the chalkboard still stood on its tripod with the final odds written on it.

But Boston Bill was nowhere in sight.

"He'll be right back," I said.

But he didn't return. Off a bit, Skruggs was unsaddling his red horse, and Engstrom was walking his bay, while Limp watched languidly. Skruggs's face was a mask. He and his cowboy buddies in the next county had hoped for a big upset, and that hadn't happened.

Sheriff Zablonski of Medicine Bow edged up to me. "It's like I figured," he said. "You'd better find

Boston Bill, and fast, and maybe put those other two behind bars."

"What?"

"Just like I thought. The three are in cahoots, along with the jockey. They pulled this one in Rock Springs and cleaned up."

"What are you saying?"

"Find Boston Bill fast. He probably skipped town. That kid there, Skruggs, he's not from Medicine Bow County. No one's ever heard of him. It's a simple deal: These three travel together. They find a county seat like this. Boston Bill sets up shop, these two run the races, sometimes throwing the race one way or another if it suits."

There were plenty of people listening, and the result was a human thunderstorm.

"Sheriff, keep order here. I'm going after him."

"Not my county."

"You're deputized. Right now."

He grinned.

I stared at the crowd, a giant thunderclap in the making, and then raced toward town. I hardly knew where to look. Boston Bill could have dodged any way, down any road. Maybe he was still there, waiting for the moment to go.

I wheeled into Sammy Upward's saloon. Sammy wasn't there, but a young barkeep was. "You see a beefy man in a dark suit and derby here?"

"Nope."

"If you do, hold him." I said.

I raced along Wyoming Street. Turk's place would be next. That's where a man could get a saddle horse. But Turk's was deserted, like the rest of the town. If Boston Bill had stolen a horse and saddle, no one was around to stop it. I stared down side streets, studied distant roads. Then I remembered the Laramie and Overland Stage. A mud wagon was due to leave about race time. That office was two blocks up Wyoming, on the west side of town, as far from the racetrack as one could get.

It was deserted, except for a clerk in a sleeve garter.

"Laramie stage leave?"

"Yep. You're too late."

"Who was on it?"

"Oh, I don't know. Couple of whiskey drummers, one patent medicine salesman."

"Wearing what?"

"Something bothering you, sheriff?"

"Tell me fast. What were they wearing? Right now!"

The feller sighed. "I don't pay much attention. Light colors, summer stuff. The whiskey drummers, tan suits, checkered waistcoats, likely. The other one, light blue jacket, straw hat."

"Any carrying big bags?"

"They all carry a samples bag, that's for taking orders. And a valise."

"The patent medicine man, what was he carrying?"

"Beats me," the clerk said. "Maybe a small case, like a sample case."

"Was he in a hurry? Breathing hard?"

"Nope, bought a ticket to Laramie, paid cash, sat down, waited for the jehu to load up, and that was that."

"How far out are they now?"

"Left fifty minutes ago. Must be four miles out."

There was a wire that went to the courthouse. I headed that way, hoping I'd find Wiley Wills, the telegraph operator. I'd telegraph Laramie, get them to hold all passengers on that stage. I huffed my way to the courthouse, but there was no one in the place. No telegrapher. I rattled around in there, looking for anyone who could tap out my message, but in fact the whole lot of people there were at the track. There were only two people in Doubtful who could tap out a message, and they were not around.

I could saddle Critter and try to catch up, and hope one of the three passengers was Boston Bill, or I could keep on looking in town. I chose to stay; there was trouble brewing right here. The whole town was like a warehouse of giant powder, ready to blow. I didn't know what would happen, but it was going to be as bad as anything I'd ever faced.

By the time I got to the racetrack, things were out of hand. A mob surrounded Zablonski, demanding that he produce Boston Bill. There were other mobs surrounding Limp and Skruggs, and about all I heard was shouting. Another crowd had corralled the judges, and were threatening to pulverize them. I looked for Rusty, but he wasn't around, and it was going to be me against not one but several mobs, all ready for a fight.

King Glad still had a megaphone in hand, so I figured I'd get to him. If I could get the mob quieted down, maybe I could keep the place safe.

But when I tried to push through the angry crowd, they simply grabbed me.

"Sheriff! Where's my money? What are you gonna do?"

"I'm going to keep the peace, and you're going to let go of me," I yelled.

But they didn't let go. In fact, they started blaming me.

"Why didn't you nab them?"

"Some sheriff! These crooks need hanging, and where were you?"

It wasn't hard to see where all this was heading. A lynching was building up, and this mob might well lynch a dozen people before it quit. They had swarmed Skruggs and Limp, and were holding both. King Glad, with the megaphone, saw what was building, climbed up on the nearest wagon and began yelling.

"Cut it out," he roared. "I'm a judge here, and I'm telling you to quiet down. Now listen to me!"

But the mob ignored him.

"Hang these bastards," yelled a cowboy. "String 'em up."

And I knew of no way to stop them, but I would try.

Chapter Forty-one

King Glad was trying to slow that mob, but the crowd turned on him and knocked him down, and started kicking him. I waded in, worked toward Glad, and found myself being yanked and hauled by more hands than I could count. Someone got my revolver, and hooted as he waved it.

"Cut that out," I yelled. "Go home. It's over."

But the mob wasn't listening. I saw a mess of cowboys catch the match race contestants, Skruggs and Limp, and wrestle them down. The two horses went berserk, kicking anyone in sight, but a dozen cowboys grabbed their bridles and hauled the horses out.

"Kill them," yelled someone, and the word spread through the jostling crowd like a tightening noose. I could see them catching the judges, Doc Harrison, Cronk, the faro dealer, and Glad himself, who ran the Admiral Ranch. The cowboys were whipping off their bandannas and using them to tie up the contestants and judges, and then they started on me.

I bucked and dodged, but all I got for it was some boots in my shins, and some yanks that nearly tore my arms out of their sockets.

I saw Sheriff Zablonski up on a wagon, yelling, but they were ignoring him, too.

"You'll hang," Zablonski yelled, but that simply heated up the game, and the mob began jeering. The mob took on a life of its own, and people knew instinctively what to do, and who to fight. I knew where this would end, and I looked desperately for help from Rusty. Or maybe the town's businessmen. Or anyone.

But there wasn't a soul except the lynch mob. The women had fled, and the businesspeople soon after, and all that remained out there, next to the horse track, was a crazed mob, bent on revenge, lawfully or not.

I saw no sign of Judge Earwig, either. He'd gotten out while he could.

The fact of the matter was that within minutes, the mob had me hogtied, Sheriff Zablonski tied up, the judges bound head to toe, and the two contestants tied up, stomped on, breathing raggedly, and fearing what would come next.

I saw Alvin Ream, an Admiral Ranch cowboy, in the midst of them.

"Alvin, stop this," I yelled. "Before something happens you'll regret."

He kicked me in the ribs. I felt my side explode with hurt.

The mob got a wagon, lifted me and the judges and the neighboring sheriff into it, and pulled the wagon into town. That was the last I saw of Limp and Skruggs. The law, what was left of it, was tied up tight. One cowboy had no trouble digging my jail key out of my pocket, and I had an idea what would happen.

Sure enough, they dragged the wagon to the jail, yanked us out—none of us could stand or walk—and dragged us into the jail, and into Cell Number Two, and locked the door.

"Where's the rope?" one of them asked.

They found it easily enough, and headed out the door. It suddenly was real quiet in there. And real quiet in town. There hadn't been a soul on the streets when they hauled us down Wyoming to Courthouse Square, and now Doubtful was dead silent.

I eyed the others, who were all wrestling with the bandannas that bound them.

Zablonski was the first to muscle his hands loose, and in short order he had freed the rest of us. Doc Harrison worked on Cronk, who was half conscious, but there wasn't much Doc could do except pump air in and out of Cronk's lungs until the man regained some sensibility. There was no water in the cell.

I hurt. The rest hurt. Some of us were bleeding, but the bandannas soon became bandages stopping the blood. My nose had taken a fist, and was swollen red and thick.

The moment came when we'd done all the doctoring we could manage in the dim light. We knew what was surely happening, not far away, in the square, where the gallows still stood. But in the cell there was only silence, and we were alone with our thoughts.

I was wondering what I might have done better, and Zablonski must have seen it in me.

"Wasn't a Ned Buntline moment, was it?" he said.

I didn't know what he was talking about, and he saw it.

"Ned Buntline writes dime novels, with outlandish heroes doing impossible things," the sheriff of Medicine Bow County said.

"Like stopping a lynching?" I asked.

"Here's how the dime novel story would go. The brave sheriff, armed with a shotgun, would stand in the path of the lynchers, daring them to walk past him, and they would see the shotgun, and see the sheriff ready to use it, and they would falter, and the lynchers would quit, and the sheriff would be celebrated as a hero."

"I'm no dime novel sheriff," I said.

We heard a faint roar from the crowd, a muffled cry in the afternoon.

I felt real bad.

"That's the dime novel world, with dime novel heroes, not the real world," Zablonski said. "You don't have to beat on yourself."

But none of the others were joining in, and I sensed they thought I'd let them down, let law and order down, let those two horse racers down. Zablonski was trying to cheer me up, but I was beyond cheer.

"A mob is an animal, and sometimes you can't stop it, and bravery isn't going to help a lawman," he said. "That's the real world, not the fictional one."

"You did what you could, Cotton," King Glad said.

But we all knew that just outside a way, there were two bodies, swinging in the breeze, live men one moment, gone the next. I had let them down, let justice down, and nothing would change my mind about that.

I can't remember a darker moment in my life. It wasn't only that I had failed; it was that the people in the town I lived in had turned savage, and had murdered two strangers as swiftly and easily as if they were shooting a deer. Something had taken hold of them, tossed all reason and restraint to the wind, fired them up, and turned them into a howling pack of killers. There were men I knew among them. Men capable of murder.

The same thoughts must have been threading the minds of the rest of us in there. They stared bleakly through the bars, waiting to be released, wondering when or whether we'd be released. Someone would turn us loose—maybe.

The clock ticked onward, and the silence outside only deepened through the afternoon, and I had a sense that people had fled Doubtful, ran as far as they could, as fast as they could from the horror.

At last we heard a door creaking, steps, and then we saw Judge Earwig, slowly lumbering toward us.

"They let me go," he said. "They still have your deputy somewhere. They're not letting him go until you promise you won't bring charges. He has the key to here; I don't."

"I'm sworn to uphold the law," I said.

He nodded. "You need food and water. I can't unlock without a key."

The others were staring at me, maybe hating me. They wanted to get out, no matter what the price.

"Find One-Eyed Jack," I said. "He can cut us out with his blacksmith tools. And see if you can find Burtell, my part-time deputy."

"Burtell's dead. He tried to stop them, so they strung him up."

"Burtell?"

"Who knows who else? I'll be back with something."

"Water now, please," said Doc Harrison.

The judge nodded, and returned with a bucket of clear water that he set just outside the bars, and a dipper. He passed the filled dipper through the bars. Harrison immediately offered each prisoner a good sip.

"Who's dead?" I asked.

"Limp, Skruggs, Burtell, and a stranger."

"The bookmaker, Boston Bill?"

"No, he's gone."

"Who negotiated with you, sent you here?"

"I don't know. They wore bandannas over their faces." He eyed the trapped men. "I'll be back shortly."

That water was manna from heaven. We drank much of what was in the bucket, which we could reach through the bars.

He returned in a while with a pot of beans from Barney's Beanery, and with the blacksmith.

"It'll take a few hours to cut you loose," Jack said. "Or I can bust the lock."

"Bust it," I said.

"It'll be noisy."

"What do I tell the mob?" Earwig asked. "I'll hang the lot?"

"Stay here. Don't tell them anything."

Jack jammed an amazingly long pry bar into the door mechanism, slammed it with a sledgehammer, and twisted. Something in there snapped. My ears were ringing. But Jack had done the job. He drew the bolt, and the door swung open. We stepped into bleakness, free at last, but my tasks had only begun.

"Arm yourselves if you want," I said to the judges.

I found a sawed-off twelve-gauge shotgun, and loaded it. The rest chose to let things lie.

We went to the door, and looked out upon a bleak scene. Four bodies hung from the gallows, swaying slightly in the August breezes. There wasn't a soul in the square. There wasn't a sound issuing from any window or building. There wasn't a horse or wagon, or cart, or ox team on the square.

"Where were you to meet the ringleaders?" I asked the judge.

"At the gallows."

"I'll go talk," I said.

I wanted Rusty real bad. He was in big trouble. I wasn't even sure he was alive. And I had no idea where to find him.

I headed out the jailhouse door, onto the lonely square, walking steadily, my shotgun cradled in my arm. The gallows loomed above me, with their dismal burden. Each man dangling, hands tied, neck snapped, head sideways, tongues bulging out of Limp and Burtell. Each body swayed slightly. Nothing under their boots but air. Once there had been the trap, solid and treacherous. But the trap hung straight down on its hinges.

I stood at the gallows, waiting, wondering whose eyes were watching me from what dark window fronting the square. There must have been a hundred windows, each hiding its own dark secrets.

No one showed up.

I sat on the edge of the gallows for a while, seeing not one soul.

My guess was that they had fled, every last one, as the reality of their crime overwhelmed them. And if so, I'd have to find and free Rusty on my own. The likeliest place was the courthouse, so I walked there, a solitary man doing a solitary task. The place was empty. I routinely checked each office as I made my way toward Judge Earwig's chamber, and when I got to the courtroom there was Rusty, gagged and tied, but alive.

He seemed plenty glad to see me. I pulled the gag off his face, and then wrestled with the bandannas that had wrapped his numb arms and legs.

Rusty, he didn't say anything. He didn't say, "Glad to see you," or anything like that. He just stared at me, and I stared at him, and some understanding passed between us.

He could name names, for sure, but I didn't ask him and he didn't volunteer any.

His holster was empty.

The judge kept a pitcher of water and some glasses there, and I poured a glass for Rusty, and he drank it greedily. When your arms are wrapped behind you, and you can't lift a glass to your lips, you get mighty thirsty, and it becomes a howling need soon enough.

"Burtell's dead," I said.

"He was trying to stop the mob," Rusty said. "He deserves a medal."

"Are we negotiating with anyone now?" I asked.

"They ran."

"Who's the stranger they hanged?"

"No one knows. They just picked on him."

"You got any notion what needs doing?" I asked.

"Call Maxwell. And cut Burtell loose first, and lay him out proper. And then the rest."

I agreed with all that.

There was something I wanted to do before we left the courthouse. I headed for the front windows, where the United States and Wyoming flags hung from staffs. I pulled both in, and folded them, and then closed the window. They shouldn't be flying in Puma County, not now.

We headed across Courthouse Square. Rusty would head for the jail and tell those people it was safe to go. I headed for Maxwell's Funeral Parlor, and told him to pay respect to the dead.

Chapter Forty-two

No one was talking. I intended to level murder charges against those who'd lynched four mortals that August afternoon. I knew plenty of the people who were rioting at the racetrack, but that didn't help. They all professed not to know who strung up the match race contestants and my part-time deputy.

Puma County had a guilty secret, and it looked like it would stay that way and that's the way they wanted it. I spent days poking and probing, and got nowhere, but I knew that someday, sooner or later, some witness would start spilling the facts. And then I'd make sure the guilty were brought to justice.

Odd how the town changed. People were afraid to talk to me. I walked around there in isolation. Maybe the ones who did the lynching were threatening those who watched them do it. Maybe the reason no witness came to me was because he feared for his life if he did. I could only wait because someday the whole story would spill, and I'd do what the law required me to do.

There was new pressure to get rid of me, too. The fastest way to bury the lynching was to oust me from the sheriff office, and sure enough, that's what happened. The county supervisors called me in one afternoon and told me they were firing me. They said I'd caused damage to county property, namely the cell door, and that was reason enough to discharge me. I stared at Reggie Thimble, and Ziggy Camp, and smiled. They smiled back. They knew what they were doing and why, and it didn't have anything to do with the wrecked cell door.

"Have a cigar on us, Cotton," Thimble said.

Rusty and I buried Burtell, since no one else was around to do it. The old deputy was a loner, with no family we could find, so we got Maxwell to dig a grave for us in the town cemetery, and we laid our friend to rest there. His last efforts were to restore peace in town, and he deserved better than he got. He took with him the secret of who strung him up. But me and Rusty, we knew we'd find out eventually.

Bad secrets always boil to the surface.

The supervisors didn't appoint Rusty sheriff. They knew he'd do what I would do, and keep after the case until he had the lynchers behind bars. Or maybe they didn't like the idea of a sheriff married to Siamese twins. By then, both Natasha and Anna were expecting, and Rusty's family would soon grow. I sort of hoped that each twin would not produce twins, but the thought was entertaining. They let Rusty stay on as deputy, mostly because the Siamese twins were becoming a tourist attraction, and bringing coin to Doubtful. And until supervisors got around to finding someone new, Rusty would be the acting sheriff.

I didn't fight the dismissal, figuring my time in Doubtful was up, and it was time to move on. But even before I collected Critter and moved out, I got word from the Wyoming Cattlemen's Association that they wanted to talk with me. So I did, and the upshot of all that was a new job, at eighty a month, as a range detective with the association, keeping rustling at bay. The cattlemen had been losing a lot of beef, and they wanted to put a stop to it, and figured I was the man. And I could stay right in Doubtful.

So I left my shiny badge with Supervisor Thimble. It was untarnished. I'd never dishonored my badge. But the county and town that employed me now had a guilty secret, and I thought it was a good thing to let go of it, at least for a while. And I had a hunch that my new job, as a range detective, would lead me to the things no one was talking about. Such as who did the lynching in Puma County that August day. The story wasn't over yet. And neither was my life.

As my ma used to say, you ain't old until you're forty.